"It's too dangerд

"Dangerous? What are you talking about? You're safer here than…" Braeden's words trailed off as he tipped his head and leaned closer.

She could nearly see the thoughts whirling behind his eyes. It wouldn't take him too long to figure out what she meant. Alexia knew Braeden was so attuned to her that it took only a look for him to know what she was thinking or feeling.

A seductive half smile curved his mouth. "Does this have anything to do with the challenge you issued? The one about not sharing my bed?"

"It wasn't meant as a challenge." It was meant to keep her heart safe. And now that she'd unintentionally reminded him, her heart might already be forfeited.

Braeden turned her face toward his. With his lips brushing against hers, he whispered, "Tell me to go away, tell me you don't want me and I'll leave, Alexia."

Books by Denise Lynn

Silhouette Nocturne

Dragon's Lair #58

DENISE LYNN

Award-winning author Denise Lynn lives in Northwest Ohio with her real-life hero, their son and a slew of four-legged "kids." Between the pages of books, she has traveled to lands and times filled with brave heroes, courageous heroines, never-ending love and the occasional otherworldly element. Now she can share with others her dream of telling tales of adventure and romance in lands filled with knights of old, or characters of the imagination. You can write to her at P.O. Box 17, Monclova, Ohio 43542, U.S.A., or visit her Web site, www.denise-lynn.com.

DENISE LYNN

DRAGON'S *Lair*

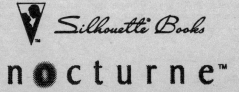

Silhouette Books

n**o**cturne™

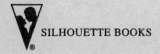 SILHOUETTE BOOKS

ISBN-13: 978-0-373-61805-7
ISBN-10:   0-373-61805-0

Recycling programs
for this product may
not exist in your area.

DRAGON'S LAIR

www.silhouettenocturne.com

Printed in U.S.A.

Dear Reader,

Thank you for deciding to spend a few hours at Dragon's Lair. I hope you find Braeden and Alexia's story enjoyable.

If anything seems remotely familiar, you aren't imagining things. Uncle Aelthed, the dragon pendants and Mirabilus first appeared in my Harlequin Historical story *Falcon's Honor.*

Their journey into the twenty-first century was fraught with danger at every turn. Of course, the danger follows them and lands at Dragon's Lair.

Enjoy your visit. Just remember to be wary of the wizards, steer clear of the dragons and watch out— the swords are real and very sharp.

Take care,

Denise Lynn

To my editor, Sally, with overwhelming gratitude.
This book wouldn't exist without her keen eye or
patience. And to Tom, with love always.

Prologue

Mirabilus Keep, Isle of Mirabilus, 1172

A young girl from the village struggled with her basket of food in the storm brewing outside Mirabilus Keep. The wind increased, forcing her to bow her head while fighting to stay on her path home.

Suddenly the storm's strength intensified. Darkness fell upon her village, blotting out the sun's light. Never in all her seven years had this happened.

Her eyes widened with fear at what she perceived as impending doom. The girl ran for shelter, but the wind blew her long hair into her eyes, leaving her unable to see clearly.

She stumbled, dropping her basket in her haste. Fear of hunger surpassed her fear of the storm and she stepped back to retrieve the basket.

An aged woman cried out from a doorway, "Hurry, child!" The girl quickly did as she was bid because the storm had come to life, taking on the form of a dragon.

All at once the wind's fury overtook her. Dust and sand stirred up by the whirlwind stung her face and eyes. She trembled with the knowledge that the storm swirling around her contained something close to human intelligence and was not mere nature.

The hag squinted against the blinding storm, her efforts to find the child fruitless. When the basket whipped across the threshold of the cottage, she slammed the door shut with a heartbroken cry.

Like the other villagers, she bowed her head in prayer, yet the heavenly appeals were unfounded, for the storm sought no more of the common folk. It had needed the life of only one innocent to complete its devilish task.

The wind howled over the dwellings, continuing its lethal path across the open field to the curtain walls surrounding the bailey. The men stationed in the twin gate towers and on the walls clung to rough-hewn beams or railings. But they were unable to stand against the blood-thirsty force.

On a near scream, the gale-strength wind hammered its way through the barred wooden shutters of the main bedchamber. Small benches, herb-strewn rushes, iron sconces and pots of medicines exploded across the floor. The heavy tapestries surrounding the bed heaved as the wind's rage came to a whirling stop.

As quickly as it had begun, the swirling wind lessened to nothing more than a misty shadow. The shadow wavered, contracting and expanding before finally it took human form at the bedside of an elderly dying man.

Nathan the Learned swallowed a gag as the thick,

cloying scents of burnt thyme and coming death invaded his nostrils. He leaned over the old man, only to be greeted with a sneer.

"You think to frighten me with mere elements?"

The wizened man's lips never moved, but Nathan easily heard his thoughts. Death drew nigh and precious time could not be wasted with banter. Nathan demanded, "Give me the manuscript, old man, and find your peace."

"Your journey is fruitless. Fire consumed the ancient book of spells decades ago."

"Perhaps." Nathan leaned further over the bed and placed his palm on the dying man's cold, withered forehead. "However, dear, dear Uncle Aelthed, all know you have spent these last years recreating the grimoire. I will have the secrets now. They are my birthright."

"They are well protected from the likes of you. The secrets go to the grave and beyond with me."

Nathan's blood ran cold. He'd not studied and worked so diligently for more than two decades only to be thwarted by death once again.

"Nigh on thirty years ago you killed my father for trying to save the original grimoire. You murdered him, your own brother, because you saw fit to claim him wicked."

The dying wizard dug his withered fingers into the bedclothes.

"I was only five years old, but I still remember the dishonor and shame inflicted on my father's dead body." He shook with growing rage. "You denied him the funeral pyre that would have permitted his soul to find peace. Instead, you placed him in cold, lifeless earth with a cross to mark his grave."

Aelthed's raspy breathing hitched. Unable to move or

escape the wrath he so richly deserved, he tried to sink down into the mattress.

Nathan curled his lip in a sneer. "Even after I remained true to the magic coursing through my veins by studying the old ways and learning the lessons set before me, you denied me the position of power that was rightfully mine."

With one knee on the edge of the bed, he bent over until his face was a mere hairbreadth from his uncle's. "You chose an uninitiated mortal to rule over the Isle of Mirabilus. *I* am the true Dragon of Mirabilus. The Dragon's blood runs in *my* veins, not his. This Norman knight bears the name only by your public decree."

Aelthed's fear swirled cold and icy about the chamber. Nathan could taste the sweetness of it on his lips. "You turned your back on the old ways and the magic of our line. By doing so, *you* lessened the worth of Mirabilus. 'Tis no longer enough to rule a magicless kingdom. I will have more."

The rise and fall of the old man's chest faltered. "Nay, Uncle." Nathan pressed his fingertips into Aelthed's temples, seeking to forestall the inevitable. "I'll not let you go until the book is in my hands."

Aelthed closed his eyes and trembled beneath the hold. He then shuddered, and after taking a gasping breath, hoarsely whispered, "Evidence of my perfidy be gone forever."

Once-dwindling powers surged forth, nearly singeing Nathan's fingertips. He stared down at Aelthed in horror as he realized the defiant wizard had wiped all memory of the book and its whereabouts from his mind.

With a single swipe, Nathan tore the bed curtains from the frame and threw them to the floor. "No!" He gritted his teeth, then tightened his grasp on Aelthed and stared into the man's paling, watery gaze.

Again he shouted, "No!" Then pressed his fingertips even harder into the older man's temples. "I'll not let you escape so easily."

He searched the chamber, his gaze landing on a small wooden box next to the bed. Nathan willed the box to come to him. But rage weakened his concentration and he was unable to bring the object to his hand.

He closed his eyes and filled his lungs with a deep, soothing breath. This time, with the power of only his thoughts, he moved the box from the table to his hand. The little cube rested on his palm. "Perfect."

He tossed the wooden cube up and down, testing its weight, then smiled and met Aelthed's wide-eyed stare. "'Tis a hollow puzzle box, is it not?"

Nathan knew by the dying wizard's silence that he'd guessed correctly. He focused on the box, finding the combination to the sliding panels with his mind. He forced his will past the magical lock, sliding one panel free, in turn releasing another, and then another, until the box opened. "Behold your new abode, Aelthed. You'll not find release in death."

Nathan tossed the cube into the air and set it spinning above Aelthed's chest, just over the wizard's heart. "Nay, powerless to escape, your soul will rot within these tiny walls. Just like my father, you shall never find peace." He laughed at the thought of the revenge he would gain. "An excellent curse, do you not agree? A fitting end for one who seeks to continually thwart me. You see, dearest uncle, I will find your ancient spells and secrets without your help."

Defiance flickered behind the old man's frightened gaze. That brief reminder of the power this High Druid once possessed gave Nathan a moment's pause. He hesitated only a heartbeat before shaking off the seed of doubt.

"No. I will not be just the Dragon of Mirabilus." He leaned down and whispered in Aelthed's ear, "In the end, your deceit will make me the Hierophant. Supreme power over all will be mine."

Thunder crashed, jolting the stone keep on its foundation. A small pun-sai dragon tree in the corner shivered. Bottles and jars crashed to the floor, shattering into countless glimmering shards.

Aelthed moaned. His last mortal thoughts sped across the short distance to Nathan. *"You waste your time. The secrets are bound by threads of love. Only the love shared between the true Dragon and his mate will set them free. You know nothing of love, or nurturing, and will never possess the power you seek."*

Lightning streaked across the sky and seemingly raced through Nathan's spine. The time was here. Aelthed's vow meant nothing. Vows were readily broken. Threads easily snapped.

Nathan closed his eyes and stretched out his arms above the dying wizard. A shaft of light radiated from Aelthed's chest, gathering into an undulating ball between Nathan's open hands.

Certain he held every last particle of being that had once been Aelthed, he thrust the shimmering mass into the wooden box, closed the panels, then sealed them with a spell.

While clutching the cube to his chest, Nathan whispered with certainty, "Immortality is almost mine, you fool. I fear not this Dragon or his mate. I have all the time in the world to find your secrets and spells. The day of my full attainment will arrive."

Chapter 1

Alexia Reve-Drake pressed her spine more tightly against the broad trunk of the tree, hoping that the tree and the darkness would hide her from the men seeking to harm her.

She forced herself to breathe slowly, trying hard to listen over the rapid pounding of her heart. A light breeze shuffled fallen maple and oak leaves, rustling them across the museum's parking lot. From a distance, the sound of traffic on the expressway hummed. It was long past rush hour, and no squeal of tires or blare of horns broke the steady whir of passing cars.

"Where'd she go?"

Alexia held the breath she'd just inhaled and fought the hysteria urging her to scream.

While the entire day had been one confusing event after another, she hadn't expected it to end like this.

"Alexia."

She swallowed the terrified cry threatening to escape. This wasn't the first time today she'd heard her name whispered.

A hushed crooning that came from nowhere to beat against the inside of her head. Even though she had never mastered the skill of telepathy, she had learned how to protect her mind from others.

But right now she couldn't concentrate hard enough to call up even an iota of protection. She was too rattled by the men after her. And this intruder was stronger, his will more powerful than any she'd encountered before.

Stronger and—not quite human. She sensed the raw, predatory power of a beast—a power that had touched her once before, sending her life into chaos. This intruder was a lethal enemy who could easily slip through her visualization of a wall closing off her thoughts to others.

"I think we lost her." Leaves crunched underfoot as the three men continued their search. She shivered, certain the masked trio would never give up their hunt.

"Alexia."

Her shivers turned to tremors of fear. She took a chance and glanced around the tree. Overhead lights glared, casting eerie shadows onto the pavement of the museum's nearly empty south-side parking lot. At this time of night only two cars remained—hers and a pale gray sedan.

The night maintenance crew and security guard parked in the lot on the other side of the building. Maintenance wouldn't reach her end of the museum for another three or four hours. And Bill, the young night security guard, would most likely be on his cell phone with his new wife.

Unless some miracle occurred, nobody would be aware that she was still here, let alone in danger.

"Alexia."

Unable to control her fear and suddenly growing anger, she silently screamed, *"What? What do you want?"*

The intruder laughed. A harsh, evil sound that nearly sucked the breath from her. Finally he answered, *"The grimoire."*

Alexia briefly tightened her hold on the padded envelope clutched against her chest. She cringed, instantly relaxing her hold when the ancient vellum pages inside crinkled like old tissue paper.

She hadn't been forced into this type of silent conversation in years. Not only was this intruder evil incarnate, the mere act of conversing without speaking dredged up memories she'd prefer to keep locked away. Yet she wasn't about to alert the men seeking her by speaking out loud. Instead, she thought, *"Then take it."*

In truth it wasn't as if the pages were hers to begin with. Someone had delivered them to her office in the museum this morning before she'd arrived. It wasn't until late in the day that she'd had time to inspect the contents of the envelope.

At first, she'd been thrilled. It wasn't every day that a medieval paleographer got a chance to research and translate dead languages. There was little she loved more than poring over words older than some civilizations—words and symbols that most members of her community had only heard or read about.

But a paragraph into the translation changed her excitement to horror. The opening of the first sentence hinted that the pages would contain secrets more powerful than the human mind could imagine.

That was when she'd felt her intruder's virtual touch. The need to physically translate the pages was unnecessary—she had only to form the words in her mind for him to have the spells.

"You never should have sensed my presence."

"If you're so damn clever, why didn't you translate the work yourself?"

His anger was hot—and swift. A wave of fire shot through her. She swayed slightly at his abrupt departure from her mind, then leaned even more against the tree for support.

"He'll have our heads if we don't find her."

This speaker was human and nearby. She tamped down the urge to curse—her intruder could have taken his cronies along with him when he'd left in such a huff.

She peered around the tree again. The men were still there. Somehow she had to get away.

"Maybe she slipped back into the building."

At last she heard two sets of pounding footsteps heading back toward the museum. What was the third man doing? She attempted another glance—he was still there.

Let him wait all he wanted. It wasn't as if she'd move from the safety of her tree before he was gone.

He turned his head in her direction and she immediately jerked back. Had he seen her?

The crackle of leaves let her know how close he was to finding her. "I know you're out here." His deep voice rasped from little more than an arm's length away. "You may as well show yourself. We aren't leaving without you."

Did he think she was stupid? She closed her eyes and fought for control as she reached into her coat pocket. She tipped her head, listening, trying to pinpoint his location.

She heard him muttering. The sound came from her right. He was too close. As slowly and quietly as possible, she moved cautiously to her left.

"We just want the translation." His footsteps stopped. "Give it to us and we'll leave you alone."

Not hardly. These manuscript pages came from more than a simple book.

The pages were sections from another manuscript, a druidic grimoire that supposedly never existed. A supposition totally off base.

She knew for a fact that the Dragonierre's Manual did indeed exist. For nearly four centuries it had been in the possession of the Drakes—her estranged husband's family. She'd seen it several years ago.

How had these pages become separated from the manual? It was kept locked away in a safe. Did Braeden know that a few of the pages had been nabbed? Or had the manual she'd seen always been incomplete?

The package's arrival before the daily mail call meant they'd gone to a lot of trouble to ensure the pages found their way to her desk. They'd somehow bypassed all the security measures and broken into her office to make the delivery.

She'd been set up. The *why* was pretty obvious—there were few people who could actually do the translation. The *who* was what worried her. Was it human or something more sinister?

Either way, was it aware of her connection to the Drakes and the value of the manual? What evil was planned with the translation?

If what she'd heard about the manual was correct, the spells and rituals were powerful. In the wrong hands the magic could be used to literally bring down nations.

"I can stay out here all night," said the man, sending her heart into another frenzy.

He was so close now that she could probably touch him. Instead, she curled her fingers around the cold, hard steel in her pocket.

After the threatening phone call she'd received before dawn this morning, she'd slipped the gun into her coat. However, this wasn't the danger she'd expected.

"It's a nice clear night. It'll get real cold soon." She heard him zip up his jacket. "It won't bother me none. I can wait."

His darkly ominous tone didn't convince her of his professed patient character.

The man sighed heavily and then said, "You're a smart girl. You know he'll eventually get what he wants. One way or another, he'll have the power with or without your help."

She clamped down on her tongue, determined to hold back the gasp trying to claw its way out of her throat. Dread crept down her spine as she realized they knew full well the secrets these pages contained.

Just as she'd feared, whoever was in charge of this venture was out for nothing more than power and evil. Offering either up to them was not an option.

"I'll make you a deal."

To her surprise, the man's hot breath brushed her ear. Alexia jerked away from him. "No."

He grabbed her arm, preventing her from pulling out her gun. "I'd say your choices are rather slim. Give us what we want, or we'll take it."

Unable to break free of his hold, she stalled for time to think. "I only received the pages today. There hasn't been time to go over them. I have nothing to give you."

He jerked her closer until she had to tip her head back to look up at him. The glare from an overhead light pooled down on them. A latex mask covered his entire head. The only part of him visible beneath the grotesque caricature of a lion were his eyes and mouth.

He stared at her through beady, bloodshot hazel eyes. His thin lips curled, his breath felt like the fires of hell against her face. "Oh, blue eyes, I have everything I need—you and the pages. He'll be more than able to convince you to finish the job."

Even with her high-heeled boots on, he towered over her. The man tightened his grasp, making her wince. She swallowed. It didn't take much imagination to guess what type of convincing they'd use.

Alexia forced down her panic. If she allowed herself to lose control, she wouldn't stand a chance of escaping.

She'd give her eye teeth for a good idea right about now, but all she could think to do was buy time. "You'll need more than just me and the pages. It's not like I have every word and symbol in every language memorized."

He dragged her behind him as he headed back toward the museum. "You just show me what books or stuff you need and we'll take 'em along."

"It's after hours. The building is locked." Since she wasn't a permanent staffer, she didn't have a key, just a small office in the basement.

"No problem, babe." He laughed. "You think a little thing like a lock will slow me down?"

She wasn't going with him. Alexia dug in her heels and fought frantically to get him to release her arm. It was like trying to shake off a mountain lion.

He stopped and faced her. "You're wasting my time." To add emphasis to his words, he tightened his grip until tears formed in her eyes. "I'm not letting you go."

Alexia gritted her teeth to keep from flinching. She was not going into the museum with him, and she had to act before he met up with his accomplices. She'd rather die.

In the end, she might die, but not without a fight. She stiffened her spine. "And I'm not going with you."

Before he could finish another laugh, she kicked him. The hard heel of her boot caught him in the kneecap. She wished it could have been higher, but she'd take what she could get.

He gasped. His eyes widened and she planted the end of the three-inch heel into his kneecap again. And that was all she needed, because he released her arm.

Before he could grab her, she whirled away, pulled the Beretta from her pocket, slid the safety off with her thumb before pointing it at his chest. Her lack of experience would require both hands for a good aim, but she wasn't letting go of the package in her other arm. No matter what her instructor insisted, one-handed would have to do. He was close enough that she only had to calm herself and hold the gun steady.

He shook his head. "That's a joke, right?"

Alexia shrugged. "It's a real gun with real bullets, if that's what you're asking."

The man took a step closer. "You aren't going to shoot me—I can see it in your eyes."

In all honesty she'd never shot anything except a target at the local gun club's shooting range. And she'd only done that out of pure necessity. Alexia suggested, "Perhaps you need to look again."

He started to reach inside his jacket.

She took a deep breath before pulling back on the trigger. The reverberation shivered through her, but she held her stance, and then heard a satisfying *whoosh* as the bullet tore through his leather jacket.

"You bitch!"

She spun and raced for her car, not caring how badly

she'd injured him. From the curses he spouted, she assumed he'd live.

His angry shouts brought his buddies to his side just as she reached the car. Before they could catch up with her, she wrenched the door open, tossed in the padded envelope and her gun, threw herself into the driver's seat, started the car and took off, tugging at her seat belt as she drove.

A quick glance in the rearview mirror revealed that while she may have shot the man, it hadn't stopped him. He held his arm and screamed at the other two as all three of them raced for their light-gray four-door.

Alexia drove with no destination in mind. There was little doubt that they'd soon be on her tail, but where could she go? Not to her sister's—she wouldn't put Maureen or the kids in jeopardy.

To the police? No. What would she tell them? That she was in possession of an ancient Druid text containing secrets to powers unimaginable? They would either ask if Halloween had arrived two weeks early or think she was a kook.

Alexia checked the rearview mirror again. No headlights shimmered off the mirror. *So, now what?* Her relief faded. Where could she go?

Outside of two twenties in the pocket of her jeans, she had no other cash on her and her cards were in her desk drawer— at home. Alexia swore. Of all times to start leaving home without plastic, why on earth had she picked this month?

She rolled her eyes. Simple. She hadn't wanted the temptation of a credit card when she was saving every dime for her upcoming trip to England.

She had to go home. Alexia frowned. What if they knew where she lived?

Sweat dampened her back from the sinking feeling that

someone might be waiting for her at her town house. But she had to take the chance.

When she pulled into her neighborhood, she flipped off the headlights before turning onto her street, then pulled into the first empty space along the curb. Heart pounding, she rolled down the window and peered toward the middle of the block at her town house.

Over the rush of her pulse she heard nothing unusual— a door slamming, a horn honking from the next street over, two cats fighting in Mrs. George's yard. Everything she'd expect to hear around midnight.

She scanned the line of parked cars. While she didn't see the gray four-door, a dark limo and a flashy red Rolls Phantom were parked outside of her place.

Neither of the two cars belonged to her neighbors. Both were too impractical, too elegant for this end of town. A pickup truck, Jeep or any SUV could've been ignored.

Then she saw a light come on in her bedroom. Scenes from every late-night horror movie she'd seen raced through her head. She'd have to make do without the credit cards, because there was no way she was going in her town house.

She rolled the window up, then eased her car out onto the street. As she put the car in reverse, she noticed two men running out of her town house. One leaped into the back seat of the limo, the other jumped behind the wheel of the Phantom. Both tore off in the opposite direction down the street.

She hesitated. Would it be safe to—

The town house exploded. A shower of glass and bricks rained on the street. She stared, frozen in shock. Torn between rushing to check on her neighbors and driving as far away as possible, Alexia remained immobile.

The Wilson family, who lived on one side of her place,

were on vacation, so that left the Hazels. The three occupants stumbled out of their home and crossed the street to another neighbor's.

A swirl of ice-cold fear snaked down her spine. She had no idea where the men had gone. No clue who they were or what they'd been looking for. If they'd been searching for the manuscript pages, why blow up her home? Surely they'd want the pages intact.

She had to get away before they found her. Mrs. George, the neighborhood busybody, would be able to tell the police everything they needed to know.

Unwilling to risk being seen, Alexia hit the gas pedal and backed down the street to the first crossroad, then took the long way around the block.

She groaned in dismay. A tank of gas and forty bucks wouldn't get her very far. There was one place she could go, and even knowing that was her only option, she had to brush away a tear. With a frustrated cry, she headed toward the expressway.

The thugs who'd attacked her probably expected her to run to Braeden. But where else *could* she go?

Nowhere.

Alexia turned onto the southbound ramp. If she drove through the night, she could be in the mountains of East Tennessee just after breakfast—assuming the men didn't catch up with her.

Even before they crawled into his office with the news, Nathan knew the three imbeciles thought they had failed. But his only intent had been to send Alexia running to Dragon's Lair and back into her husband's arms. With a little prompting on his part, it'd succeeded. Where else could she go once her home had blown up?

Still, there was no point in letting anyone else in on his scheme. So he waited, knowing they'd eventually summon up the courage to tell him that three strong men had been unable to kidnap one small female.

Nor was there any point in slipping into her mind again. When she did finally make her way to Dragon's Lair, he didn't want to risk the Drakes knowing who was behind their troubles. No matter how carefully he covered his tracks, it would be far too easy for one of them to go traipsing through Ms. Reve's mind and catch a trace of him.

That was the last thing he wanted. Too many mistakes had already been made through the centuries. People had paid with their lives for errors in judgment.

His eldest son, Marcus, had been so certain that the Drakes of the sixteenth century were the ones who would translate the book that he'd gone against Nathan's wishes. That mistake had sent the book deeper into hiding.

However, watching his brother's execution had done little to stop another son from repeating the same mistake a generation ago.

Jason had taken it into his head that the previous Drake couple had been the ones who would finally grant the Learneds what they had waited for so long.

And yet again Nathan had tried to convince the dimwit of his error, to no avail. In the end he'd had to kill not only his wayward son, but the Drakes, too. He couldn't risk them living with the certain knowledge of his existence.

Not yet. Not until the grimoire was in his hands.

After all the planning and work he'd done, Nathan was unwilling to be caught now. He'd nearly risked detection himself years ago when he'd conjured up a winged beast to force Alexia's car off the road.

That petty, yet necessary, act had served two purposes. She'd lost the child she'd been carrying, ensuring that the Dragon wouldn't pass on his power to his child. As an added bonus, her husband's disbelief at her explanation of the accident had driven a wedge between them.

The timing had not yet been right. While he'd been certain even then that these were the two who would eventually give him what he needed, neither of them had possessed the skill at the time to do so.

While he'd been smugly satisfied when she had gone back to school, he'd been forced to kill again. Rumors of the grimoire's existence had been passed down through the generations much like the book itself. Most people scoffed at the rumors. But some, like Ms. Reve's professor, were far too curious.

The man had been too sly for his own good. He'd taken advantage of Ms. Reve's connection to the Drakes and her eagerness to obtain her degree to convince her to do a paper on the grimoire.

Nathan had been slightly amused at Ms. Reve's attempts to change her professor's mind. But in the end, she'd been unable to do so.

The man never lived long enough to discover that Ms. Reve's paper was nothing more than speculation containing nothing of the facts.

Now Alexia had the ability to translate the grimoire. And Braeden Drake, High Lord and Wizard of Mirabilus, was indeed the Dragon that Nathan had long awaited. The Dragon and his mate would renew their love…at least long enough for the grimoire to be translated.

Nathan shook his head. If they knew how much he had dabbled in their love life, they would be horrified. He'd torn them apart, pilfered letters, waylaid phone calls to keep them from each other long enough for the wheels to turn.

And now, just when each thought their separate lives were finally on track, he would toss them back together.

Never in all his years of waiting had he expected love to be the most evil, albeit strongest, tool he'd employ.

Nathan opened a desk drawer and pulled out a small wooden cube. He rubbed a finger across the smooth worn oak before sitting it atop his desk. "Ah, Aelthed, our time has finally arrived."

The box vibrated, clattering across his desk before levitating. Nathan easily reached out and captured the cube. "No, not this time, my friend." He'd been caught unaware the first time this had happened and sported a black eye for days.

"I would think that after eight centuries, you'd be thrilled at the thought of freedom." He placed the cube back in the drawer and shrugged. "But perhaps you've come to enjoy your solitude."

He slammed the drawer shut before turning from his desk to face the makeshift altar behind him. Since the hard part of the ceremony had already been completed, he only needed to finish the remainder now—then he'd know for certain that Alexia went to Braeden.

After righting both the small amethyst and sapphire dragons stationed at the rear center of the wooden ledge, he began to chant. Slowly, methodically, he lit two of the candles, then the incense.

He picked up a figurine, the flame from the candles bouncing off the red wax. An image of Alexia came easily to his mind as he lit the figure. "Here burns the Spirit and the Power of Alexia."

Nathan lit the remaining candles, then completed the

chant. He leaned back in his chair before swiveling to face the desk once again. He stared into the free-standing mirror perched in the corner and focused on Alexia.

The mirror clouded. Fog swirled in the smooth glass, setting his heart racing. "Ah, yes. Appear—"

A sharp knock at the office door interrupted his scrying. With an exasperated curse, he called out, "Enter." He turned and gazed ardently at the dragons before extinguishing the candles. "Soon, you and all else shall be mine."

Chapter 2

Alexia gripped the steering wheel of her ten-year-old Thunderbird tightly enough to dig her fingernails into her palms, then leaned closer to the windshield. This seven-hour drive had turned into the never-ending journey.

A rockslide just over the state line had held her up for more than four hours. Then it had started raining about the time she'd hit the foothills. The downpour worsened with each passing mile until she'd had to pull over until it let up enough for her to see the road ahead.

She couldn't help but wonder who would be more upset by her arrival—Braeden or his aunt Danielle. With any luck, his aunt had stayed behind in Boston and she wouldn't be around.

To keep boredom at bay and the family coffers filled, so to speak, Braeden and his brothers designed and built resort hotels around the world. Alexia knew from news articles and recent television interviews that the current work in progress was a secluded resort in the mountains just outside Gatlinburg, Tennessee. While she could envision Braeden and his brothers there, she couldn't imagine Danielle Drake leaving her high-society life in Boston for the mountains.

On the other hand, since Braeden was cursed, it was a safe bet his aunt wouldn't let him get too far away from her. Why the woman thought she still needed to protect her *boys* was beyond Alexia's comprehension. Danielle may have raised them after their parents died, but they weren't boys any longer.

Braeden had evoked the curse himself. As had been done in previous generations, he'd made the mistake of marrying an uninitiated mortal. In an attempt to keep their line of wizards pure, a curse had been placed on the eldest son. Supposedly any mortal the son married would be able to drain him of his powers.

While Alexia had never seen any indication that was true, Danielle Drake took the curse seriously. The woman had taken every opportunity she could to drive Alexia away.

Hopefully, Danielle thought Braeden would be safe without her help this time and had stayed behind in the comforts of Boston. It was something Alexia knew she'd discover soon enough.

Since she didn't have directions to the Drakes' resort, the clerk at the convenience store on the edge of town said it'd be impossible to miss Dragon's Lair as long as she stayed on this road.

The rain had finally stopped, but now the typical Appalachian fog coated her car like a layer of frost. As the wipers fought the thick dew, a country ballad crackled from the radio. Something about lost love and pain. If she weren't so afraid of lessening her death grip on the wheel, she'd turn the radio off. Music that had once soothed her jangled her last nerve.

The closer she got to Braeden the more nervous she became. Between the rockslide, rain and fog, it seemed as if even nature itself was against this trip. Not a good omen, but she had to ignore it.

What she couldn't ignore was the feeling of approaching disaster that clung to her skin like perspiration on a muggy summer day. Except it wasn't summer, nor was it hot. This sensation was frigid, making her shiver in spite of the air blasting from the car heater.

She hadn't seen another car in more than an hour, yet her senses warned of someone—or something—following her. Constant checking in the rearview mirror revealed nothing but an empty road.

Not seeing anything could be meaningless. Alexia knew from past experience that otherworldly creatures existed. One such creature had forced her car off the road, causing the accident where she'd lost her unborn baby.

Her heart flinched at the reminder. And her arms ached with emptiness. Sometimes, like now, Alexia wondered if she'd ever get past that horrible moment.

The accident and loss had led to the breakdown of her marriage. Her disbelief upon learning that she'd married a wizard had been hard to overcome, but she had. She'd loved him with all her heart and had accepted who and what he was. Yet Braeden hadn't returned the same level of trust. He hadn't believed her explanation of the accident.

At first his adamant disbelief angered her. Then the realization that he didn't trust her broke her heart. She could have lived with his anger, but not his lack of faith. So she'd left and never expected to return.

Especially not under these circumstances.

Alexia steered around another curve and slammed on her brakes. Could that be Dragon's Lair? She leaned sideways and tipped her head to better see the monstrosity.

A medieval castle rose out of the Appalachian mists, totally out of place in this environment. Its towers were starkly outlined by the glare of spotlights mounted at the base of the walls.

It was as if Mirabilus Keep, the Drakes' ancestral home, had been transplanted stone by stone from its island in the Irish Sea to East Tennessee.

Resort, castle or medieval keep, Dragon's Lair was aptly named. With the dark sky and steadily thickening fog, the hulking structure loomed over anyone approaching its gates.

Alexia straightened, fighting the sudden urge to turn the car around, floor the gas pedal and head as far away from Braeden's home as possible.

Instead, she took a deep breath and inched the car forward. He wouldn't be happy to see her, not after the things she'd done to him. She had the sinking feeling he would still be angry.

She didn't blame him, but she had no options.

She wasn't running to him because she *wanted* to—she did so only because she *had* to. The pages belonged to his family. Maybe returning them would in some way make up for breaking her vow of silence about the book.

Even though the choice of writing the paper on the manual had been taken from her, guilt for doing so still plagued her.

Perhaps the book would be safe at Dragon's Lair. Perhaps, somehow, even she'd be safe—if not from her husband's anger, then at least from those after the book.

* * *

Braeden Drake shoved away from his desk, rose, then crossed the office to once again stare out the tall, narrow window. Fog blanketed the mountains, giving life to the murkiness of his mood.

She was out there. And he could feel her getting closer. That one thought—Alexia's returning—had jolted him awake just before midnight.

Since then he'd waited, his anger growing with each passing hour. He hadn't felt this level of rage in years. The mere fact that he was still this angry with her irritated him to his marrow.

There were legitimate reasons to despise his wife. She'd lied about the accident that had killed their unborn child. She'd left him. Then, to make matters worse, she'd used confidential information about his family's secrets to further her career.

Her speculations about the grimoire, the Dragonierre's Manual, had resurrected debates about its existence. Not only debates, but also the increasing number of those seeking to gain fame, fortune and power from discovering the truth about the grimoire.

Somehow she was involved in the recent events at Mirabilus Keep. It was obvious by the timing that her paper on the manual had triggered an avalanche of disasters.

In the months since her work had been published, there'd been four break-ins. During the attempts, four of his employees and an intruder had been killed, a hired carpenter was still in the hospital and another intruder had been seriously injured.

As the ruler of Mirabilus Isle, he was responsible for his employees' families. He didn't care about either criminal. However, no clues were found at the scene and the intruder's prolonged coma made it impossible to get the information he needed.

He'd tried using every ounce of power he possessed to get inside the intruder's mind. But the attempts had proved useless. He'd received only distorted images of the man's childhood.

Dragon's Lair was almost ready to open. He didn't have the time or the energy required to make the repeated trips to Mirabilus, open the resort and keep both his family and the people under his protection safe against those seeking to harm them.

He slammed his fist against the wall. He didn't want Alexia here. Didn't want to deal with the anger and lack of concentration her presence would create.

The sight of headlights stopping just outside the gates warned him that whether he wanted to deal with her or not, she was here.

Far from a hotel, Dragon's Lair looked more like a movie set for an old horror flick. A gloomy castle complete with towers, parapet and arrow slits for windows, it'd probably even have a dungeon outfitted with a torture device—in her size.

Braeden would never go that far. Would he? Alexia shook her head and answered her own question. No, he wouldn't.

Even with people he didn't like, he was always formal, polite and able to keep things impersonal. He wouldn't be any less formal or impersonal with her.

Impersonal. Great idea, but could *she* keep it that way? The years hadn't dimmed her memories. She still remembered everything. The whirlwind courtship that brought them breathless to the altar. The deep timbre of his voice, his caressing touch, the heat of his kisses. The memories twisted in the pit of her stomach, consuming her with despair.

To keep this dire visit impersonal, she needed to remember what had driven her away in the first place. Even though she'd been forced, it had been her unhealed anger and pain that had made it slightly easier to write the paper on the Dragonierre's Manual. Her conscience still niggled regretfully. But there was little she could do about it now other than return the missing section to its rightful owner.

She pulled through the open wrought-iron gates and around the circular drive to the front of the castle. She grabbed the envelope off the seat, then stepped out of her car. The hair on the back of her neck rose. Someone was watching her from one of the many narrow windows.

It would do her no good to put her fear and worry on display. She kept a firm grip on her package, squared her shoulders and opened one of the oversize entrance doors.

Her breath caught in her throat.

Antique iron wall sconces had been outfitted with flame-shaped lightbulbs. Suits of armor flanked all three of the arched doorways. Tapestries covered some walls, while murals of medieval hunting and jousting scenes graced the rest. It would take just a dusting of dried herbs on the rough, planked floor to complete the transformation to the Middle Ages.

Alexia shivered. The enormous lobby was empty and as cold as it looked. If the Drakes had been looking for the dank, dark atmosphere of a medieval keep, they'd succeeded.

Only the registration desk and lobby bar anchored the hotel in the present day.

She crossed to the desk. When no one came out to greet

her, Alexia peered over the counter and picked up a map of the hotel from behind the counter. Management offices were down the hall to the left.

Certain she'd find Braeden's office there, she headed down the long, dark hall stopping at the first set of huge, metal-studded double doors. If the Lord of the Castle had an office, this had to be it. A quick glance at the brass wall plate confirmed her guess.

Should she march right in, knock or turn around and leave? Her stomach somersaulted. Her heart raced. She couldn't decide.

Why? After all this time, why? She'd successfully squashed her feelings for him—her anger and near hatred had made it easy enough. So why now had her legs turned to jelly?

She sensed him just beyond the door. The spicy scent of his aftershave swirled beneath her nose, awakening more intimate memories. The gentleness of his large hands brushing against her cheek. She shivered, remembering the feeling of his warm breath against her neck.

Those tangible memories could easily be pushed back. It was the others, the more recent ones, that threatened to bring her to her knees.

Her chest tightened as she remembered. When he'd lifted her from the car wreck, his voice had been husky and deep with concern. But when she'd lost the baby they'd both longed for, he'd blamed her.

And when she'd tried to explain, he'd insisted that her mind was playing tricks on her.

Alexia lifted her hand to the throbbing in her chest. She couldn't do this. She couldn't face him. Not even after all this time. She'd have to find some other place of safety—because Dragon's Lair wasn't safe, after all.

Quickly, before she was discovered, she turned and headed back down the hall toward the lobby.

The door behind her groaned. She clutched the package in her arms to her chest, hoping the pressure would slow her pounding heart.

"Leaving already?" Braeden's deep voice rippled over her, stopping her escape.

"I don't know."

The carpet beneath his feet silenced his footsteps, but she sensed his approach. And to her horror her body warmed in welcome.

Obviously perceiving her body's response, he rested a hand on her shoulder. Then quickly withdrew his touch as if he'd been burned.

The brief contact had been enticing, yet at the same time it had proved baffling. The sudden urge to run from desires and longings she thought safely put to rest collided with the need to lean into the chest so close behind her. It would be, oh, so easy to relax against his broad chest, tuck her head beneath his chin and let his strong arms enclose her in still-familiar warmth and safety.

"Made up your mind yet? Staying or leaving?"

Far from inviting, the coldness of his tone suggested her best choice would be to leave. She stepped away and faced him. Without the heat of his body against her back, she could almost breathe again.

She looked up at him, then swallowed a gasp. Instead of impersonal, the hard, chiseled planes of his face spoke volumes of his anger. But it was the animalistic glitter in his narrowed eyes that threatened to steal the last remaining thread of bravery she clung to so desperately.

There was no doubt in her mind that safety at Dragon's Lair would come at a high price. How much would she have to forfeit to the Master of the Lair for protection against the evil seeking her? Would facing the unknown evil be less dangerous than facing the heartbreaking rage of the Dragon standing before her now?

Alexia wasn't at all certain she was up to the challenge of either choice.

Braeden stared down at her. "Why are you here?" Before she could answer, he stepped aside and motioned toward his office. "I'm not going to stand out here in the hallway. Make yourself comfortable, then we'll talk."

Comfortable? She doubted if she'd ever be comfortable in his presence again. Still, she accepted his suggestion and stepped into his office.

Her feet sank into the thick midnight-blue carpet. She tried to ignore her innate urge to investigate the dragon statue and swords adorning the room. How many of the swords were real and how many were excellent replicas?

Without being too obvious, she slowed her pace as she walked by a dragon statue perched on a pedestal. The column was marble—that much she was certain of. What about the dragon? Glass or gemstone? Sapphire? Blue topaz? Imitation? Real?

Braeden walked behind the dragon on the way to his desk. "Sapphire. Twelfth century. The amethyst one in Cam's office is identical, even down to the scratch on the beast's belly."

Heat rushed to her face. "That obvious?"

He said nothing. But his quick glance at her sent goose bumps racing down her arms. They instinctively tightened, crushing the package. Feeling like a fool, she relaxed her hold and sank into one of the leather armchairs facing the desk.

While Braeden stared out at the fog, she studied the man she'd once called her husband. He was still everything she'd fallen for the moment she'd first laid eyes on him. He was tall enough that she had to tip her head up to look him in the eye. But it wasn't his chiseled face or full lips that had first captured her attention.

With his hands in his pockets, his suit jacket hiked up, he gave her a view that made her cheeks flush with warmth. Even now, the sight of his long, muscular legs and tight ass still set her heart fluttering in her chest.

The well-tailored jacket clung smoothly to his back. She knew full well that there wasn't any padding in those shoulders.

Three years wasn't a long time, but where his muscles had filled out to near perfection, hers had become more rounded and soft.

It simply wasn't fair.

Finally Braeden turned and sat down. He leaned back in his seat, giving her the impression of the Lord of the Castle seated on his throne.

"What do you want, Alexia?"

She cringed before making the mistake of looking more closely at his face. A frown marred his forehead. Dark amethyst eyes stared unwavering back at her. If his tone in the hallway hadn't warned her that he wasn't thrilled about seeing her, the coldness of his eyes and the hardness of his square jaw clued her in.

When had he stopped wearing tinted contacts to hide the color of his eyes? He silently waited for her to tell him why she'd come. Uncertain where to begin, she asked the first thing that came to her mind, "You didn't tear down Mirabilus, did you?"

"No. But that's not why you're here."

"I, um…" She fumbled with the package, hating how spineless she suddenly felt. Despite her vivid imagination of him as a dragon and what he could do to her, she had no reason to physically fear the man across the desk. Lifting her chin, she forced her shoulders back. "Don't glare at me."

"What?"

"If you're trying to intimidate me, it's working."

"We've shared a bed and a life together and suddenly you feel intimidated?" He shook his head. "I would think guilt would be a more suitable emotion."

"Guilt? For what? For losing our baby?" A knife ripped through her chest. She swallowed down the searing pain. "It wasn't as if I'd planned it. I had help, whether you believe me or not. Or do you mean guilt about leaving your home? I wasn't welcome there any longer."

He leaned forward and opened his mouth. But before he could speak, she barreled ahead. "Why didn't you come after me? Braeden, you could have contacted me at your will, anytime, anywhere, and you never even called or wrote or—"

"Enough." He cut her off, then asked, "Are you finished?"

No, she wasn't finished. She wanted to lunge across the desk and throttle him until he gave her the answers she needed.

Braeden laced his fingers together until his knuckles turned white. Apparently he was as angry as she was. Good. It served him right.

"In the first place, did we or did we not agree that I would never use an ability you did not possess?"

Alexia looked down at her hands for a moment. Yes, that was true. He'd vowed not to force his thoughts into her mind and not to use any form of magic to locate her. But there were other methods of communicating. She lifted her gaze. "You could have picked up a phone, or a pen, or sent an e-mail."

"I wrote to you. I called you. You never responded."

He briefly closed his eyes. His frown deepened. Alexia waited while he concocted another story to appease her.

"I did call, but Maureen told me I'd done enough damage and to leave you alone. I most certainly did write."

Alexia groaned. Leave it to her sister to protect her, whether she wanted the protection or not. She paused. While she could see Mo stepping in to field a phone call or two in the beginning, she didn't think her sister would go that far afterward, nor would Mo dispose of letters unread. What did Braeden think to gain by lying?

Before she could ask, he hit her with questions of his own. "What do you want? Why are you here? Are you ready to file for a divorce?"

Alexia cringed, ignoring his last question to push the package across the desk. "This is yours."

He slid a letter opener across the top of the envelope like he was slicing into someone's body. She was pretty certain that someone would be her.

Braeden slipped the contents out onto his desk and stared at the manuscript pages. "Where did you get these?"

"Do you even know what they are?" She picked up the sealed packet of acid-free gloves that'd been inside the envelope. "Put these on, please."

To her surprise he did so without question, then he ran a gloved finger over the entwined Celtic dragons on the front page. "It doesn't take a degree to suspect these could be from the grimoire."

"Could be? No, I'm certain they are from the book."

"Impossible." Braeden leafed through the highly ornate pages, disbelief widening his eyes a little more with each flip. "It's still under lock and key." The corner of one faded page crumbled beneath his touch.

She grimaced at the sight of flaked vellum. "Braeden, be careful."

He returned the pages to the envelope, put it in his desk, then took off the gloves. Once he'd locked the drawer, he asked, "How did you get them?"

"They were on my desk when I got to work yesterday. I don't know how they got there."

"How can you be certain they're part of the Dragonierre's Manual?"

"How could I not be certain?" Surely he knew she'd done a paper on the manual. Alexia laced her fingers together and looked down at her lap.

"Touché."

His clipped reply surprised her. She'd expected a rant about her paper. When she raised her head, she was startled by the fury etching his face. Perhaps she should be afraid.

"Why did you—" Braeden was cut off by the buzz of his phone. He hit the intercom button. "Yes, Harold?"

"Mr. Drake, there's some waxy stuff on the roof of your visitor's car. Want me to wash and polish it?"

"Waxy stuff?"

"Sounds strange, but I'd say candle wax."

Alexia stared at the intercom. "Candle wax?" Then she looked at Braeden, mouthing, "Harold?"

"The chauffer, mechanic and sometimes valet. I had him park the car in the garage." Braeden tapped his desk a couple of times before asking, "Is there a pattern?"

Harold answered, "Could be. Looks like something your aunt might do."

"Don't touch it until Ms. Drake sees it." Alexia's hopes about his aunt remaining in Boston were dashed by his direction to Harold.

Braeden punched a button and got Danielle Drake on

the line. After explaining the situation and asking her to look at it, his focus returned to Alexia, making her squirm.

He said nothing.

"Braeden?" Alexia's pulse raced faster with each second of silence.

She recognized his expression. His forehead creased with concentration. He clenched his jaw, making the already squared shape more intense. He turned his head, causing a dark blond hank of hair to fall across his face.

For some men the unkempt, wayward look required expert work. For Braeden it was natural. It also meant he needed a haircut before the back started to curl. And when had he shaved last? Her sister loved the rugged stubbly look, but Braeden's faint beard only made him look tired. He wasn't taking care of himself, which meant he was still working too hard. Alexia frowned. What difference did it make to her?

Trying to get his attention, she smacked the desk. "Braeden!"

The tactic worked. But the cold stare he turned toward her seemed filled with hate. Instinctively she leaned away.

While the hatred vanished, she could still feel his anger.

"How did you say you came by these pages?"

"They showed up on my desk yesterday morning."

"Why didn't you just mail them? What prompted you to come here in person?"

Had his silent concentration moments ago been focused on her? No. Alexia doubted if he'd give her that much energy.

She wished she could trust him enough to tell him everything. But she didn't. He'd destroyed her trust years ago, and Alexia knew in her heart that hadn't changed. "I wanted to make sure the pages got into your hands."

"You could have sent them with a signature required." He leaned forward. "Want to try again?"

"I wondered how you were doing."

He hiked an eyebrow, echoing her opinion of that lame answer. Braeden raised two fingers. "That's two. Want to try for three?"

Something in the back of her mind told her to lie. She bit her lip. Why? Unable to justify her reasoning, she shrugged. "I needed to get away."

"From what?"

"My job."

He shook his head. So she offered, "Mo."

"Not likely."

Not wanting to see his response, she closed her eyes before saying, "The men trying to kidnap me."

"You mean someone other than a Drake wants a piece of your hide?"

Chapter 3

Braeden didn't seem the least bit surprised by her confession, almost as if he already knew. A knot formed in her stomach.

Instead of expressing concern, he repeated his original request. "Start at the beginning."

To keep her focus away from her increasingly queasy stomach, Alexia ran a fingertip along the beveled edge of his desk. "The package was waiting on my desk when I got to the office yesterday. Inside was a note asking me to translate the pages and a very lucrative offer I couldn't pass up."

"If you were broke you could have called me."

"Called you?" At least a thousand sarcastic comments tripped over each other on their race to her tongue. She swallowed them. "I never said I was broke. I don't need or want your money."

"You're still my wife." Braeden reached into a drawer

and pushed a bankbook across the desk. "The money's yours for the taking."

Intentional or not, the insult stung. He didn't believe she could take care of herself. Worse, she wondered if he was right. She pushed the offending bankbook back to him. "If I remember correctly, you paid for my degree. That more than covered our short marriage."

"You're right, I did. And yet you saw fit to bring the Dragonierre's Manual into the limelight." He stared at her, his eyes darkening even further. "In case you've forgotten, we're still married."

Alexia wanted to explain. But as the words teased her throat, she knew he wouldn't believe her. Braeden would never understand being forced to do anything. The concept of not having a choice would be too foreign, too easily brushed off by accusing her of putting her priorities in the wrong order.

He took a deep breath, then asked, "Why were you so desperate for cash?"

To prove I could make it by myself. Alexia clasped her hands in her lap. "The necessities of life—rent, utilities, food…research…" Why was she explaining this to him? "Actually, it's none of your business."

"None of my business?" His tone was flat and far too steady not to be forced.

She'd always needed the physical signs—the clenched jaw, blazing eyes, thinned lips—to let her know when he was ticked off before. But now his rage wrapped around her heart like a vise. Had time and distance made her more sensitive to his moods? Or was Braeden finally breaking his vow to her and calling on the magic running through his veins to convey his anger? Alexia waited silently for the eruption.

"I'll tell you what *is* my business." He glared at her. "Men dying or ending up in an emergency room because of your complete lack of integrity." He slammed a fist on the desk. "It's my business when Mirabilus Keep is broken into and defaced because you couldn't keep a sworn secret."

Confused, she asked, "What are you talking about?"

"I'm talking about two employees and an intruder who died during the first break-in. I'm talking about a carpenter who barely clings to life after trying to stop a second break-in. I'm talking about a groundskeeper who was fatally shot by yet a third intruder. That intruder is still comatose. And let's not forget the hired gun that died in the last break-in. All after you got even with me by writing your paper on my family's secrets."

"Oh, my God, Braeden. I never thought—"

"You never thought? I'm supposed to believe that you never realized what chaos your hints, insinuations and speculations would create? You aren't that stupid."

People dying and getting hurt had never been her intention. She had to explain. "Braeden, I—"

The ringing of the phone cut her off. Braeden hit the intercom. "What?"

"Braeden?" Alexia recognized the youngest Drake brother's voice. Sean sounded a little hesitant, but said, "We need you down here in the garage. And bring your...guest along, too."

Those brief seconds had given Braeden the time he needed to pull his detachment firmly back in place. She grabbed his arm, stopping him as he walked past her on the way to join his brother. "Wait for me."

He shook off her hold and headed for the door without saying a word.

Since he didn't tell her not to come with him, she sprinted to keep up with his long strides. But she refused to give up. "Braeden, I never intended to harm anyone. Surely you know that."

He shook his head, but kept up the pace. "Except me?"

"Well, not intentionally. I am sorry."

"How convenient."

"Convenient?" Alexia had had enough of his foul mood. Yes, she'd expected him to be angry, to be distant and remote. She hadn't expected curt sarcasm. "Look, now that you have the pages, I'll be on my way." To where, she had no clue.

He stopped in front of a mural. She thought maybe he'd halted to finally say something *to* her, instead of *at* her. When the mural parted in the center, she realized it was an elevator.

Since they were heading to the garage and her car, she followed him inside and stood at the far corner. What was she going to do now? She sure as hell couldn't go home— she no longer had a home. How could she go anywhere? It would take at least a day or so before the credit-card company sent a replacement card…and that wouldn't happen until after she called them.

She squeezed her eyes closed. *Don't cry. Don't you dare start crying.* The more she repeated her silent order, the harder it was to obey.

"Where will you run to this time?"

The emotionless tone of his question stole her breath. It sounded as if he didn't care at all. The lump forming in her throat would soon make it impossible to speak. So she answered quickly, "What does it matter to you?"

"Damn it, Alexia." The elevator bounced to a stop, but before the doors could open, Braeden hit the close button on the panel, sealing the two of them inside.

He moved in front of her, so near she could feel the

warmth of his body and hear the unsteadiness of his breathing. When she pressed her back against the wall of the elevator, he inched closer.

"What do you want me to say?" he asked. "*You* left *me*, remember? No explanation, just a note telling me to leave you alone."

"You know why I left."

Braeden placed his hands on the wall behind her, effectively trapping her between his arms and chest. "You left because it was easier to run away than face what had happened."

"No." She paused, hoping to steady her voice. "I left because there was nothing else for me to do."

He leaned even closer. His breath hot on her face only conjured up the image of a dragon in her mind once again. "There was a lot you could have done or said. But instead, you chose to punish me for the loss of our child."

"I never—"

He stopped her denial with his lips. It was an effective tactic he'd used more than once during their marriage. Yet Alexia gasped at the contact. Shock, fear, anger, unbidden desire…all warred within her. Before she could act on any of the emotions setting her heart to race and knees to tremble, he broke their kiss.

"And now you've returned." He spoke as if his kiss had never happened. But the lingering tingle on her lips let her know that she hadn't imagined the searing caress.

She pushed against his chest. "I said I'd be on my way."

"No." He didn't move a muscle, except to narrow his eyes. "You came to me for protection. You'll stay until I know you're safe."

Alexia didn't need more than a heartbeat to realize he wasn't kidding. Braeden didn't tease about anything.

"You can't force me to stay."

"Don't bet on that, Lexi."

His use of the nickname he'd given her gave her pause. Maybe she'd been alone too long. Or maybe she'd thought she hated him for too many years.

No. Something…a strange flash warned her to be careful, not to let lingering feelings and memories cloud her better judgment. He was too close to the Dragonierre's Manual not to be part of recent events. A sudden fear sent ice through her veins.

She took a deep breath to steady her nerves, then looked up at him. "Why? Why would you force me to stay?"

He silently returned her scrutiny for a minute before saying, "Because I want you close, right where I can see you." He moved away, then smacked the open button on the panel, adding, "And you might prove useful."

His admission sent her thoughts into a whirl of confusion. Had her flash of warning been correct? Did she have more to fear from this dragon than the evil she'd encountered at the museum?

I might prove useful?

How?

Before she could ask, she heard footsteps approaching the elevator.

"Took you long enough. Thank God it wasn't a real emergency."

Alexia couldn't help shaking her head. Sean was just as impatient as ever.

Braeden moved aside, waving her forward. "I'm sure you remember my guest." She darted around him and out of the elevator.

"What is *she* doing here?"

Danielle Drake's voice dripped with all the hatred Alexia remembered. The unwarranted tone set her teeth on edge. She'd never seen any indication that the curse Danielle feared so much had been true. Not the tiniest speck of Braeden's power had been drained from him during their marriage. What would it take to make his aunt see reason?

Alexia hadn't the faintest idea. Since she had no plans to stick around for long, she really didn't care what Danielle thought or felt.

"Don't start, Danielle." Braeden's exasperated sigh reminded Alexia of how many times he'd been forced to come between her and his aunt before—and of how many times he'd failed to do so.

She studied Danielle. His aunt, a petite woman, hadn't aged at all in the past three years. The jet-black hair flowing over her shoulders and her unblemished, wrinkle-free skin made the woman all that much easier to dislike. How did a woman professing to be as old as dirt retain such a youthful appearance?

Even though Alexia wasn't telepathic, she'd learned the hard way that Danielle Drake was more than able not only to read her mind, but also to send thoughts to her. The only thing Alexia needed to do was let down her guard, and Danielle would see to it that they held a full conversation without saying a word out loud.

Intentionally letting down the wall surrounding her mind, Alexia mused, Danielle Drake didn't look a day over…eighty.

Aunt Danielle's instant glare momentarily pinned her in place. *"Eighty? Quite a compliment coming from someone the other side of…forty."*

Alexia narrowed her eyes against the expected intrusion and returned the nasty stare, thinking, *"I see you haven't*

*lost your ability to stick your nose where it doesn't belong.
Stay out of my head, Danielle."*

"Seems you invited me in." Danielle tossed her head.
*"What the hell are you doing here in the first place?
Haven't you caused Braeden enough grief? Or are you
looking to finish him off?"*

"It doesn't take a psychic to know what the two of you
are doing." Braeden grasped Alexia's arm and pulled her
to his side while ordering his aunt, "Enough."

Instead of goading Danielle further, Alexia turned her
attention to Sean. He'd introduced her to Braeden. She'd
known Sean at college. They'd been friends and she'd
gone with him to a weekend party at the Drake mansion
in Boston. He'd only asked her because his girlfriend had
stood him up, and arriving alone would have only made
him a target for his aunt's matchmaking.

Braeden had also been at the party. As if bewitched,
they'd been drawn to each other. It took all of ten minutes
for her to lose her heart and soul to him. They were meant
for each other. How had things turned out so wrong
between them?

Unlike the rest of his family, Sean was *uninitiated.* He
was normal. Safe. She smiled at him and asked, "How are
you?"

For the first time since they'd met, Sean's smile didn't
reach his eyes. While he returned her greeting, his guarded
look and narrowed gaze made her want to escape. She
shouldn't have expected anything different. Uninitiated or
not, Sean was still a Drake.

Braeden released her, only to drape his arm possessively across her shoulders while he caressed the side of
her neck with his thumb. Surprised, she flinched. What
was he up to with this sudden display of affection?

Between the heat of his body against her and the shivers of awakening desire shooting down her spine, Alexia wondered if coming down here with him had been a wise decision.

She tried to step away, but he merely settled his arm more firmly around her. Had her move only been seen as a challenge to him?

Somehow challenging a dragon didn't make a lot of sense. She rolled her eyes at the thoughts running unchecked through her mind.

He was a man. Not a mythical beast, just a man. He stroked the soft spot beneath her ear. And she swallowed a groan as heat pooled low in her belly. Oh, yeah, he was just a man all right. One who knew every inch of her body almost better than she did.

More than anyone else alive, Braeden Drake, the Dragon of Mirabilus, possessed the power to melt her resolve to be impersonal with nothing more than a simple touch. A gentle stroke, a mind-numbing kiss, a lingering caress, and if she wasn't careful, she'd fall to her knees with hungry wanting.

And he knew it.

"Was there a reason you asked us down here?" Braeden said to Sean. His breath rushing hot across her ear fed the hunger she fought to control.

"You mean other than to explain what's on your woman's car?"

Alexia froze at Sean's remark. She hadn't been Braeden's *woman* in years. The implication would only force her husband to behave even more possessively.

Instead, he lowered his arm. For less time than it took her to gasp, she missed his touch.

As if nothing were amiss, Sean headed for the car. "You're going to like this."

Braeden placed his hand at the small of her back, urging her along, and they fell into step behind Sean. "Considering your obvious sarcasm, I'm sure it'll be something interesting."

As they approached her Thunderbird, she noticed an older man standing off to the side. Braeden waved him over. "Harold, this is my wife, Alexia."

Danielle sighed loudly, but said nothing. The valet frowned, but extended his hand. "Good to meet you…Mrs. Drake."

The unfamiliar greeting felt strange. Harold's hesitation made it obvious he didn't know Braeden was married. "Nice to meet you, too, Harold. Thank you for taking care of my car."

"No problem, ma'am."

Danielle motioned to the roof of the car. She waited until the three of them stood alongside the vehicle before explaining, "This wax pattern is from an ancient ritual."

Braeden said nothing, but Sean barely concealed a choked cough. He'd always found Danielle's fascination with spells and rituals a waste of time.

So had Alexia—until she'd started translating ancient texts. Now she wasn't so certain.

Blunt as usual, Danielle asked, "Why did you come here?"

After ensuring her mental wall was firmly back in place, Alexia asked, "What business is that of yours?" She couldn't help herself. When it came to Braeden's aunt, it was easier to be rude.

"Your reasons might assist me in determining which ritual was being performed."

"She brought me some pages from the manual." Braeden looked at Alexia. "Did you ever meet the man who wanted to hire you?"

Meet him? "Not in person, no."

"Hired her for what?" Danielle's voice climbed half an octave.

"To translate the pages."

"I suppose you gave him what he asked for just to spite us even more." The woman's loathing was palpable—that hadn't changed. She'd gone out of her way to prove that more times than Alexia could count.

Braeden intervened. "No, she didn't."

Alexia put her hand on the car for support. Otherwise, she would have fainted at his defense of her.

Braeden directed Danielle's focus back to the car. "So, what's this?"

After glaring at Alexia one more time, Danielle said, "A ceremony to track her. The white, orange and purple candle wax point to a scrying ritual." She touched the red spot in the middle. "Obviously whoever did this was doing so for a female."

Alexia knew that much by the wax—red for a female, black for a male. "Didn't they need some personal effect?"

"Was your car locked?"

"No." They all looked at her like she'd just admitted to a crime, so she explained, "The lock broke a few months ago and I haven't gotten around to getting it fixed yet. Nobody breaks into cars back home." Apparently that assumption was wrong.

Danielle shrugged. "Then access to a strand of your hair would have been easy."

"Yeah, but why go to the trouble of performing a ritual out in the open? They could have been caught. Wouldn't it have been easier to use an altar somewhere private?"

Braeden asked, "Where was your car parked?"

"At the museum, near the college."

"It's nearly Halloween." Sean added, "This time of year, who would think twice about some student burning candles on top of a car?"

"But we're talking about a small town in the Midwest. It's not exactly a hotbed of wizards and witches."

"You'd be surprised," Danielle muttered under her breath. "It doesn't need to be a hotbed, just takes one—"

"One who wants the manual," Braeden finished his aunt's sentence.

Danielle touched the melted wax, then shook her head. "But I don't see how this particular ritual would have helped. It was most likely repeated at an altar, with a crystal ball, bowl or mirror."

"Then what was the point of doing this to my car?" Alexia chipped off some of the wax with a fingernail.

"To let you, or us, know you would be followed."

Braeden asked, "If you didn't meet the person, did you ever talk to who wanted to hire you?"

Alexia glanced at the wax and shivered. "Not on the phone or in person. But yes, we did…chat, so to speak."

Danielle's sharp gasp drew everyone's attention. "You let down your guard to a stranger?"

"Not on purpose. But it didn't matter, he slipped through quite easily."

"One of the Learned sent her here." Danielle gasped and raised a hand to her chest as if protecting her heart. "You've brought danger to us all."

"That was probably the idea to begin with." Braeden put an arm around his aunt, pulling her close. "But don't worry, it'll be fine."

"Fine? How can you even think that? They killed your parents. They'll not rest until they rid the world of Drakes. You know that, Braeden." She pointed a shaking finger at

Alexia. "Get rid of that woman once and for all. She's nothing but a curse personified."

Alexia had to hand it to Danielle—her theatrics had greatly improved over the years. Or *was* it theatrics? Was Danielle going overboard out of guilt? Or to cover her steps. When it came to spells, potions and invading someone else's mind, there was no one better than Danielle Drake.

"She can't stay here, Braeden. Surely you see that. Look at what's happened at Mirabilus. She's nothing but trouble. We'll all end up dying." Danielle slid a measuring look toward Braeden. Was she baiting him or gauging his reaction?

"You're seeing things that aren't there." Sean's tone was sharp.

Danielle tore out of Braeden's embrace to confront Sean. "You may not have honed your powers, but they do exist. Have you forgotten the things that have happened to this family? The things she's done to this family? I haven't. I want her gone. Now."

"Done." Alexia opened her car door, then looked at Braeden. "Sorry to have bothered you."

"No." Braeden grasped her arm, pulled her away from the car, pushed the door closed, then glared down at her. "Perhaps you didn't understand what I said. You aren't leaving here until I say you can."

She jerked free of his hold. "You can't stop me."

"I could stop you physically if I so desired. But I don't need to use brute force." He crossed his arms over his chest. "You won't get too far without finances."

Had he slipped into her mind without her knowing it? No. She'd have felt his intrusion. Since he didn't know for certain that she was broke and had no credit cards, he planned something else.

Alexia dredged up what little bravado she had left and returned his glare. "Do you always resort to magic to get your way?"

"Magic?" To her complete shock, he laughed. "It's the twenty-first century, Alexia. We have these little boxes called computers. I can close your nearly empty bank account and cancel your credit cards with the push of a finger."

"You wouldn't."

A challenging smile crossed his mouth. "Try me."

Certain he was overestimating his power to keep her in place, she retorted, "You don't have that kind of capability."

"Don't I?" He frowned as if thinking, then spouted off her checking account number and miserable balance before adding, "Your last credit purchase was three days ago at the bookstore down the street from your town house. You paid $24.99 plus tax for a book called *British Folk Tales*."

Alexia nearly choked on a scream of outrage before shouting, "You've been tracing me?"

He shrugged. "Obviously, not closely enough."

Sean whistled softly. "Good God, Braeden."

"What?" Braeden turned his attention to his brother. "You don't find it a little odd that people started dying after her paper was published?"

"What are you saying?" Alexia grasped the sleeve of his suit jacket. "Are you saying that I'm to blame?"

He looked down at her hand. When she released her hold, he asked, "Can you prove you aren't?"

She had no way to prove it except by her word. And she knew how much he'd trust that. While she wasn't personally to blame for what was happening at Mirabilus, she was indirectly at fault. She had to find a way to right what had gone wrong. But how?

"Then she needs to leave here." Danielle repeated her suggestion.

"No." Braeden glanced from her to his aunt. "No. If it is a Learned, she's in way over her head. She's staying. We can use her knowledge."

Danielle visibly bristled. She literally shook from her toes to the top of her head. "What can we possibly use from her?"

Good question.

"None of us can change the fact that the paper on the Dragonierre's Manual is out there. We know what trouble it's already caused. There's no telling what else will happen before this is all finished."

Alexia flinched.

"Just burn the thing and get it over with." Sean's suggestion sounded so simple.

"No." Braeden was adamant. "That was tried centuries ago and somehow it turned up again—bringing more grief along with it."

Apparently he'd already thought this out. The realization only fueled a throbbing in her head. Had he calculated everything every step of the way just to get her here?

He reasoned, "If it's translated, we'll learn why people are willing to kill for it."

"And you want *her* to do it?" Danielle pointed one long, red-nailed finger at her.

"Who better? She knows her job and she's here."

"Isn't that convenient?" Alexia cringed at Danielle's bark of laughter. "Oh, yes, she knows her job. At whose expense?"

Braeden drew in a deep breath, then let it out slowly. "I've already made up my mind. She stays." He looked pointedly at Danielle. "And you will leave her alone. Am I understood?"

Immediately, his aunt's entire countenance changed. She came forward and placed a hand lightly on Braeden's chest. "I only want what's best for you. Don't get involved with her again."

"And I want what's best for Mirabilus and Dragon's Lair. Anything beyond that is between Alexia and me."

Alexia's heart thudded heavily in her chest. *Anything beyond that—such as?*

Danielle glared at Alexia before promising, "I'll leave her alone. Just be careful, Braeden."

He waved Harold over. "Put her car in with the family vehicles."

The family vehicles? Alexia scanned the garage area. "Where's that?" Not that she was planning a hasty exit, but she'd like to know where her car was going to be parked—just in case.

"Right over here, ma'am." Harold held out an automatic garage-door opener and hit the button.

A huge door slid up, permitting entrance to a private garage within the larger parking area.

Alexia's breath caught in her throat. The hairs on her neck and arms rose.

Her mind flashed back to her town house and the explosion. Perspiration formed above her upper lip.

Parked inside the Dragon's Lair garage was the same flashy red Rolls Phantom that had raced away from her home earlier.

Chapter 4

Alexia's stomach clenched as if she'd been slugged. Fear and confusion swirled icy cold around her.

Had she not seen a Rolls Phantom at a car show a few months ago she wouldn't have known what it was—or how rare it was to see two within a twenty-four-hour time frame. The vehicle was too new for many to be on the road yet—unless you had enough cold hard cash.

Slowly, hoping he wouldn't notice, she stepped away from Braeden.

Would he have gone this far to get even with her? Was Braeden the one behind everything, including blowing up her town house? Had he expected her— wanted her—to be inside? Or had he done so knowing full well that he would be the only one she'd run to when she had nowhere else to go? The thought that Braeden could possibly be behind all this dried her throat. She tried to swallow the bile that made its way up from her stomach.

To her horror, it all added up. He had the manuscript. Obviously he had the wheels, too. He also had the ability to dance around inside her mind. Surely it'd be easy enough for him to change the sound of his voice so she wouldn't recognize him. But wouldn't his presence have felt familiar to her, instead of frighteningly strange and inhuman?

Harold opened the trunk of her car, snapping Alexia out of her shock. She'd pulled over at the first rest stop on the expressway to exchange her boots for the sneakers in her workout bag and to unload and stow her gun in the trunk. "No, wait, I'll—"

Too late.

He'd already pulled her gun from the holder anchored inside her trunk and handed it to Braeden while asking, "Your bags, ma'am?"

"I…don't…have…any." Teeth gritted, she enunciated each word. The man had no business handing her weapon to Braeden.

Danielle shot Braeden a look Alexia couldn't decipher before muttering something unintelligible under her breath and storming from the garage.

Harold looked from Alexia to Braeden. He cocked an eyebrow before turning to close the trunk. "I'll just go park the car."

Braeden stared at the Beretta in his hand. "What is this?"

While that most likely wasn't what he'd meant to ask, she refused to supply him with any information other than the obvious. "A gun."

Braeden's lips thinned and his frown deepened. Apparently her answer didn't meet with his approval. She didn't care. Right now, gaining his approval was the least of her concerns.

She took another step away from him. "Where…" She swallowed again, trying to calm her voice. "Where were you yesterday?"

"Yesterday?" He moved toward her, slowly, as if stalking prey.

"You heard me." Again, she inched away.

"Here." Again, he followed. "Why?"

"All day?"

"Yes." He stared at her intently as she took yet one more step backward. "I've been here all week."

She narrowed her eyes. "What about everyone else?"

Sean approached, stopping at her side. A frown of confusion marred his forehead. "Alexia, we're trying to open Dragon's Lair. Everyone has been right here."

Her brother-in-law's voice was steady and seemed sincere. She longed to believe him, but before she could swallow her still-growing fear, Braeden moved quickly and grasped her wrist. He pulled her away from Sean and headed toward the elevator with her in tow. "We need to talk."

"We've talked enough. There's nothing else to say." Alexia tried tugging her arm away. "I think I'd rather just stay here right now." Until she was certain he had nothing to do with her town house or the thugs after her, the last thing she wanted to do was be alone with him. "Let me go."

Sean stepped in front of them, halting their progress. "Braeden, you heard her. Let her go."

Confused by his action, it took Alexia a minute to realize Sean was doing what he always did—protecting someone he deemed weaker. Back in college, she'd witnessed this behavior from him many times. But why would he think it necessary to come between her and Braeden?

"Back off, Sean."

Alexia's eyes widened at the deep, sinister tone of Braeden's warning. His words echoed in the cavernous garage, making them sound even more deadly, but Sean barely flinched.

"She's obviously spooked by something and you're doing nothing to put her at ease. Let me show her to a room where she can rest while you calm down. *Then* you can talk."

Alexia didn't argue. She welcomed the idea of having time to sort things out. Before she could take Sean up on his idea, Cameron's voice broke the deafening silence that had fallen between the brothers.

"Braeden, you around?"

Still glaring at Sean, Braeden released her, then slid his cell phone out of his pocket and flipped it open. "Yes, I'm here."

"Checked up on your wife lately?"

Obviously Cameron had no idea she was at the Lair.

"Why?"

"Seems her town house was blown up—the authorities think it was arson. They haven't found any bodies and can't seem to find her, either. Did you want to take a run up there—"

Alexia cut him off. "No need, Cam."

"Alexia?"

Braeden answered, "Yes, it's her."

"Ah. Then I won't waste your time." Braeden's twin brother paused a moment before adding, "We do still need to discuss the chief-of-security position."

"I'll be up later." Braeden's glare turned toward her as he snapped the phone closed. "Nothing else to say?"

"No." She shrugged. "Not really." At least not to him.

He glanced back at his younger brother. "Don't you have something else to do?"

"Yeah." Sean nodded. "Security. Computers." When he didn't leave immediately, Braeden cocked an eyebrow, silently questioning why Sean wasn't moving.

She had no wish to see the brothers get into it, so she said, "Go, Sean. I'll be fine." The tension in the air eased slightly. Sean glanced at her one more time before leaving the garage.

Looking for a way to buy time, Alexia touched Braeden's forearm. "Please, I've been up all night. Can I get some rest and then we'll talk?"

His gaze fell on her hand. "Nice try. We'll talk now."

This time when he headed toward the elevators, Alexia followed. What else was she going to do? It wasn't as if he was about to leave her alone. The doors hadn't completely slid closed when she found her voice. "We're done talking."

Braeden shook his head at her statement. She didn't really think it was going to be that easy. He leaned against the far wall. "We haven't even started."

Alexia backed into the opposite corner and crossed her arms. Any other man would take that as a silent signal to keep his distance. But he wasn't any other man, and she had little hope that he'd take the hint.

"Tell me what's going on," he said.

"There's nothing going on." When he glared at her, she added, "I'm fine." She'd reached the point of exhaustion. Between her rising temper and the sick fear twisting in her gut, she was ready to scream.

"Fine?" Braeden narrowed his eyes. "Terrified is not fine."

She hated that he could still read her moods. It only infuriated her more. "Just stop it. I said I'm fine, so let it go." Alexia nearly hissed.

He held up the Beretta. The magazine was still in the trunk, but he retracted the slide to make sure the chamber was empty before handing it to her. "Here."

His actions backed up his attitude. He really didn't trust her. She dropped the gun into the pocket of her jacket.

"Why are you carrying a weapon in the first place?"

"None of your business."

Braeden curtly reminded her, "You came to me for help. Or was that just another lie?"

She raised her head, bringing her gaze to meet his. He wouldn't believe her, but it was the truth. "I've never lied to you."

"I'm amazed you can say that with a straight face." He edged closer, then leaned his shoulder against the back wall of the elevator. "Why did you bring a gun along? Who did you plan to shoot?"

Shocked that he could ask such a question, she let her jaw fall open for a brief moment before she sputtered, "I didn't plan on shooting anyone. My God, Braeden, I don't hate you or your family that much."

"So why do you have it?"

"It isn't important." More to the point, it wasn't any of his business.

"Alexia, you came here for protection. How am I supposed to protect you if I don't know what's happening?" His cold eyes glimmered as he asked, "How do I even know you actually need protection if I don't know what's going on?"

She'd had enough of his questions and insinuations. Her sigh hissed in the confined space before she asked, "Why do you bother asking me questions when you can get the answers yourself?"

"You *want* me to get to the bottom of this myself?"

"It wouldn't be the first time."

Her sarcasm only served to fire his anger. Jaw clenched, Braeden leaned away from the wall, hit the stop button on the elevator, then closed the narrow distance between them.

She felt the warmth of his body. He was too close. He loomed over her like a dark, threatening beast. She pressed her spine hard into the corner.

But he wasn't backing off. He only leaned closer. She was unable to draw a breath. Whether she meant to or not, she'd goaded him with an invitation he obviously wasn't about to ignore.

"If you're so damn eager to feel my presence, look at me."

Resisting the urge to push him away, Alexia lifted her gaze to his. And her breath came at last, long and shaky. It had been years since she'd let anyone this close to her—physically or mentally.

She gasped as his will immediately penetrated her protective wall, forcing it to crumble. Alexia shivered at the ease with which he skimmed beyond her shock at seeing his Phantom, then past the conversations in the garage and his office.

He drifted over the frustration she'd felt during the trip to the Lair. Visions of the rockslide, rain and fog sprang to life. As did her fear of being followed. The wax on her Thunderbird gave justification to that fear.

Braeden coaxed her mind further back and Alexia saw the envelope on her desk, the attack in the parking lot and her shooting the one man.

She relived seeing the limo and Phantom pull away from her town house right before the place exploded. The intensity of her fear escalated.

But the sudden trembling of her legs wasn't from fear of those who were after her. Her roiling emotions whipped back and forth between her memories and the realization of how her earlier fears of him were mere imitations. Now, with every beat of her heart, true fear slammed at her.

He could kill or harm her with nothing more than a thought. She'd always known that. But until today, she'd feared the harm he could cause her emotionally far more than the threat of any physical danger.

"Stop it."

The deep commanding timbre of his voice flowed into her veins like molten lava, heating her blood, bringing memories of a kiss, a touch, entwined limbs, flooding to the forefront of her mind. The memories converged with her fears—then mastered them. Their attraction had always been strong, but now it was deadly.

Long-forgotten senses and feelings came alive too suddenly to control them. Her knees nearly buckled as a path of fire snaked the length of her body, then returned to throb low in her belly.

His eyes widened, then narrowed as her mind tripped unbidden over memories best left undisturbed. But when he leaned closer and his unsteady, warm breath feathered across her cheek, she realized that he, too, was captured by the current of what bound them together. And she knew the power she held over his intrusion into her thoughts.

Alexia moaned softly and purposely remembered a time they'd been too angry at each other to sleep or even talk. Instead, they'd taken their frustration to bed.

That particular sexual encounter had been anything but gentle or loving. But it had been downright breathtaking and one of the most erotic nights they'd shared. His hands had held her steady. Her fingers had dug into his arms yanking him closer…closer.

It wasn't hard for her to awaken not only the visual memories, but also the sensations and emotions she'd experienced. Her body had burned with lust. Every muscle, every tendon strung as tight as a bowstring, straining for fulfillment.

Braeden had set any semblance of civilized man aside and become the beast he was named for. Her dragon came to life and scared the hell out of her. For the first time she'd felt pure fear slink cold and deadly through her body.

She wanted to run away, but the glitter in his eyes mesmerized her and promised her untold passion. Held enthralled by a promise she couldn't fathom, she remained… terrified and intrigued.

Removing her cotton summer dress proved no obstacle, as the thin fabric tore easily in one fluid rip from hem to neckline beneath his two-handed grasp. Emboldened by the action, she'd shouted at him.

Before the first curse fully left her mouth, Braeden threaded his fingers through the hair at the back of her head and jerked her closer, cutting off her words with his mouth. The unyielding kiss curled her toes.

Alexia sighed raggedly at the memory as her toes now curled inside her sneakers. She'd meant to set Braeden's mind awhirl. But her own heart hammered and the sound of her unsteady breaths mingled with his.

He'd claimed her that night. The Dragon of Mirabilus had marked her as his mate. Ignoring her unvoiced fear, his hands, lips and tongue had set fire to every inch of her body until she writhed on the bed unabashedly begging him for more.

Alexia closed her eyes against the spinning in her head. The memories, the feelings, came faster and faster. Her cheeks burned. Her tongue stuck to the roof of her mouth as she tried to swallow. What had she done? The loneliness and longing she'd locked away inside burst free, nearly knocking the wind from her.

Braeden now groaned with frustrated rage before sliding his hand to the back of her head. His touch tingled hot and cold down her neck. Yet a part of her welcomed it, yearned for more.

Lowering his mouth to hers, he whispered on a near growl, "You should have stayed away."

He was right. She should have stayed away. She'd been insane to come here.

His lips covered hers and Alexia's heart pounded so hard she truly thought it would burst. She swallowed his warning and clutched at his shoulders for support. She knew he didn't want her here—any more than she'd wanted to come to the Lair.

She should pull free of him and leave. It would be better for everyone. And much safer for her.

But the desperate need created by her memories wiped away any rational thought of self-preservation. Even as confusion washed through her mind, her body suffered from no such confusion.

He'd been angry at her that night, too. But while his demanding touches had surprised her and drawn cries from her lips, they hadn't harmed her. In truth, she'd done more harm dragging her fingernails across his flesh.

Braeden flinched beneath her touch. He *was* sharing her memories.

Did he see how much that night meant to her? To them? Did he know how much she'd loved him then? And trusted him? She'd known full well the magic he possessed and yet she'd given him free rein to do whatever he wanted.

Her throat tightened. Regardless of the danger—physical or emotional—the need to feel his touch, to lose herself in his kiss, urged her on. Alexia leaned against him.

Braeden pulled her close. His arms wrapped around her like bands of steel.

Nearly drunk with the headiness of her first taste of power over him, Alexia teased him deeper into her memories. No matter how rough their lovemaking had been that night, the next morning he'd awakened her with gentle strokes and near-reverent kisses.

And she'd—

Braeden froze. He tore his mouth from hers and slammed the palms of his hands against the wall of the elevator on either side of her head. "Enough."

Alexia swayed from the harshness of his exit from her thoughts. But she stared up at him, refusing to be bullied by his nasty tone of voice or the evil glitter in his eyes. "What?"

"Don't you ever try anything like that again."

She raised one eyebrow. "Then stay the hell out of my mind."

Braeden lowered his arms and stared down at her. How had she learned to intentionally direct her thoughts in a manner that beckoned him to follow? When had she become so calculating?

He stepped away. While he now knew what had driven her to the Lair, not once had he sensed the presence of another. If someone had sent her the pages, or as she'd insisted they'd magically appeared and the sender had broken through her wall of protection, she'd managed to bury that information so deep he couldn't find it.

Before she could sense his growing unease, he pressed the button to restart the elevator. "I'll show you to your suite."

As the elevator came to a stop, Braeden heard her sudden intake of breath and turned to see her crumple. Without a second thought, he caught her.

"Alexia?"

He frowned at her unfocused gaze and when her head lolled forward, spilling long, blond waves over her face, he lifted her into his arms. Silently cursing himself for probing her mind to the point of exhaustion, Braeden headed toward his suite and paused briefly at the door.

His original plan had been for her to stay in the suite next to his. But he wasn't about to leave her alone until she'd had enough rest to function normally.

Since the key card to his door was in his jacket pocket, Braeden quietly ordered, "Open up." He heard the latch click before the door silently swung open.

Alexia jerked awake, struggling in his arms. "Put me down."

He tightened his hold and ignored her until reaching his bedroom.

She took one look at his bed, gasped, then asked, "What are you doing?"

"Taking you to bed."

"We may still be married but—" Alexia pushed against his shoulder "—I am *not* sharing your bed."

"You're right." He held her over the bed a moment and stared into her near-wild gaze before dropping her the short distance onto the mattress, then heading toward the door.

Over his shoulder he said, "I'll be sleeping on the sofa." He didn't bother to mention that it was the middle of the afternoon and he wouldn't be sleeping anywhere for quite a while.

He paused in the doorway. "There are T-shirts and sweats in the dresser—help yourself." He hitched a thumb at the door on the far wall. "The shower is that way."

"Braeden?"

He turned to look at her. "What?"

Alexia frowned, looked away, then shook her head. "Never mind, it was nothing."

Her hair hung about her slumping shoulders in disarray. And her normally bright blue eyes were drained of their brilliance. She looked so damn weak that it was all he could do not to cross the room and gather her into his arms.

He quickly reminded himself that she'd brought this current fear and confusion on herself. He wasn't about to get so wrapped up in his attraction to her that he lost sight of the simple fact that because of her, good people had died. He didn't trust her, especially not after that little game in the elevator, and he couldn't let himself forget that, not even for a moment.

Yet it was beneath him to torment someone who couldn't fight back. "Alexia, that wasn't my Phantom. Mine was delivered early this morning. Go to sleep."

Nathan leaned against a tree and shivered from the cold damp of the mountain fog. He hated the damp. But he didn't want to risk detection by the Dragon, so entering the Lair hadn't been a consideration.

Instead, he'd taken the form of an inconspicuous squirrel and hidden in this tree to watch events unfold against the face of a smooth-polished scrying mirror.

Not only hadn't the Dragon detected his presence outside the Lair or in Alexia's mind, Drake had fallen prey to an uninitiate's manipulation. A woman, no less.

Amazing.

But truly excellent for him.

A cold breeze ruffled his fur, making him shiver again. Why anyone would want to build a resort in this godforsaken land was beyond his understanding. Why not someplace warm and sunny? Someplace with a beach and the pounding ocean.

Although he had to admit, the rugged terrain and the forest provided excellent concealment.

In truth, the climate didn't matter in the least. Because if all went according to plan, Braeden Drake wouldn't be opening his resort anytime soon—at least not in this lifetime. However, at the moment things were not exactly going according to his plan.

Certain the Dragon was too engrossed with Alexia to sense him, Nathan morphed back into his normal form and dropped lightly to his feet at the base of the tree.

What was he going to do with these two?

He hadn't thought for a moment that they'd fall into each other's arms. In the past he'd put up too many roadblocks to keep them apart for that to happen.

But he hadn't expected quite this level of confusion, anger and mistrust. Nathan patted the box in the pocket of his cloak. "Damn you, Aelthed, for binding such nonsense about love to the grimoire."

When the elder wizard had set the binding into motion, Nathan had laughed, thinking it would be a simple spell to break. Now it seemed the laugh was on him. But soon he would have his way.

He was tired of waiting. This had to be the right couple.

Every instinct he possessed told him that this was finally the generation that would give him what he sought. He didn't want to wait yet another lifetime before gaining the power he deserved.

If this plan failed, if he did not gain the knowledge of the grimoire, there was only one way he could be Hierophant, the most powerful Druid alive. The Drakes and their kin would simply have to die.

He'd been denied the position of High Druid far too long now. Unable to change the course of history, he'd spent all these centuries watching one Drake after another attain what was rightfully his.

The thought of killing gave Nathan no cause for concern. They would die just as easily as the others. With one major difference—if he killed them slowly enough, Nathan knew he could drain them of their powers, absorbing the energy, the strength, from their souls until they heaved their last breath.

The entertainment value alone almost made forgoing the translation worth it. But he'd waited too long for this chance. He would try once more before ridding the world of the last remaining Drakes.

Silently reaching up, Nathan snatched a dove from its perch and slit the bird's belly with a fingernail. He let the body fall from his hand, then squatted to read the entrails.

A hushed sigh of relief whistled through his lips. Yes, he most definitely had the right dragon and the right mate. They needed only to rediscover the love they'd lost.

Unfortunately matchmaking wasn't his forte. So there had to be another method to get the Dragon and his wife in bed together. Surely if they renewed their physical lust, they would soon come to recognize their love.

But how—

A smile slowly curved his lips. He stood up, then chanted a spell before stepping off the side of the mountain path into the mist-laden air.

Chapter 5

Alexia jerked awake and sprang upright on the strange bed. She stared nervously around the semi-darkened room. Her pulse beat rapidly as she tried to clear the fog of sleep. Where was she?

A quick study of the room revealed heavy, dark furniture. Extremely masculine, suited to a man. And as an all-too-familiar spicy scent rose from the bed, it came flooding back.

This wasn't just any man's bedroom. It was Braeden's.

She groaned and shoved the covers aside. The cool air raced across her skin. Her...very...naked...skin. Alexia didn't remember undressing herself. Actually, she didn't remember anything after Braeden dropped her on the bed and left the room.

"Why that..." She swallowed her curse at the sound of someone moving around on the other side of the closed bedroom door.

"Are you awake?"

She glared at the door a minute before answering, "No." She didn't want to deal with him right now. She was tired of being angry, frightened and confused. And he'd only intensify those emotions.

"There are clean towels in the bathroom and a robe hanging on the door."

Warmth flowed into her limbs at the gravelly sound of his voice. Alexia frowned. More than anything else, she was extremely tired of *that*.

How was it possible that a grown woman had no control whatsoever over her physical responses to a man she disliked so intensely? She wasn't at all certain she could even trust him not to harm her. Why couldn't her head explain that to her body?

Until the past couple of days, she'd done just fine without him—most of the time. After a while she'd even been able to put thoughts of him from her mind—more or less. But the second she saw him again, her body went into some lust-crazed overdrive mode she couldn't seem to control.

Whatever happened to keeping this impersonal?

With an exasperated sigh, Alexia rose and headed to the shower. There was no need to put herself through this turmoil any longer than necessary. She would just translate the manual, then get away from the Lair and Braeden as soon as she could.

Tripping on what felt like clothes, she reached over and flipped on the overhead light. Her clothes were strewn on the floor.

Braeden hadn't undressed her. Unless something had changed, and she doubted it, he never would have tossed clothes on the floor. Not even if they were dirty. He would have folded them up and stacked them neatly on the dresser.

In a strange way, it was nice to know that some things never changed. She scooted them into a pile and went into the bathroom.

To her surprise a small basket on the double sink held all her usual toiletries. Braeden had obviously gone shopping while she slept. Or he'd sent someone.

Either way, she now had her brands of shampoo, conditioner, deodorant, toothpaste and even lavender soap. She rooted through the basket and found a wide-toothed comb, a purple, soft-bristled kid's toothbrush, body lotion, powder and a pack of various sized barrettes for her hair.

This wasn't fair. He couldn't go and get all domesticated on her now. She didn't want to owe him anything more than what was absolutely necessary.

She rushed through her shower, then slipped into the robe before going back out to the bedroom—and coming to a rocking stop. Light streamed in from the doorway and a shadow stretched across the floor.

The rustle of bags preceded Braeden into the room. Without looking at her, he dropped the bags on the bed, the contents spilling out onto the covers. "Get dressed. Dinner is waiting."

When he turned and paused to stare at her, Alexia recognized the anger etching frown lines across his forehead. Yet, while he was no less mad at her, something else simmered beneath the rage. An emotion she recognized, because it flared to life within her, too.

She swallowed past the dryness in her mouth as heat flooded her body to settle between her thighs. Her cheeks burned, and from the hungry look darkening his eyes he knew they shared the same response.

Before this unwelcome desire could convince her to do something she would only come to regret, Alexia searched for something to say. "I…thank you for the…shower things…I…" She ran her tongue over lips trying to ease the growing tingle as they anticipated his kiss.

He didn't say a word. His steady stare didn't waver. It felt as if he pierced the thick fabric of the robe with his gaze.

The cool air shifted against her belly, bringing with it the realization there was no fabric to pierce. The robe had fallen open.

She should pull the robe closed. Order him to leave. But she couldn't make her hands and voice obey. Instead, she stood there, her heart pounding, her breath ragged, frozen in place by the heat of his gaze.

He walked slowly toward her. Steadily, purposefully, like a beast intent on obtaining its prey.

The fire on her cheeks burned hotter. The maddening pulse low in her belly beat harder, faster.

Braeden curled his fingers through her still-damp hair and tugged her head back.

Alexia closed her eyes and parted her lips, intent on telling him to leave. But as he caressed her breast, his strong fingers expertly stroking and teasing the already tightening tip, the only sound that escaped her throat was a soft moan.

His lips covered hers, accepting the wordless invitation.

Breathless and on fire, she grasped his shoulders, not caring what tomorrow would bring. This moment was the only thing that mattered.

The buzz of a cell phone cut through the thickness of lust. Braeden tore his mouth from hers on a groan. Without releasing his hold on the back of her head, he whipped the phone from his chest pocket and flipped it open. "What?"

Alexia's pulse slowed at the sharpness of his voice.

What the hell was she doing? Had she lost all ability to think rationally?

This was not the way to keep herself safe. Giving in to uncontrollable lust would gain her nothing more than heartbreak.

Braeden's frown returned as he nearly snarled into the phone, "It'll keep until later." He snapped the cellular closed and slid it back into his pocket.

Her knees shook when he looked back down at her. It would be, oh, so easy to ignore the warnings of her mind and let her passion retake control.

Braeden stared at her for just a moment before relaxing his hold on her head and stepping away. On his way toward the door, he pointed at the bags. Without pausing, he said, "Get dressed and come eat."

Her knees shook so badly and her legs felt so rubbery it was all she could do not to slip to the floor. But she was afraid that if she didn't get dressed and go out to the other room to eat, he'd come back in to see what held her up.

That was the last thing she wanted. She didn't have to think twice about it, for she knew that her response would be the same and that he'd not make the mistake of letting anything interrupt them.

Alexia hesitantly tipped the bags upside down and watched the garments tumble onto the bed.

It appeared he'd purchased everything she would need for at least a week, if not longer.

Everything was there—jeans, blouses, sweaters, socks, a pair of hiking boots, bras, panties, pajamas, two pairs of sweats, a heavier jacket than what she had with her, a robe and slippers.

She didn't know whether to laugh or cry. Everything he bought was something she would have picked up for herself.

How dare he have such a good memory! She rolled her eyes. The man filed away every little thing. If he couldn't instantly remember something, all he had to do was search his own mind and whatever he wanted would be there.

After slipping into some underclothes and socks, she pulled on a pair of sweats and a long-sleeved shirt before putting the other items back in the bags.

Alexia turned to pick up her dirty clothes from the floor and saw that they were now folded and stacked on the dresser. He just couldn't help himself. The man was a neat freak, methodical and predictable. Too bad she couldn't predict anything else about him.

She paused at the bedroom door and took slow, deep breaths, trying to find a way to calm the uneasiness washing over her.

Not a few hours ago she'd wondered if this risk was worth the pain it could cause. She still didn't have the answer.

Although now she knew exactly how much pain and heartache this trip would gain her. She desperately needed to find a way to shield her heart from what Braeden did to her.

She wished they could be like two normal acquaintances—polite, yet distant from each other. But that would never happen. There was far too much between them to maintain any measure of distance. And too many unsolved issues for them to be polite to each other.

Why hadn't she realized that before pulling through the gates?

Simple. Because she hadn't considered how much she had missed his kiss, his touch and the very sound of his voice. She hadn't considered everything they'd once shared—the passion, the love or even the pain.

If nothing else, she needed to be honest with herself. This man, her husband, could crush her heart more easily than anyone alive, simply because a part of her still cared far too much.

He said she couldn't leave and Alexia believed that he would stop her. So that stripped away the option of getting into her car and driving off. Even if she did, where would she go?

As far as she could tell, she was left with only two options. Either let things continue the way they were and remain silent, as the passion, the caring and the longing tore her apart.

Or face the past head on. Yes, Braeden would then know how much she still cared, leaving her wide open for the heartbreak she dreaded. And yes, she would be forcing herself to relive the pain of the accident, losing the baby and her husband all over again.

And in the end she still might find herself facing the loss one more time.

But if it was all out in the open, wouldn't she be better able to make her peace with the past and move on?

Alexia shook her head. All her wonderings and all her silent questions only left her with more unanswerable questions.

She jerked open the door and wandered toward the living room. She stopped in the center of the room and stared at the view before her.

The panoramic vista of fog-shrouded mountains wiped away her confusion, anger, fear and still-lingering desire. Untamed wilderness tumbled into the room through the floor-to-ceiling windows.

Had Braeden not moved forward to slide open the door and step out onto a balcony, she wouldn't have realized anything existed beyond the sheer wall of glass.

To her it appeared the view was unobstructed. What would most likely be a spectacular panorama on a clear day was now veiled by mist as the sun began to set. The murky view added new depth to her sense of foreboding.

The fog swirled around Braeden. While seated behind his desk, he'd been the picture of Lord of the Castle. He swung his gaze to her and Alexia's breath caught. Now he looked every inch the High Druid. As uncivilized and wild as the untamed nature surrounding them, Braeden could easily have stepped out of the Dark Ages.

Beneath his tailored suit, expensive shoes and the businessman's polish beat not only the heart of a dragon, but the soul of a warrior—a warrior trained in wizardry.

If the academic world knew half what she did, the history books would need to be rewritten. There was so much she could have included in her paper, but she'd held back purposely. Knowing what chaos could be created by the truth, she'd intentionally danced around small lies and half-truths.

And she'd done so without guilt—at least, none where the university was concerned. They'd coerced her into writing the paper to begin with by dangling her degree just out of reach. They'd been desperate. So desperate she'd chosen lying and concealment, instead.

In her what-if scenario on the Dragonierre's Manual, she'd not mentioned that the book did indeed exist, nor had she even hinted that the Druids of Gaul had not fallen into extinction.

Had she claimed either to be true, Alexia knew that her life and the life of the man now staring at her so intently might have been over. A risk she'd been unwilling to take.

She'd thought she'd held back enough. She'd worked so hard to edit out any line, any word, that might have hinted at the truth.

But her painstaking work hadn't been enough. Now, she and the Drakes were all in danger—from an enemy she knew nothing about. Abruptly she asked, "Who is the Learned?"

He didn't turn around, but said from over his shoulder, "You're working with them. You tell me."

She flinched. "They may have left me the pages, but I am not working with them. You know that."

"Do I?"

"You saw what happened." She ignored the flush warming her cheeks as she remembered the episode in the elevator. "How could you think I'd work with someone who threatened me?"

Braeden leaned on the railing, his mood as murky as the fog. "I saw what brought you here, nothing more."

"What else is there?"

"The being who left the pages, the one who wanted the translation, the one you said got into your thoughts."

"I *said?* You think I made it up?"

"It's possible." After a few moments of silence, Braeden beckoned her out into the mist. "The Learned are a long-lost part of the Mirabilus clan."

Drawn by the view and his apparent willingness to talk, she forced down the impending doom clutching at her and joined him on the balcony, making certain to stay out of his reach. "Why would someone in your family kill your parents? Why is Danielle so afraid of him?"

"Them, not him. It's more than one person. Although if Nathan still lives, he'd be more than enough to deal with."

A damp mountain breeze wafted cold against Alexia's cheeks. But she'd gladly suffer the chill. It helped to clear her head. "How so?"

Braeden leaned on the railing. "He was born in the twelfth century and rumored to be immortal. If that's true, it might be a little hard to defeat him."

She closed her eyes and rubbed her temples. She'd come to accept many otherworldly abilities since meeting Braeden and his family. But it was hard to believe what he'd just told her. Looking back at him, she said, "Immortal? Braeden, please."

"I grew up hearing tales about Nathan and his brood." He shrugged. "I've never met him or any member of his family. I assumed the tales were just that—tales, nothing more. But Danielle is certain he killed my parents."

"I take it he's a wizard, too?"

"So I'm told. He was supposed to have been named the High Druid at one point in time, but that position was granted to a Drake."

She shook her head. "So he's waited this long to take his revenge?"

"Unlikely."

The cry of a hawk soaring somewhere above them caught her attention and she craned her neck to follow the sound. Unable to see through the wall of mist, she closed her eyes and let the mountain's breath wash over her. It seeped steadily into her veins, soothing her jagged nerves, calming her riotous heartbeat.

Alexia sighed. The fear that had been building since yesterday began to fade away in the fog.

The hawk screeched loudly, breaking the silence as if in warning. The hair on her arms stood on end. She frowned, then opened her eyes. What danger had the raptor sensed? She glanced at Braeden. He still stared off into the fog as if his attention was directed as hers had been—on the fog and mountain air.

She could see nothing on either side of the balcony that would cause alarm. But the fog was so thick she couldn't see more than six feet in front of her.

It felt as if someone watched her. Even through the mantle of mist and smoke, the being studied her with a focus so intense it set her stomach churning.

Alexia stilled her mind but could find no hint of intrusion. Still, the sense of being watched was as tangible as the balcony beneath her feet.

She went back inside. While the feeling lessened, it didn't go completely away.

"What's wrong?" Braeden followed her back into the suite, closing the door behind him.

She brushed her hands up and down the thin sleeves of her shirt. "Nothing, I was just getting cold."

He sat down in one of the chairs flanking the stone fireplace and pulled the coffee table between the chairs. "Sit down and eat."

"I'm not hungry."

"You haven't eaten since yesterday. Sit down and eat."

Had he always been this demanding? She sat down in the other chair. Arguing with him over food wasn't going to get rid of the anger still evident in his eyes.

She met his gaze, and noticing the laugh lines around his mouth, she wondered when he'd last laughed about anything.

Braeden handed her a glass of wine, removed the domed covers from the plates of salad, then unwrapped a basket of rolls.

She drank half the wine, then set it down to pick up a fork and stab at her salad before taking a bite.

One swallow later her stomach growled, letting her know how hungry she was. Braeden shook his head, but thankfully didn't say a word.

While they ate their meal in silence, Alexia wondered why she felt the need to goad him the way she did. If being overly contrary with him was some strange way of protecting herself, it was senseless. Feeding his anger would get her nowhere.

She hadn't always been like that. So when had she started? She paused, midbite, frowning. *After the accident.* Before Braeden noticed her hesitation, she brought the fork to her lips.

Why? She swallowed her bite of salad and nearly choked as the answer tightened her throat.

He handed her the half-empty glass of wine. Their fingers barely touched, yet the unexpected jolt of electricity made her gasp, lodging more salad in her throat.

She downed the remaining wine and gestured for more. Braeden handed her a glass of water as he refilled her wineglass.

Alexia gulped the water, clearing her throat in the process. She drew in a deep breath of air.

The only reason she'd started goading him was to intentionally get him angry so they wouldn't talk. If they didn't talk, she didn't have to admit her fears or her agony. She didn't have to tell him of the guilt she bore or of the blame she placed on him. She didn't have to verbalize her despair or the grief that trailed her even today.

Her stomach knotted and she set the water down before retrieving the glass of wine. Staring at him, she tried swallowing her guilt along with the wine. It didn't work, so she held out the now empty glass.

But instead of filling it again, Braeden plucked the goblet from her fingers, set it on the table, then pushed the table aside.

"What's going on?"

She had known this was coming. Just like the clothes on the floor, it was another quirk. He wasn't going to stop until he had an explanation for everything he'd seen in her mind. It was all she could do not to huff in resignation as she leaned back in the chair. "You already know why I'm here."

"I know some men attacked you." He ticked off the items on his fingers. "That your town house was blown up and that you thought it was my Phantom parked in front."

With three fingers raised in the air, he said, "Those three things don't explain why you're here or why you're packing a gun." He lowered his hand. "As I already told you, my Phantom was just delivered this morning. I haven't even driven it yet."

Something in the tone of his voice made her believe him. Perhaps he didn't want her dead. If he did, he could have pushed her over the balcony. Except that would have been a little obvious.

However, someone had forced her into the position of coming to him. The why was fairly obvious—they wanted the whole book translated and Braeden had the book. Still, the question was who. Was it this Nathan?

Or was it Braeden? Would he have gone to such lengths for the translation? No. It would have made more sense for him to seek reconciliation with her, even if only temporarily, to get what he wanted.

"Quit thinking and tell me what's going on."

A telltale flush heated her cheeks. After all this time it was still so easy for him that he needed no special powers to decipher her expressions or body language. At times she nearly hated him for that skill.

"I already told you all I know. Someone wants the manuscript translated."

"You just discovered that yesterday morning. You had no clue that they meant you harm, so why were you carrying a gun?"

"To protect myself."

He laced his fingers behind his head and leaned back. "From?"

Alexia stared at him. With his arms pitched at that angle and his chest expanded, he looked like a dragon with its wings spread. Worse, he looked like some primitive warrior. A powerful man, strong and sure of himself. Someone who could protect her from any danger. She cleared her throat. If she weren't careful, she'd be throwing herself at that muscular expanse.

When she didn't answer, he asked, "Who is Jack?"

Damn. How had he made that connection? She nearly gagged on her curse.

"Nobody."

"A boyfriend?"

"*A* boyfriend? You make it sound like I have a dozen on a string."

"Is he?"

"God, no." She wanted to disabuse him of that notion right away. They had enough between them without the added complication of an imagined lover. "No. He was just someone I worked with. We had coffee a couple of times, but that was it."

"How is he connected with the gun?"

She should have known Braeden wouldn't give up. She rose, unwilling to look at him, thinking it easier to pace the floor instead. "He wanted to be more than a fellow employee. I explained to him that I was married, but he didn't seem to hear, or want to hear me."

"I'm surprised you remembered."

This was something else she should have expected—his pointed jabs. Trying her best to ignore them, she continued, "One of the employees held their wedding reception at the museum. We went together—"

"On a date."

Again she paid no attention to his tone, responding, instead, to his comment. "All of us were there. Jack and I only drove together because my car was in the shop."

"Not a wise move on your part."

No kidding. She'd figured that out far too late, though. "Yes, well, he proceeded to get drunk, so I took a cab home."

"Something you should have taken to get there."

Ready to scream, she glared at him. "I made a mistake in judgment. That's all."

Braeden lowered his arms. "The gun?"

Alexia took a deep breath. "Jack was busted for drunk driving on his way home."

"And?"

She stopped in front of him. Something wasn't quite right. While his comments made it sound as if this was all news to him, his expressions, his tone of voice seemed more bored than anything else.

She narrowed her eyes and tapped one foot. "You already know the *and,* don't you?"

"You mean the part where he was busted for drug possession?"

Alexia flinched. "So you've tracked more than just my spending habits. Did you pay someone to watch me?"

"No, but from now on it's a given that you'll have someone shadowing your every move. The arrest was in the paper."

"I doubt if Jack getting busted made the newspaper down here. What'd you do—run a search on my name every day?"

"Ah, Alexia, your life wasn't that interesting. Once a week was enough to keep tabs on you."

Fervid tremors coursed hotly through her. Alexia curled her fingers into fists, closed her eyes and tried her best to count to ten.

When she opened her eyes, she found herself nose to collar bone with Braeden. He'd risen soundlessly and now loomed over her.

"You can't hide anything from me." He cupped her chin and tipped her head back. "Do you understand that? It doesn't require magic to know where you go or what you do. If you don't just tell me what I need to know, I will find it out myself. And I won't have to delve inside your head to do so."

"You pay people to watch me?"

"When I need to, yes."

She didn't understand why he would go that far. "I left you. There was no reason for you to concern yourself with me."

"You still use my name. You are still my wife."

"And you were worried that I would embarrass you or disgrace your name somehow?"

He leaned closer. "Don't be a fool."

Alexia groaned. Every logical thought in her mind screamed, *Push him away, don't keep letting him do this to you!* But her heart urged her to lean against him, to let his lips and hands remind her again of the magic they'd once shared.

She uncurled her fingers and placed her hands against his chest. "Don't. Braeden, please, don't."

His mouth hovered a breath above hers. "You want this as much as I do." His lips were warm as he brushed hers with a kiss. "Can you deny that?"

Alexia did her best to ignore what his touch did to her. She knew that the sudden difficulty with breathing could be calmed. The urge to thread her fingers through his hair and draw his mouth back to hers would be quieted. The heat flaring to life in her blood would cool.

Yet while she could eventually steady the erratic pounding of her heart, she would never be able to rid herself of the desperate longing his caress produced.

"No, damn you, I can't deny it."

He released her. "The gun?"

Alexia nearly groaned at the loss of his touch. She closed her eyes tightly while a shiver raced the length of her body. Finally she looked at him asking, "Gun?"

"The Beretta."

How could he stand there and act as if he wasn't bothered in the least by what had just happened? She sat down and forced herself to fake a calm she didn't feel.

There was no point lying about it. As he'd warned her, if she didn't just tell him, he'd find out himself. "While Jack was in jail, he called a couple of times threatening to get even with me for testifying against him, so I learned how to use a gun just in case. The gun-club instructor said the Beretta was pretty accurate and it was small enough to fit my grip. I figured it'd be easy for me to handle."

"Small isn't necessarily easy to handle."

"I figured it'd be easier to handle than, say—a tank."

Braeden crossed to the glass doors. "Jack is out of jail?"

"Yes, he called yesterday morning before I left for work, promising to show up at the museum." She'd started the day out thinking her only worry would be Jack, so she'd slipped the gun into her jacket pocket.

"Did he?"

"Thankfully, no."

Without turning around, Braeden asked, "Did you kill the man you shot?"

Kill him? Just the thought made Alexia feel ill. "No, I couldn't do that. I just winged his arm."

"So he's still out there."

It wasn't a question, so she didn't answer. But he was right. The men were still out there.

"Would you recognize him?"

"No. They all wore face masks."

Braeden muttered something under his breath that sounded suspiciously like a curse before turning away from the view.

He pointed toward a hallway to his right—the opposite direction of his bedroom. "There's another bedroom with a master bath that way."

Completely businesslike, he nodded toward what looked like a wet bar. She could see the kitchen beyond it from where she sat. "There's a dining room and laundry room at the rear of the kitchen."

"The den is there." He pointed at the French doors at the front left of the living room.

She'd come to him for help, for protection, not to play house. "There aren't any other rooms available?"

"Of course there are. There are 220, to be exact."

"Then—"

He stepped in front of her. "No. You'll stay here."

"In your suite?"

"Yes."

The idea terrified her, turned the blood in her veins cold. "Why?"

Without any trace of emotion, he said, "Because I don't trust you."

"Am I your—prisoner, then?"

"No. This time when you decide to run away, instead of coming to me, I will be there to stop you."

He's gotten too good at second-guessing her. "I didn't run away. I just left."

Braeden turned and walked to the entry door. With his hand on the knob, he asked, "Who do you think your lies hurt more? Me? Or you?"

Before she could respond, the door slammed closed behind him.

Chapter 6

"My lies?"

Braeden heard Alexia's furious shout through the closed door.

The door handle jiggled and he stopped, turned around and waited for her to barge into the hallway. A shouting match in the middle of the family's private floor would be the final straw to this already wasted day.

When the handle didn't turn, meaning she was too irate even to notice that she had to push the button to turn it, he took a step in the opposite direction—toward the elevators.

With any luck he could get out of the hallway before she figured out how to open the door. He wasn't escaping. He had a business to run, a resort to open. Cam wanted his input on the candidates for the chief-of-security position. He'd already put his brother off twice today.

Behind him, Alexia pounded on the door, shouting, "Damn you, Drake, get back here!"

At the same moment, Sean sauntered around the corner at the other end of the hallway. He'd obviously heard Alexia, because he crossed his arms and leaned against the wall with an arrogant smirk on his lips and an amused gleam in his eye.

Ten or so years ago, Braeden would have wiped both the smirk and the gleam from Sean's face. If Sean wasn't careful, he still might.

Braeden turned back to his suite and thumped the door, giving Alexia warning that he was coming in. Again, instead of retrieving his key card, he just waved the door open.

It slammed against the inside wall hard enough to leave a dent in the drywall. And slammed again when he stepped into the suite and waved the door closed behind him.

Alexia wasted no time. She rushed at him, stuck out her hand and poked her index finger against his chest.

"Don't you dare slam a door in my face again!"

He grabbed her arms and pushed her away. "You don't want to do this."

"I don't?" Alexia's voice raised half an octave. Her breathing was heavy and hard. "How dare you tell me what I do or don't want to do!"

"Alexia, don't."

His softly spoken warning would have made a sane person think twice. It was apparent Alexia currently had no illusions of being sane. "Or what?" She stood toe to toe with him, glaring up at him. "What will you do, Braeden?"

She really didn't want an answer to that. Her eyes shimmered like sapphires against the flush of her face. Her chest heaved, and her lips parted with the force of her breathing.

What he wanted to do was kiss her until her breathing turned ragged with lust.

Braeden paused at the turn his thoughts had taken. Following that road would gain him nothing but trouble. And he had enough of that right now.

She poked him again. "Answer me."

Oh, he had every intention of answering her—in his own time and in his own way. It was obvious she was going out of her way to make him angrier than he already was.

What sort of game was this? What benefit did she think to gain from making him totally lose his temper?

"Are you listening to me?" She raised her hand toward his arm.

Braeden stepped out of her reach. Since she wasn't going to let it go, he pulled out his cell phone and buzzed Cam. "We're going to have to put this off until morning."

Cam laughed before saying, "I'm shocked."

Braeden didn't bother to reply. He turned the phone off, tossed it onto the bar, then took off his suit jacket and loosened his tie while heading toward the bedroom.

"Don't you walk away from me."

He stopped, but didn't turn. "Since you're so damn anxious to have a fight, I'm going to get out of these clothes first."

"Oh, we have nothing to fight about. I'll just leave."

At that he did turn around. But instead of going to Alexia, he made a show of snapping his fingers at the door. She started this. And this time she wasn't walking away. "Go ahead, try."

She did, but after tugging at the door, yelled at him, "Why, you—"

Before slamming the bedroom door, he shouted back, "Hold that thought."

Alexia stormed to the bar. She jerked open the small fridge beneath the counter. The selection included regular beer or light beer. She kicked the door closed.

What she wanted was a double shot of scotch. Anything that would help lessen the pure fury pounding in her head and chest.

But the scotch would only make her sick, and that wouldn't do much to improve her mood.

Why was she so livid? She poured a glass of water and stared at Braeden's bedroom door. Her rage only grew the longer it took him to reappear.

Three years ago she'd have backed down. But she was done backing down. This moment had been a long time coming. Years, to be precise.

She was tired of being called a liar. Whether he did so outright or in so many words, the accusation was there. And it stung more than she could say.

The sound of running water from his shower dragged a frustrated scream from her throat. If he thought taking his sweet time was going to calm her down, he was wrong.

It only fueled her desire for a good, old-fashioned argument. The kind they'd never had. She snorted and raised the glass of water toward his room in a mock salute before leaning her elbows on the countertop. This time neither one of them was walking away.

By the time she swallowed the last of the water, his door opened. Alexia set down her empty glass and turned to meet him head-on.

In his usual brusque manner, he stalked toward her wearing nothing but a pair of baggy sweatpants.

Expecting him to stop in front of her, Alexia planted her feet and lifted her chin.

But he didn't stop, he walked right up against her and

kept pushing her backward until she was pinned by the hard wall behind her and the solid wall of muscle in front.

"Get away from me." She lifted her hands to push him away. But he easily grabbed her wrists and dragged them above her head.

"You were saying?"

She tried pulling her wrists free, but he held them pinned against the wall with one hand. "Let me go."

Braeden shook his head. "No."

At his cold, emotionless tone, icy dread seeped into her anger. The need to get away helped feed the now growing fear. She struggled against him, but he only pressed his chest harder against her.

Her heart pounding desperately, Alexia bent her leg, but before she could plant her knee in his groin, he kicked her legs apart and stood between them.

That attempt for freedom thwarted, she did her best to throw herself against his chest.

But when that move only drew a sigh from Braeden, she glared up at him and sucked in a heavy breath at the darkening of his narrowed gaze.

"Let me go. Please, let me go." To her horror, her voice quavered and she bit her lower lip to keep from saying anything else. She wasn't going to cry in front of him. It didn't matter that the tears were those of rage. She wasn't about to give him that kind of satisfaction.

Braeden relaxed his hold slightly. "Finished?"

Nearly exhausted, she nodded. He released her wrists, but before she could move away, he picked her up, threw her over his shoulder and headed back to the bedroom.

"What the hell are you doing?" She kicked her legs, but he only wrapped an arm around them. "Braeden, put me down."

He did, but not until he'd closed the bedroom door behind them and dropped her onto the mattress. She scrambled to the far side of the bed. But he grasped her ankle and pulled her back, ordering, "Stay there."

"I'm not your lapdog."

"No, you're my lying, back-stabbing wife."

Alexia flinched. "I am not."

"Not what? My wife? Or not a lying back-stabber?"

She slid to the far side of the bed. "Neither." He was going to make this as hard as he could.

"I told you to stay put." He reached out to grasp her arm.

She slapped at his hand. "Leave me alone."

Braeden caught her hand midair. "You don't want to make this physical."

Alexia eyes widened at his warning. She raised her other hand.

In the blink of an eye, he had her pinned flat on her back. He straddled her, his feet hooked over her ankles and his hands holding her wrists to the bed alongside her head. Looming over her, he said, "I warned you. I'm stronger and quicker than you. You can't win a physical battle with me."

"So, instead, you'll bully me."

"If that's what it takes to keep you from getting hurt, yes."

"As if you care."

"Is that what this is all about? Why should I care? You left me."

"You quit caring long before I left."

"I did? When?"

Her throat closed. She couldn't do this. Not staring up at him. Not calmly, not rationally. Not without sobbing.

"Let me go, Braeden. Just let me go."

"No. I told you not to do this. But you started it and this time we're going to finish it."

She squeezed her eyes closed and felt a tear slip down the side of her face.

"Cry all you want, Alexia." He bounced her wrists on the bed. "But, damn it, tell me when I quit caring."

"A lifetime ago."

"Melodrama will get you nowhere. Answer me."

"Before the accident." Her chest constricted. Everything was measured by that twist of fate.

"What gave you that impression?"

"You were never around."

"I was working all hours trying to open the ski resort in Switzerland."

She knew that and she also knew it had been petty to have been so hurt by his absence, but... "Even when you were home all we did was argue."

"Even when I tried to ignore you, who started those arguments?"

She had, but that was beside the point. "It was the only way I could get your attention."

"You could have come with me. You knew that. But you insisted on staying in Boston."

"I was pregnant."

"You were hormonal."

She opened her eyes and glared up at him. "That's low. I couldn't help it."

"Low? I'd say running away was farther down the scale."

"What did you want me to do?" Alexia's voice echoed in her ears. She was nearly screaming. "You blamed me for the accident."

Braeden released her wrists and sat up. "I never blamed you."

"Yes, you did. You accused me of killing your child."

"What the hell are you talking about? I never said that. I never thought that."

The tears she had been fighting to keep inside slid down her cheeks. "Yes, you did. In the hospital. I heard you tell Danielle that I'd killed your baby."

He moved off her and got up from the bed. "The only time Danielle was at the hospital was when you were still in the emergency room. Alexia, you were too out of it to even know your own name."

"What's that got to do with anything? My hearing was fine. I know what I heard."

"No. What you heard was me telling Danielle that you were nearly killed. When you heard the words 'my baby,' it was Danielle asking me about the baby. At the time the doctors weren't yet certain if he could be saved or not."

Was he telling her the truth? Alexia tried to focus on that night. But everything was jumbled.

Before she could figure it out, he asked, "When you were released from the hospital, you shut me out completely. Is that why?"

"Partly. Yes. But—"

He walked toward the bedroom door, holding out his hand. "Enough. No more."

Alexia stayed on the bed while he left the room. She didn't know what to say or do. From the brief glimpse she'd had of his face before he turned away, she got the impression he was as upset as he was angry.

About what? Maybe if she gave him time alone, he'd be able to figure it out. She tossed the covers aside. No. Over and over again they'd let time alone come between them. He said they were going to finish this, and while he may have changed his mind, he was right. At the very least, they should try.

She quietly walked out to the living room and came to a dead stop when he walked out of his office with a sword.

Braeden caught the look of pure terror in Alexia's wide-eyed gaze and lowered the sword to his side. "It's not for you."

She shook her head. "I didn't think it was."

Like hell she didn't. "Go to bed."

Without taking her eyes off him, she walked into the kitchen, putting the bar between them. "I thought you said we were going to finish this."

He had no desire to continue the conversation. If he had any hope of getting the manual translated, he needed to maintain some level of distance from Alexia.

There was too much between them. Even just standing here in the same room with her, emotions threatened to choke him. He'd been through this once before. He wasn't about to lose control and do something they'd both regret.

Braeden paused at the entry door. "I'll be back later. Go to bed."

"You're just going to walk away?"

"Yes." Without turning around, he added, "I had a good teacher." Then he walked out the door and headed down to the basement.

He knew from past experience that some physical exercise would go a long way toward taming his growing unease. There was nothing like a sword fight to clear his head, even if it was with an imaginary foe.

As his vaporous wings glided through the wind, Nathan dismissed the previous coldness. One benefit of taking the form of an elements dragon was that he felt neither heat nor cold.

A quick sweeping circle outside the suite was all he needed to do to know that the Dragon had left Alexia alone. Nathan needed only a few moments to set the next phase of his plan into motion. He decreased his speed to a gentle drift until he landed on the balcony outside the bedroom.

Even though he risked detection by the mortal, he was confident she wouldn't be able to see him. Once he shifted back to a more human, albeit invisible, form, he silently ordered, *"Elsbeth, come to me."*

In less than a heartbeat his wife curled her arms about his neck. *"You called, my love?"*

He jerked her arms from around him and set her aside. *"I need only a spell. One to make these two fall into each other's arms."*

Haughty as ever, Elsbeth lifted her chin a notch and looked out toward the forest, asking, *"And what do I get in return?"*

Nathan narrowed his eyes and smiled. In his mind he conjured the image of him choking his darling wife to death. The vision instantly took form and the woman beside him gasped. When her eyes nearly bulged from her head and she clawed at the unseen hands around her neck, he whispered, *"You get to live."*

Elsbeth nodded frantically and he released the spell. She quickly caught her breath and waved her hands in the air, chanting some nonsense about love, desire and devotion.

When she was done, he patted her hand. "You better hope that your spell will send these pawns into each other's arms."

Instead of answering, Elsbeth disappeared into the mists.

* * *

Braeden slipped back into the suite a couple of hours later, grateful that Alexia had gone to bed. While exhaustion made him less willing to argue, his workout had done little to quell the urge to pull her into his arms.

Unfortunately he couldn't decide what he'd do once he got her there.

After cleaning and putting away his weapon, he approached the bedroom. If she was asleep, he knew that he could set a bomb off next to the bed and she wouldn't wake up. But he also knew that if she'd waited up for him, she'd be good and riled.

He paused outside the open door, breathing a sigh of relief. Alexia was sound asleep.

Once he'd showered and slipped into a clean pair of sweatpants and T-shirt, Braeden paused at the edge of the bed.

Soft light from the bedside night-light fell across Alexia's face. The puffiness of her eyes caused him the first pang of guilt since she'd arrived at the Lair.

She'd cried herself to sleep. Braeden stroked a knuckle gently across the velvety softness of her cheek. Still sleeping, Alexia turned her face into his touch. He reluctantly withdrew his hand.

He didn't doubt for an instant that she, too, carried plenty of demons inside, old and new. While he admittedly was partially to blame for the old ones, she was the only person responsible for the new ones.

Alexia rolled over, snuggling deeper into the blankets. Unwilling to wake her up, Braeden quietly left the bedroom, leaving the door ajar behind him.

After getting something to drink, he stretched out on the sofa, thankful that Cam had talked him out of leather. Braeden wasn't certain exactly what the fabric was, but at least it was soft and, as Cam had insisted, it was comfortable enough to sleep on if necessary.

At the time Braeden had laughed at the thought. Why would he ever need to sleep on the sofa? He frowned. Had Cam known this was going to happen?

No. His brother wouldn't withhold that kind of information. Would he?

Braeden shook his head. Obviously he was more tired than he thought. He had no reason to doubt his brother. His distrust was reserved solely for Alexia.

What was he going to do about her? He didn't trust her at all. And while he was angry and frustrated with her and her actions, he realized that he didn't exactly hate her, either.

No matter what, in the end, this maddening woman was still his mate. Logic railed against that fact. A part of him wasn't yet willing to let go completely. He needed to find a way to shut off that part of him.

But until then and until they could change their situation, he would protect her—even if she didn't like his methods. Her likes or dislikes weren't his concern. His most pressing priority was the safety of those on Mirabilus.

If, as he believed, that safety was dependent on translating the manual, he would keep his anger reined in as best he could until Alexia finished the work.

The sound of muffled crying reached him. Unable to ignore the unwanted tugging at his heart, he got up and glanced into the bedroom.

Since she appeared to still be sleeping, he backed away and paced the living room, waiting for her cries to cease.

How many times had he done this before? After the accident he spent many nights pacing the floor outside their bedroom, uncertain what to do. He had tried to be understanding and kind, but since she'd refused to talk to him, it had gotten him nowhere. So he'd tried to be demanding and forceful, gaining only an empty house.

Once Alexia quieted, he went back to the sofa. Stretched out on his back, staring up at the ceiling, he dozed on and off, wondering how to keep the warring inside him at bay.

He needed to stay angry for his own self-protection and sanity.

"Braeden."

He jerked more awake at the whisper in his ear. "Alexia?"

"Braeden, I need you." Her breath was hot against his skin. Her touch skimmed down his chest, setting his blood on fire.

"What are you doing?"

She kissed his cheek and slid her hand further down his stomach. "Don't you want me?"

His physical reaction had nothing to do with it. Of course he wanted her. What man wouldn't? But what he wanted more was to know why she was acting so strangely.

Instead of following logic and pushing her away, he made what he knew could be the biggest mistake of his life—he closed his eyes and rolled onto his side to make room for her on the sofa. "More than anything. Come here."

She lay against him, her legs entwined with his, her lips against his. He slipped one arm around her and the other beneath her, then stopped.

Something didn't feel right. He stroked a hand down her back, across her hip. It was his wife, all right. He'd long ago memorized every hill and valley of her body. Yet his wife never would have come to him like this.

He searched the suite with his mind. While he found no one, his senses warned of an intrusion.

Braeden frowned. Had someone been here while he'd been in the basement?

He focused on Alexia. Her subconscious was sound asleep. Yet her physical body performed flawlessly. Her expert touch as she slid a hand beneath the loose waist of his sweatpants drew a gasp from him.

Braeden sucked in a breath in an attempt to calm his raging libido. Alexia was rarely this demanding. And considering that neither one of them was too thrilled to see the other, he doubted his wife was acting under her own volition.

He ignored his oath to stay out of her mind and probed quickly, catching the hint of an unfamiliar power coursing through her. Alexia was completely and totally uninitiated. She had no powers other than those he gave her on occasion. He'd given her nothing since her return.

Meaning someone else had.

There was one way to find out. He leaned into her. "Oh, baby, I want you so bad."

Tipping her head up, she pressed her lips to his, "I want you, too."

Braeden groaned, then whispered, "There's not enough room here."

She laughed softly. "There's always a bed."

He paused. It would be so easy to take advantage of the offer. Even though his tightly strung body was more than ready to oblige, his stomach clenched at the idea.

This was not his wife. He needed to remember that this was nothing more than someone using his wife for their own ends.

If he wanted to free her of this spell without causing any lasting harm, he needed to make certain he didn't do something they would both regret later. Somehow he had to get her back into her bed and slip away before she awoke.

While he hesitated Alexia slinked down his chest, her lips teasing as she went.

He swallowed a curse. Were they watching? Listening? Waiting to see what would happen?

Regrets be damned. He wouldn't be bested in his own domain.

He sat up, drawing her with him. "It's been too long. Let's go." He rose, picking her up as he did so, cradling her in his arms. He could feel her breath on his neck, her fingers in his hair. If he wasn't careful, he could easily fall victim to the lust flaring to life inside.

As quickly and quietly as possible, he walked down the hallway and into the bedroom. With luck and a little manipulation on his part, none of this would pass to her conscious mind in the morning.

When he bent to place her on the bed, she clung to him, pulling him down alongside her. Before he could extricate himself, she jerked at his sweats and ran her tongue across her lips.

Sweat beaded on his forehead. If he yelled at her, it would only awaken her and then he'd have to admit that he hadn't kept her safe—and give an explanation he didn't want to give at the moment.

Mustering all the thought processes he still had, Braeden pushed her onto her back, pinning her to the mattress with his body. "Slow down. We have all night."

His assurance did little to soothe her. "I need you. Now." Before he could form an answer, she caught his lips with hers.

She tasted like Alexia, smelled like her. He cupped her cheek, and the flesh beneath his touch was just as soft. Braeden fought the groan building in his chest.

She uncurled her arms from around his neck and shimmied her silky camisole up her body, breaking their kiss long enough to slide it over her head before dropping it on the floor.

He took the opportunity to push himself upright. Straddling her on his knees, Braeden silently ordered, *"Release my wife. Now."*

Without warning the being lashed out, using Alexia as a weapon. She clawed at his face, her fingernails gouging the flesh. Before he could grab her wrists, she clawed him again. This time his blood trickled hot from the deep gashes on his cheek.

In mere seconds Alexia fell back onto the bed. Remnants of a shadow swirled from her, then raced toward the balcony door to disappear into the darkness of the night.

Braeden did a quick check to make certain that whatever presence had been in the suite was now gone. He glanced at the balcony, whispering, "I'll deal with you later."

Right now he needed to get out of the bedroom before waking Alexia. But as he moved to get up from the bed, she gasped. "What are you doing?"

Not wanting to make this memory any more tangible than it was, he leaned over her, stroked her cheek and lied, "Hush. It's just a dream, Alexia."

Easily susceptible to his powers, she closed her eyes, giving him the chance to make a hasty exit.

Chapter 7

Alexia opened her eyes and groaned. If she didn't know better, she'd swear that somebody had used her as a punching bag last night. She ached from head to toe.

She sat up slowly and squeezed her eyes closed against the pounding in her temples. She hadn't had that much wine. There was no reason for her to feel this bad.

With an effort she rose. Feeling drugged, she staggered to the bathroom. After flipping on the shower, she rested her forehead against the cool tile and let the hot water pour over her.

Obviously something had happened last night, but for the life of her she couldn't remember what. Braeden had brought her bags of new clothes. They'd eaten. Talked. Argued. After he'd stormed out with his sword, frustration and confusion overwhelmed her until she'd cried herself to sleep.

While that might account for her headache, it didn't explain the rest.

Strange and distorted memories flitted through her mind. Her breath hitched. What had she done? Taking a slow, deep breath, she calmed her racing heart. Nothing. She hadn't done anything except sleep.

Then why did she vaguely remember bits and pieces of joining him on the sofa? And later of scratching his cheek?

Alexia shook the water from her face. No. It was nothing more than a strange dream.

It had to be.

Otherwise she wouldn't be able to face him again.

What in the world would have made her do anything that…stupid and outrageous? How was she going to find out if she even had?

Alexia nearly choked on the answer. The only way to discover if it had been a dream or an act of insanity was to do the unthinkable—go and find Braeden.

The thought made her stomach roll and head pound even harder, but it wasn't as if she could hide from him forever.

Quickly stepping out of the shower, Alexia dried off, dressed and got ready to leave the bedroom. She paused at the door and wondered how she was going to explain her actions if she discovered it hadn't all been a dream.

Braeden stepped out of the elevator. Picking up his pace, he passed his office and headed for his brother's. He'd managed to dress and leave the suite before Alexia awoke.

He hoped she would sleep late so he could get some work done uninterrupted. He entered Cam's office without knocking, then barreled right into the topic he'd unintentionally put off yesterday—candidates for the security-chief position. "How many choices do we have?"

"As many as you want." Cameron swiveled his chair away from the laptop to look at Braeden across the desk. "What's Alexia doing here?" His eyes locked on Braeden's face. "Who were you fighting with?"

"Nobody, it's just a scratch." Leave it to Cam not to beat around the bush. "She needed a place to stay." Braeden dropped into a chair. "I'd like to have at least three choices to start with."

"Scratch?" Cam shook his head in apparent disbelief. "From what? A mountain lion?" With a quick push, Cam slid three folders across the desk. "Here, start with these. Is she back for good?"

"No. Just a couple of days." Braeden reached for the folders, only to have them moved beyond his fingers by an unfurling, gnarled branch of the dragon tree on the corner of Cam's desk.

Braeden hated that damn miniature tree—almost as much as the aberration apparently hated him. He stared at his brother. "Move it, or I'll kill it."

"That's brave of you." Cameron rolled his eyes before moving the ancient pun-sai tree out of reach to the credenza behind him. "You act as if it's some beast out to do you harm."

"A tree that moves at will is a beast." Braeden snagged the folders and leafed through the top two, dismissing them with little more than a glance. "Not enough experience." It was too bad he couldn't deal with Alexia in the same manner—just run through her résumé without any preconceived notions or feelings.

Cameron slid two more folders toward him. "Any idea why someone would blow up her town house?"

"Other than to send her running here? No idea." Braeden set one folder aside as a possible interview candidate.

"Should I avoid Danielle for a while?"

"That's up to you." He ignored Cam's snicker and slid one folder back across the desk, adding the other one to the "possible" pile.

"These last two are it." Cam handed the final two folders to him, asking, "So where's Alexia now?"

"Sleeping."

Cameron leaned back in his chair. "In your suite?"

Braeden ignored the question. It was none of his business.

At Cam's soft laugh, he looked up from the folder he held. "What?"

Cam tilted back his chair. "I wonder if you'll answer my next question."

"Which is?" He hated it when Cam played these little games. Occasionally, instead of just saying or asking what was on his mind, Cam liked to drag it out. Thankfully, it didn't happen too often.

"What do you intend to do about your marriage?"

"Nothing."

"Yeah, right."

Braeden frowned. He didn't want or need his twin's interference. "I'm not going to argue with you about this."

"I have no intention of arguing with you about it." Cameron shrugged. "I just want you to get your head out of your ass and fix your marriage like you should have done years ago."

Only his twin could get away with saying something that blunt. Anyone else would have had to call 9-1-1 after picking themselves up off the floor. But he and Cam had been together literally from the moment of conception. Only a few minutes separated the heir from the spare.

Still, having shared a womb didn't lessen the impact of Cam's brutal bluntness. "Why don't you keep your mouth shut and let me worry about Alexia and my marriage?"

Instead of taking offense or hounding him further, Cameron tapped the top folder. "I think we should call this guy in."

"Then call him in. We need to get security personnel in here as quickly as possible."

"Why? What's up?"

"Dani thinks Nathan might be involved." Braeden wasn't certain. Obviously someone had put a spell on Alexia last night, but he didn't know if it was Nathan.

Cam leaned back in his chair and whistled. "Nathan the Learned?"

"Yes."

"And you think some mortal security guard with a gun will keep him at bay?"

Braeden rolled his eyes. "Of course not. But the security force will be able to handle the normal day-to-day details while we figure out what to do about Nathan."

Cameron didn't look as if he agreed, but he said, "It's worth a shot, I guess. I'll bring this guy in."

"Good." Braeden rose. "I'll be in my office if anything comes up."

Since it was already after nine, Alexia wasn't surprised to discover that Braeden had already left the suite. So she headed down to the offices.

She stopped before his slightly open door to knock. Voices raised in anger made her pause.

"I told you she was nothing but trouble."

Alexia shook her head. Of course Danielle Drake would say that.

"I doubt if she even knows what happened last night."

Alexia swallowed her groan. Great, it hadn't been just a dream.

"And I wouldn't be surprised if she'd instigated it herself."

Alexia blinked at Danielle's assumption. Even if she did have any powers, she wouldn't have used them to seduce a man who had the ability to crush her heart.

"No. Alexia wouldn't go that far. Besides, she doesn't have the ability."

She frowned. This wasn't the first time since arriving at the Lair that Braeden had defended her to his aunt. While she appreciated his effort, she wasn't a child anymore. She could defend herself against Danielle.

Alexia rapped on the door before pushing it open further. When both Braeden and Danielle turned to stare at her, she shrugged. "The door was open."

"Eavesdropping?"

"No, Danielle, though I'm sure a deaf person would have heard you."

Braeden sat on the edge of his desk. "How are you feeling?"

She turned her attention to him and gasped at the gouges on his face. She'd envisioned scratches. But the marks on his cheek were a bit worse than simple scratches. He looked as if he'd fought with a tiger and lost. "Miserable." Especially now that she'd seen him.

Danielle smirked at Braeden. "See, she knows what happened. She probably planned it."

Alexia kept her gaze locked on Braeden. "Discussing last night?" The thought that he would discuss her with his aunt made her skin crawl.

"No." He nodded toward a chair. "You better sit down."

Instead, she headed over to the small bar. "Coffee?" she asked.

"Help yourself."

Once she'd poured a cup, she took a seat. "What's going on?"

"So you do remember last night?"

"Unfortunately, yes, but just bits and pieces." She paused, then tried to explain. "I don't know what came over me. Most of it's like a foggy bad dream."

"A spell gone wrong."

He'd said it as if he was talking about a lightbulb going out, as if it was a common occurrence. But a conversation about spells was far from common for her. Afraid she'd spill the hot coffee, she held it away from her lap and asked, "Beg your pardon?"

"You were under the influence of someone's spell. Either the being doing the casting did something wrong, or something inside you fought against it."

"I acted insane."

Braeden ignored Danielle's snort, saying, "That's what happens."

After taking a long swallow of the coffee, she sighed. "I really didn't come here to bring you trouble."

Braeden didn't acknowledge her statement, but said, "We just have to work on making sure nobody can do that again."

"Do you think it was this Nathan?"

"No clue." He shrugged. "At first I wasn't certain it was a who."

Alexia took a breath. She'd been sure that the voice she'd heard in her head had been much more than human. No mere human could possess the amount of evil she'd felt from his presence. Even though she didn't want to, she forced herself to ask, "If not a who, then *what* did you think it might have been?"

"This is why you could never be a true Drake." Danielle's hard glare pierced her. "You're far too single-minded in your belief that only humans walk this earth."

"Actually, I was very aware that the thing I heard in my head was more than human. Just as I knew Braeden wasn't a normal human when we got married." Alexia couldn't resist adding, "I never was too sure about you, though."

The floor beneath their feet shook momentarily, cutting off their verbal sparring before it went any further. Danielle narrowed her eyes, but closed her mouth.

Alexia whistled softly. Not one item had fallen off a shelf. No picture vibrated out of place. Her coffee hadn't sloshed and nothing on his desk had even quivered. Her husband had obviously refined his powers.

Braeden crossed his arms over his chest and asked, "Are you ladies done?"

He didn't appear angry, so Alexia said, "This spell caster wouldn't have been—" she hesitated, but couldn't help glancing at his aunt "—anyone here?"

"No." Danielle answered. "I wouldn't have botched a spell that badly."

It was nice that Danielle Drake thought so highly of herself.

Watch your sarcasm, Ms. Reve. Danielle's thoughts rasped against Alexia's mind.

Alexia set her cup on the desk and rose. She looked pointedly at Danielle. "I'm only going to say this once. Stay out of my head. Do you hear me?"

"Is that a threat?"

"Take it any way you want. I'm not putting up with your games this time."

Braeden swore before physically coming between her and his aunt. Alexia waited for him to berate her for talking to his aunt that way. But to her surprise he looked at Danielle. "Leave her alone."

Danielle gasped as if she'd been deeply insulted. "She brings us nothing but trouble and you defend her?"

Instead of going into any detailed explanation, Braeden simply said, "I'll deal with her myself—later. Right now I'm telling you to back off. Like it not, she's still my wife."

Alexia nearly fell back onto her chair. To cover the lack of grace, she picked up her cup and finished off the coffee.

"She's dangerous, Braeden, don't you see that?"

He put a hand on his aunt's shoulder. "Dani, I can handle this. You have nothing to worry about."

"You just feel sorry for her because she needs you right now. What about later, Braeden? When she's back on her feet and no longer needs or wants your help? What then?"

Alexia blinked. Is that what everyone thought? That she was just using Braeden? Granted, she had come here because she had no place else to go, but she hadn't done so with the idea of using Braeden and then leaving.

She heard Braeden's sigh. Didn't Danielle realize that meant he was losing patience?

"You have too many other things to deal with. You shouldn't have to deal with her and her problems, too." Danielle's overprotectiveness set Alexia's teeth on edge.

"She's still my wife," he repeated.

"Fine. Have it your way. I have warned you since the first day you brought her home that her soul was black and dangerous. But you wouldn't listen then and you aren't listening now." Danielle headed toward the door. "Have you considered what'll happen if she leaves you powerless this time?"

She slammed the door behind her before Braeden could respond.

He ran a hand through his hair and sat down behind his desk. "How are you feeling?"

Alexia tried to dismiss his uninterested tone, but it still stung. "I'll be fine."

His frown deepened. "This shouldn't have happened."

Whether it should have happened or not, it did. And it had left her humiliated and him bleeding. "How am I going to know if it happens again?"

"It won't."

He said it with such forceful confidence that Alexia believed him.

"Either way, under someone's spell or not, there was no excuse for my actions last night." She nervously traced a finger around the rim of her coffee cup before adding, "I am sorry, Braeden, and I wish you'd accept my apology."

"If it'll make you feel better, I accept."

His tone was clipped, as if he was unwilling to discuss the incident. Did he think she lied about even this? "You don't think I had any part in what happened, do you?"

He stared at her as if contemplating his answer. Unable to stand the silence any longer, Alexia leaned forward, prompting, "You said yourself that I have no powers."

"That doesn't mean anything. You could easily be working with someone."

A shudder of disbelief, anger or both rippled down her spine. Before giving it any thought, she replied, "It would take a lot more than magic to get the two of us in bed together."

Horrified at her own stupidity, Alexia closed her eyes and prayed for the floor beneath her to open up and swallow her. There was nothing like offering Braeden an open invitation to see exactly what it would take.

"Sure about that, are you?"

Fortunately he didn't elaborate on his response. She hoped that by ignoring it, the subject would be dropped.

Alexia stared mutely into her nearly empty coffee cup. A nerveracking silence filled the space between them. The longer it lasted, the more time Alexia had to think of what might have been.

She needed a diversion before she got lost in memories and dreams that would do nothing except stab at her heart. "I know it's Sunday. But I'm willing to start working on the Dragonierre's Manual."

"Good." Braeden unlocked a desk drawer. "I don't think it wise to do this in here. Come tomorrow there'll be people in and out." He pulled a leather satchel from the drawer. "There's a well-equipped office in my suite."

"Wouldn't it just be easier if I had a suite of my own? Then I wouldn't be taking up your office—"

"We've already had this discussion. You're staying put."

The urge to argue was overwhelming. But she managed to bite her tongue. "Fine. Since you're better able to protect the manual, your suite will work."

He closed and locked the drawer before heading toward the door. "The rest of the pages are up there in my private safe."

"Do you want something to eat before we get started?"

"No." Alexia's stomach rolled at the thought. "The coffee was enough."

She followed him out of the office, down the hall and across the lobby. Her thoughts, which should have been focused on the task ahead, were, instead, riveted on his tight jeans.

Braeden was dressed less than casually by his standards, but the jeans and T-shirt look worked well for him— and better for her.

Did he keep himself so trim, firm and muscular by working out or by magic? And when had his legs gotten so long? He'd always been tall, but for some reason she'd never noticed them quite so vividly before, not even when they'd first married. Why her attention was drawn so acutely to his body now was a mystery she didn't wish to solve. Alexia resisted the urge to fan her warming cheeks.

"Alexia?"

She caught herself right before literally running into his chest. When had he stopped and turned around? Hesitantly lifting her gaze to his, she felt her face warm even more.

He lifted one eyebrow.

"I…uh…" She took a breath and gave up. "What?"

His deep laugh rumbled through her like a lingering caress, sending a shiver through her. The fact that he so obviously thought it amusing only embarrassed her more.

"I assume you'll want to take notes. On the computer or on paper?"

She shook the budding passion from herself. "Actually, both, and a tape recorder if there's one available."

"No, but there's a mic on the computer."

"That'll work."

To her relief the elevator ride up to his suite was uneventful. He opened the door and waved her inside.

The office was through the double doors off the living room. A conference area took up one end of the room. A mahogany desk, credenza and file cabinets were in the other end. About midway down the side wall was a long, narrow worktable.

Alexia slid the pages from the satchel onto the worktable while Braeden retrieved the others from the safe behind his desk.

She stopped. "I need the case from the back seat of my car." She didn't want to handle the fragile pages without gloves. The acid and sweat from her hands could damage the parchment.

"I'll get it." Braeden paused at the door. "Do you need anything else?"

Without taking her fascinated gaze off the pages, she sat down in the swivel chair before the table and answered, "No, that should do it."

While most of the words appeared to be gibberish, or some strange code, the drawings were exquisite. There was a drawing of a dragon pendant. The fine detail made it so lifelike that Alexia was drawn to gently touch the winged creature.

She stroked from the beast's head to its tail and felt the creature stretch beneath her touch. "What the—" She jerked back her hand.

"Bugs." It had to be bugs. She lifted the page and found nothing underneath.

Certain the impression of movement was because of the intricate detail, she picked up a magnifying glass and leaned over the page.

The pointed barb at the end of the tail seemed to vibrate. She hadn't realized she was shaking. Steadying her wrist with her other hand, she moved her gaze up the tail. Instead of just an outline drawing with some details etched in, each individual scale had been recreated on the page.

She jotted a few notes on a pad and continued to study the dragon. The wings had been drawn in a manner that mimicked movement, another technique she wouldn't have expected from something done in what was supposed to have been the twelfth century.

The magnifying glass jumped as if it had been tapped

from below. She leaned away, frowning at her carelessness. It wouldn't do to get so carried away that she accidentally damaged the page by scraping her hand or the glass across it.

With more care, she bent back to her task. Alexia studied the dragon's back and neck before moving higher up the drawing. She positioned the glass directly over its head—and froze as she stared into the dragon's blinking eyes.

She dropped the glass and shoved away from the table, nearly tipping the chair backward in her attempt to get away.

Alexia raced out of the office to the front entrance door, but it wouldn't open. She opened her mouth to scream, but nothing came out. Her heart threatened to pound out of her chest as she fought to calm the frantic beating. *Braeden! Braeden, I need you. Now!*

He materialized at her side immediately and pulled her into his arms. "What?"

Unable to speak, she pointed at the table in the office.

Braeden saw nothing unusual, but Alexia's fear was too real. He moved toward the table and she pushed free. He left her by the door and went to see what had caused such a reaction.

He stood over the page and stared down in amazement. "Well, I'll be."

The drawing of the dragon was seeking life. The end of the tail and part of its head had already freed itself from the page. He hadn't been this excited about something magical in ages. Braeden reached toward Alexia. "Come here. Look at this."

"No."

"You've got to see this before I put it back."

She pressed herself against the doorjamb. "No."

He wasn't going to argue with her. Braeden stretched out his arm, extended his hand and ordered, "Come."

Her eyes grew large as her body obeyed. Levitated a few inches off the floor, she closed the distance between them until he grasped her hand and she lowered to her feet.

"Now, look at this."

He could smell her fear as she stared down at the table.

"It's not going to harm you, Alexia." He leaned closer to the dragon. "Look at the color."

The sections of the beast that had come free from the page were turning amethyst.

"Make it go away."

He glanced up at the sound of her strangled voice. Her eyes were huge and bright against the paleness of her face. Alexia wasn't just afraid—she was absolutely terrified. He realized that if he didn't do something, she would faint.

Reluctantly he put his hand over the page. "Remain the drawing you were meant to be." The dragon melted back into the book.

And behind him, Alexia hit the floor with a thud.

Nathan strangled on a laugh and dragged his shaking wife more tightly to his chest. He enjoyed the pureness of the fear racing through her body. She knew well the price she'd have to pay for casting a failed spell. But he intended to enjoy her terror in a way he'd not enjoyed their long marriage.

Without taking his eyes off the scrying mirror, he stroked the soft flesh on the side of her neck. "Your spell didn't work. They have not made love."

Elsbeth tried pulling away, but he held her fast. "You know what that means, don't you?"

Nathan grabbed her chin and forced her to look at him. "Kiss me, my love. Let my lips be the last thing you feel."

He captured her scream with his mouth sealed firmly over hers. She trembled beneath his deadly touch. Slowly, with near reverence, Nathan literally drew the breath from her body. He inhaled her life force and, along with it, the meager powers she possessed.

After dumping the now lifeless body to the floor, he pulled the wooden box from his desk drawer. "Nice trick with the dragon, Aelthed. How did you do that?"

Not that it mattered in the least. Nathan was certain he'd learn that secret when he gained control of all the others.

Excitement thrummed through his veins like a drug. Soon, very soon, he would have all he ever wanted.

Now that Drake and his wife were finally getting around to the grimoire, his wait would soon end. He'd give them a few days. If they made little or no progress, he'd be forced to prompt them into action himself.

Quite a few of the Drake kin lived on Mirabilus. The untimely death of one or two of them should be enough to speed things along.

Nathan whispered a curse as Drake turned his head and seemingly stared directly at him. He waved a hand before the mirror, darkening the image.

He'd have to be more careful in the future and be satisfied with nothing more than a quick glimpse now and then.

Chapter 8

"Alexia." Braeden knelt beside her. "It's gone."

She came to with a jerk, swinging her fists and catching Braeden on the shoulder.

"Stop." He grasped her wrists. "It's gone." When she uncurled her fingers and relaxed her arms, he released her and rose.

"What *was* that?" Pushing up from the floor, she stood with Braeden's help, then moved behind him.

"I'm not sure, but it was easy enough to quell."

Alexia headed for the door. "I need some air."

"You don't want to get back to work?"

"Sure." She narrowed her eyes. "Right after I get my heart rate down around aerobic level."

He didn't want to stay in the suite. There were at least two dozen things on his desk that needed to be completed. But he didn't want her left alone, either. She was upset enough to take off. "Just a few minutes so I can check this out, too, and then we'll go for a walk."

She stayed by the door and waved a finger at the pages. "Fine, but turn that one over."

Braeden reluctantly conceded and flipped the dragon drawing facedown. Hands resting on the table, he leaned down and studied the next page. "What do you make of this?"

Slowly, as if uncertain she wanted to get much closer, Alexia asked, "There's no drawing?"

"Nothing like before. A swirl at the top-right corner and the rest is just letters—words, maybe."

She joined him at the table. "Any you can make out?"

"Actually, yes." He pointed at what looked to him like a fancy swirl. "This is on my and Cam's dragons."

Alexia jotted a few things on her pad before holding the magnifying glass over the symbol. "Well, of course it's on your dragons."

"Of course?"

She put the glass on the table. "It says 'dragon'."

It was all Braeden could do to keep his lips from twitching. Apparently Alexia was going to get more than her fill of dragons today.

She picked up her pad and scribbled something on it before handing it to him. "The letters DRACA are written on top of each other. Each letter smaller than the last."

"Draca is…?"

Alexia took the pad from him. "Old English."

"Why would a Druid be writing in Old English?"

She shrugged, wondering the same thing. Why hadn't the author followed the methods of the church at the time and created an illuminated manuscript? Perhaps they hadn't wanted their text tied to the church. "Because they didn't commit their secrets or lessons to writing?"

"Are you asking me?"

"No, just wondering out loud. With no written language, illustrations could have been used. It would have made more sense. Or they could have reverted to the Greek alphabet of the Gauls. Either way, Gallic Druids did not hand down their lessons in writing." She tapped on the table alongside a page. "So what is this?"

He reminded her. "You're the one who did the paper on this book that doesn't exist. You tell me."

She flushed, but said, "I hope to."

Braeden grasped two chairs and dragged them over to the worktable. "Here."

Without comment she sat down and pulled a pair of gloves from the case he'd brought in from the car. Alexia refocused her attention on the pages.

He took a seat next to her and watched as she stared at a page, made some notes, then went back to staring and frowning at the page.

Someone who didn't know her might think she was performing a task that frustrated or bored her. But he caught a glimpse of the bright shimmer in her eyes. And the way every now and then she would pause, chewing on her lower lip before scribbling another note on her pad.

A stranger wouldn't notice that the tiny pulse in her neck would suddenly speed up when she discovered something new to jot down.

But he wasn't a stranger. And he noticed every little nuance whether he wanted to or not. Each movement, even just the rise and fall of her chest as she breathed, beckoned him to remember what they'd once shared—and what they'd both lost.

He frowned, knowing he had a choice to make. He could either make her life miserable, or he could call a truce at least until this manual was translated. After that she would once again leave to make her own life without him.

The knowledge angered him, but he wasn't certain why. As he'd declared more times than he could remember, they were still married. But his life was easier without her around. Calmer. Less tense.

Boring.

He shook the thought from his mind. Just take one thing at a time. Right now his responsibility was to ensure her safety. He thought that would be easy. Obviously he hadn't counted on the strength of the outside force following her.

For now he watched, fascinated by the play of emotions racing across her features as she became lost in her work. Braeden remained quiet, oddly content to do nothing more than sit here on guard in case another mystical creature decided to scare her half to death.

Almost two hours flew by before Alexia leaned back in her chair. She rubbed her neck and arched her back.

"Figure anything out?"

"I can only assume this is the beginning of the manual. It seems to be telling a story, or relating events about the Mirabilus twins. I think they were women, but I'm not sure. It's as if there are words missing."

"Missing? As in faded out or as in intentionally not written?"

Turning her head from side to side to stretch her neck, she answered, "I'm not certain."

Without thought Braeden stood behind her and kneaded her shoulders. He suggested, "Let's take that walk I promised, then we can grab some lunch."

She leaned back into his hands. "In a minute."

He pressed his thumbs into her neck before leaning down to whisper in her ear, "You said it would take more than magic. Is this something more?"

To demonstrate what he meant, he slid one hand over her shoulder and across her collarbone. The tips of his fingers grazed the swell of her breasts.

Alexia gasped softly before sitting upright and swiveling the chair away from him. She shook her head, whispering, "No. No, it's not."

She lied badly. He read the look in her eyes. How could he not recognize the glimmer of desire? But he wasn't certain if the desire was real or just the lingering remains of last night's spell.

Braeden stepped back. "A walk in the fresh air will do you good."

She nodded. "Let me note where I left off, then we can go."

The late-October sky was clear and bright. Alexia lifted her face to the sun, glad he'd suggested a walk. The fresh air did more to clear her head than the aspirin she'd swallowed this morning.

They walked side by side along a well-kept path around the Lair. It led them alongside, then behind the resort before passing a large outbuilding that looked like a garage of some type.

Harold yelled from the doorway. "May I have a minute, Mr. Drake?"

Braeden nodded at the man and looked at Alexia. "This won't take long."

"That's fine." Alexia pointed up the path where it led into the woods. "I'll wait for you up there."

"Don't go too far."

She heard a vague warning in his tone and asked, "It is still your property, isn't it?"

"Yes. You'll be fine, just stay on the main path, and if you get to the fence, stop. I should catch up with you well before then."

After Braeden headed off to talk to Harold, she ambled up the path, following it into the woods. The sun filtered through the mix of pine and oak trees, but it wasn't enough to provide much warmth beneath the denseness of the trees. Alexia buttoned her jacket and stuffed her hands in her pockets.

The path angled up, but the freshness of the air, the freedom of being outside, made the hike worth the effort. And the scenery went a long way toward making the journey enjoyable. She was at an elevation where the evergreens and deciduous trees grew together. The darker green of the evergreens provided a contrasting canvas for the palette of colored leaves still hanging tenuously from the deciduous trees.

When the path forked, she paused, wondering which branch was the main path. If guests were going to use these trails, the Drakes might want to think about marking them.

Before she could decide left or right, Braeden came up behind her. "This way." He took the trail heading off to the left.

Alexia followed him more deeply into the forest. "What's on the other trail?"

"Nothing."

He answered too quickly for her to believe him. But she wasn't going to call him on it now. They had to work together and it'd be easier to do if they weren't at each other's throats.

They hiked in silence until the path led up to a grassy knoll. A light breeze rustled the long, brown grass. She climbed onto a large boulder to survey the scenery.

Alexia sighed as all her cares and concerns faded away beneath nature's calming touch. She could live here without hesitation. She could once again be Braeden's wife with little coercion.

Alexia blinked. Where had that thought come from?

Braeden Drake didn't need a wife. He needed nothing more from life than the rush of the next challenge to meet and conquer.

Her gaze wandered over the mountaintops and the hollows before coming to rest on Braeden.

She felt his return stare and turned away from the questioning look in his eyes.

Alexia didn't want to face the questions. She didn't want to search for the answers. Not right now. Not when his nearness made rational thought almost impossible.

No. All she wanted to do was finish this translation and get as far away from Dragon's Lair and Braeden Drake as possible.

Quickly, before the hunger and need gnawing at her caused her to do something her heart would later regret. She didn't think she could survive losing him again.

She bent her legs and rested her forehead on her knees. Coming here had been stupid. The threat at home had been physical, but here, at the Lair, her heart and soul were in grave danger.

The grass surrounding the boulder rustled. Yet no breeze had set the long blades moving. Alexia shivered as a finger of ice traced down her spine.

Braeden glanced around before joining her on the boulder. Kneeling beside her, he whispered, "Stay still."

His softly spoken order made her nerves twitch with dread. Just as quietly, she asked, "What's going on?"

He pointed at the still-moving grass. Her gaze moved in that direction and she held her breath.

Like undulating waves, the grass rippled in the stillness. Each wave was broken by a thin curving line racing toward them, breaking only at the base of the boulder then continuing around.

Alexia closed her eyes and tried to swallow the cry in her throat. She grabbed Braeden's arm.

"They're just garter snakes, Lexi. Stay calm."

"Calm?" She didn't care what kind of snakes they were. They were slithering creatures with fangs and they were nearly upon them. He wanted her to be calm? The threatening cry escaped with her question. She snapped her mouth closed and dug her fingers into his arm. "Get me out of here."

"In a minute." Braeden pried her fingers from his arm, then rose.

Careful to keep her gaze on him and not on the still-rustling grass, Alexia opened one eye. "What are you doing?"

He nodded toward the other side of the knoll. "We have company."

Alexia hazarded a glance and saw a wispy, nearly formed figure levitating at the edge of the forest. With his dark robe and wild hair he had the appearance of someone who'd just stepped out of the Middle Ages—or off some movie lot.

"Who the—"

"Nathan. That is Nathan the Learned."

She stared up at Braeden. "So he is real."

"Obviously."

Alexia shivered. Then he was also probably the voice of evil she'd heard in her mind.

Nathan looked straight at them, without any acknowledgment, then disappeared. Taking his snakes with him.

"Did he see us?"

"Oh, he saw us." Braeden jumped off the boulder and held out a hand to help her down. "We need to get back to the Lair."

"What are you—" Before she could finish her sentence, she stumbled over the thick carpet in Braeden's office. Quickly catching her balance, she took a seat. "A warning would have been nice."

He shrugged. "Walking back would have taken too long." Without waiting for her reply, he tapped a button on the phone. "Cam, Sean, Dani, in my office."

Something was dreadfully wrong, but from the frown of concentration on Braeden's face as he sat down behind his desk, she wasn't at all certain she wanted to know.

Cam blew through the door connecting their offices with a stack of papers in his hand. "What's up?"

Sean walked in the other door with Danielle on his heels. Once they were all seated, Braeden leaned forward. "Nathan is here."

Danielle's ragged gasp and theatrics nearly had her on the floor. She pointed at Alexia. "It's her fault. She brought him here."

"Most likely, yes."

Ignoring their aunt, Alexia slowly swiveled her chair around, looking at the brothers one at a time. "So what now? Can the three of you defeat him?"

Cam answered first. "If it's just him, perhaps."

She could tell by the flat, serious tone of his voice that he wasn't joking. She glanced at Sean, who only shrugged in response. Alexia swiveled back to face Braeden. "Well, can you?"

"I don't see where we have a choice in the matter. If you do, please share it with us."

Everything that had happened the past couple of days exploded. Rising, Alexia glared at Braeden. "Between being threatened, my home blown up, the pages of that manual just appearing, a dragon coming to life and rituals being held on top of my car, I've had more than enough. I don't have any magical skills you can use, so I'm not needed here. And I sure as hell don't need your sarcasm."

Her pulse racing in anger, she headed for the door. Before she got within arm's length, the door slammed closed.

"Sit down."

"Don't tell me what to do." She put her hand on the door, waiting for Braeden to release the spell holding it closed.

Instead, he repeated, "Sit down."

She turned around and studied each of the faces now staring at her. Not one hint of sarcasm met her perusal.

Fighting the sudden churning of her stomach, she took her seat and asked, "What kind of powers does this Nathan have?" She paused and looked at Braeden. When he shrugged, she continued, "So how do you even know if you can defeat him or not?"

It was hard to imagine that she'd just asked those questions, so the next one was almost impossible to fathom. "This is going to end up being a war with an unknown force isn't it?"

This was turning into a nightmare, one she hoped to wake up from soon.

Danielle waved an arm in the air. Her flowing sleeve billowed. "He's a Learned. A wizard like Braeden. At one time he'd been trained to be the High Druid of Mirabilus, but that was denied him. Who knows what he can or can't do?"

"He can't translate the manual."

Alexia looked back at Braeden. "Obviously." She took a breath. "Where has he been hiding all this time?"

Braeden raised his hand. "Hold on a minute." He directed his attention to Danielle. "I want amulets for everyone."

She nodded in agreement.

He then focused on his brothers. "See that the Lair and the perimeter is secured." He pointed at Sean. "Physically." Then he pointed at Cam. "And magically."

Leaning back in his chair, he frowned before adding, "We'll meet at dinner."

Alexia watched in amazement as the other three took their leave. "They take orders well."

"Too bad you don't."

She glared at him. "I'm not one of your serfs."

"But you are my family and that puts you under my protection whether you like it or not."

His family. Funny she hadn't felt like a member of his family in years. And right now, she actually preferred it that way.

Alexia stood up. "If I try to walk out the door, will it open?"

"Of course it will. But you aren't going anywhere until I'm ready."

If he was trying to piss her off, he was succeeding. "Excuse me?"

"Don't play dumb. You said yourself that you have no powers. Until Nathan is dealt with, you aren't going to be left alone. You pose too much of a risk."

Alexia crossed her arms. "How so?"

He rose and shook his head. "Please, the role of dimwit doesn't suit you. What do you think would happen if Nathan captured you?"

She shivered. "He'd kill me."

"No. That would be the last thing he did. First he'd use you to get the book and Mirabilus."

"That choice would be yours. And I don't see you giving up Mirabilus for me."

She'd forgotten how quickly Braeden could move. Before she could take a step back, he came around the desk, grabbed her arms and pulled her hard against him. "Then you are a fool, Alexia."

Her hands resting on his shoulders for support, she stared up at him. She could see his intent in his overbright gaze. He was going to kiss her again, and this time she didn't think she'd come away unscathed.

"Braeden, please, don't." Her trembling voice disgusted her, but she was unable to stop the shivers racing through her body at his nearness.

He threaded a hand through her hair and lowered his head to brush his lips gently over hers. "Don't worry, I won't let him harm you."

She closed her eyes on a groan. "I'm not afraid of *him*."

Nathan tipped his vaporous wings and circled the Isle of Mirabilus far below. He glided lower until rivers, mountains and valleys came into sharp focus. Someday soon it would be his—along with the rest of the world.

The certainty that he would succeed excited him, leaving him with a hungry need. A hunger so intense that it drove him into the currents of autumn air swirling about the island. It'd been nearly eight hundred years since his last visitation upon the inhabitants. They wouldn't know what hit them.

But the Dragon would know. Between the death of an innocent and another orchestrated break-in, the Dragon of Mirabilus would rush home, leaving his lair—and his mate—unprotected.

Chapter 9

Maybe it was nothing more than the rush of adrenaline at the thought of the coming battle with Nathan, but she tasted so good. Braeden pulled her closer against him as if holding her would keep her safe.

He broke their kiss and stared down at her. A trace of tears shimmered in her eyes and he cursed himself for being such a fool.

Slowly he released her. And even more slowly she backed away. Her hesitancy showed that her body wasn't as averse to his touch as her words claimed.

Alexia turned toward the door. "There's work to do."

A slight tremor was still evident in her voice. Braeden narrowed his eyes. There were too many things left unsaid. Not just about their past or present. He was positive Alexia still withheld information he needed to know.

If he waited for her to tell him about her dissertations

on the manual and her involvement with Nathan, they could all be dead. But Braeden also knew that if he approached those topics head-on, she would clam up.

There were other methods. Some mortal. Some not.

He waited until she was a few feet away before saying, "The good news is you're right. We do have work to do."

Without turning around, she stopped and asked, "And the bad news?"

"We need to solve *us,* Alexia. One way or another." He waited for the eruption.

"Why? Just let it rest."

He didn't like the sound of defeat in her tone. Alexia didn't talk when she was upset. Instead, she sought solitude by climbing into a cave, then pulling a rock over the entrance.

But when her emotions ran high, with passion or anger, she had a tendency to talk—sometimes too much. Her anger or passion would serve him better right now. "For how long? Another three years?"

"We tried to talk about this yesterday and *you* walked away."

It galled him that she was right. "Yes, for once *I* walked away." He couldn't tell if the flush reddening the tips of her ears was from guilt or anger.

"If I apologize for leaving, will you stop throwing it in my face?"

He stared out the windows at the swaying pines. It probably would be easier to take her advice and just let it rest. He could obtain the information about Nathan from her any time he wished. But something inside struggled with the idea of taking anything from her mind without her permission.

Some nearly forgotten sense of chivalry demanded he play fair. He had to get her to talk. First, they needed to get beyond that one moment in time—the one that tore their world apart. And the only way to do that was to shove the doors open and face the monster on the other side.

Was he ready to do that?

Braeden clenched and unclenched his fingers before turning toward her. "There's no need for you to apologize for leaving a situation you couldn't bear."

Alexia blinked as his words sank into her mind. She turned around and looked at him. Frown lines creased his forehead. His eyes darkened, glimmering with an emotion she couldn't quite put her finger on. It wasn't exactly anger, but neither did he appear to be willing to have this conversation.

She sighed and waved absently toward the door. "We don't have to do this now." In all honesty, as far as she was concerned, they *never* had to have this conversation.

He stepped closer. "Someday soon we'll have no choice."

Her pulse quickened. She wasn't at all certain she was ready to hear or say things that would only bring the reason for her departure back into sharp focus.

Before she could fully decide, the warmth of his hand on her shoulder made her knees sickeningly weak. He traced the side of his thumb along her neck, making the urge to lean against him almost impossible to resist.

Alexia swayed. It would be so easy to accept the gentleness he seemed to offer. *No.* She pushed him away. "Braeden, don't."

He lowered his hand. "Go back to the suite. I'll be up…later."

His slight hesitation let her know there was more than

angry frustration driving him. She looked away. "I'm sorry. I just…"

Braeden shook his head. "Save it."

"I just…I don't…" She took a deep breath. "I don't want to share your bed."

"You say that like it's a challenge." He reached out again and stroked her cheek.

"No." Alexia backed away. "I mean it, Braeden."

He didn't say anything. He simply stared at her lips, making her mouth go dry. Then he lowered his gaze to her breasts, causing her nipples to harden. Between gritted teeth, she ordered, "Stop it."

"Fine. I will."

She headed to the door. Before leaving the office, she heard him add, "For now."

Braeden paused just inside the door to his suite. It hadn't taken him long to come to a decision. Before this day ended, he'd have all the answers he needed, one way or another.

Alexia stood before the worktable in the office, staring down at a page of the manuscript. Without turning around, she asked, "Did you move these?"

"No." He hadn't been in here since they'd left earlier. Walking up behind her, he asked, "Why?"

She picked up her notes. "According to my notes, this is the page I was working on."

He glanced over her shoulder. "Isn't that the same swirl at the top?"

"Yes, but doesn't it look…different to you?"

"It could be smaller than I remembered."

"And look at this." She pointed at the first line.

He moved to stand beside her, remaining silent when

she put a little distance between them. She'd obviously understood his silent warning—he wasn't going to let her challenge go unanswered.

He shifted his attention to the page. A frown marred his forehead. "Where is that *draca* symbol?"

"Oh, it's still there, but it's extended out now, letter by letter, instead of all four letters on top of each other."

"How?"

"I'm only in charge of translating." She glanced up at him. "Anything magical or mystical is your responsibility."

"Are you positive this is the right page?"

She handed him her notes. "Yes."

Braeden studied the crude drawings on her pad, then looked back at the page. He handed her back the pad. "What else is different?"

"There seem to be more words on the page."

"Can you make anything out now?"

She sat down, put on her gloves and picked up a pencil. "The writer is telling the story about the Mirabilus twins who existed at that time. They were women and had been separated at birth. One was raised by her mother, a Druid priestess, while the other was raised in Normandy by her titled Christian father."

He sat in the chair next to her, leaned back and seemed to absorb her recital.

"Look! Braeden, they were each given a dragon pendant. The girl raised by her father was given an amethyst pendant that matched the color of her sister's eyes. The Druid sister owned a sapphire pendant that matched her Christian sister's eyes."

She turned to him. "You and Cam even have the right dragons in your offices. You have the sapphire one, and didn't you say he has the amethyst one?"

"Yes. Any particular reason that seems right to you?" She was so engrossed in her discovery that she didn't appear to notice how easily she shared the information, or her excitement with him. Nor was she aware that he'd moved closer.

"Well, other than what I've just read, not really."

He waved her back toward the manual. "What else?"

Alexia tried to write as quickly as she talked. "The Druid sister was called Evonne, queen of Mirabilus. The other was Rhian of Gerviase. They were brought back together when their father died shortly after his wife."

"Had the parents lived apart all that time?" Braeden stretched his arm across the back of her chair.

"It appears so. There's no mention on this page of them reuniting."

She paused, studying the words on the page as they seemingly became clearer before her eyes.

"After returning to Mirabilus, Rhian soon married Gareth of Faucon—the man who'd escorted her to her sister—and then she moved to England with her husband."

Braeden intently studied a gentle wave in a section of Alexia's hair. He trailed a fingertip through the soft wave, letting it curl around his finger. "And the queen?"

"Her first husband died a week after their wedding. Eventually she wed…" Alexia shook her head, pulling her hair free of his touch. Then she continued, "She wed an earl, Jared of Warehaven. He was known as the Dragon. He gave up his lands and title to move to Mirabilus, where he and Evonne eventually took on the surname of Drake."

"Ah, the beginning of my family."

Alexia set the page aside and pulled the next one forward. She groaned in dismay.

Braeden stroked her neck and watched the goose bumps race along her flesh. "What?"

"It's garbled, like the other one used to be. I don't understand this."

"How do you think the first page changed to something coherent?"

"If I knew the answer to that, don't you think I'd use it again?"

He ignored the sharpness of her tone and suggested, "We could sit here and watch."

"Watch what?"

"Just simply watch to see what happens, if anything."

Alexia sat back in her chair and stared at the pages. Minutes ticked by and nothing happened. Braeden's even breathing was the only sound to break the silence of the room.

He caressed her shoulder, making her heart momentarily kick into higher gear. When it settled into a more stable rhythm, she glanced at him and noticed that he'd narrowed his eyes.

Whether he was aware of it or not, his breathing had quickened before falling back to normal.

With his arm still slung across the back of her chair, she knew he'd taken her comment about not sharing his bed as a challenge.

That was typical of Braeden. How could she have forgotten that? Yet it was his quiet contemplation that had her on edge. Why did his next move require so much thought? It was doubtful that whatever plans he made would benefit her.

She wished things were different. It would be easy to accept his closeness, even to swallow her challenge if she wasn't so certain he was actually plotting to get her into his bed simply to prove her wrong.

Why couldn't there be more? Alexia wondered if the same memories ever ran through his mind. Did he occasionally wonder what it would be like if things had been different? Did he ever find himself mourning what they'd lost?

Her breath lodged in her throat. She wished she didn't still care about Braeden. If only she could find a way to make her heart forget that she'd ever cared, that she'd ever loved him—or that he'd once loved her, too.

Braeden leaned forward and stared at the pages. "Look."

She leaned forward, too, and looked at the manuscript. The top quarter of the page had filled in with readable writing. "How?"

He stood up and paced the floor. "A spell binds the book."

Alexia didn't tell him how obvious that was because she knew he was just thinking out loud and she didn't want to interrupt his thoughts.

He frowned. "What were you thinking about just now?"

Heat fired her cheeks. "Nothing." She turned away, hoping to hide the flush.

Braeden stared at her. *Now* what was she hiding? He'd had enough of wondering what she hid, and more than enough of her half answers.

If there was a time to coax her into providing answers, now was it. She was flustered, embarrassed and still excited about the manual.

He could take her up on her unwitting challenge, make headway before she'd realized what was happening. While seduction might not be considered fair play, it was useful. And right now there were too many loose ends, too many questions unanswered. He needed to employ every tactic in his arsenal if he was ever going to obtain the information he sought.

Without drawing her attention to what he was doing, Braeden willed the bolt on the entry door to slide into place. Just as silently, he willed the double doors to the office closed.

Since she appeared not to notice either action, he moved behind her, asking the obvious, "Was Nathan the one who contacted you to begin with?"

Her shoulders tensed. "Maybe."

Even though he was certain Nathan was involved, Braeden refused to settle for her half answers. He placed a hand on her shoulder, brushing his thumb along the side of her neck, and coaxed, "Maybe, as in yes, or maybe, as in you aren't sure?"

"I'm pretty sure, yes. When we saw him in the forest, I got the same sickening feeling. The man who'd mentally harassed me had left the impression of pure evil."

Braeden's eyebrows rose at the ease in which she'd answered, so he continued, "The men after you, were they sent from him?"

"Yes. But he's got lousy instincts when it comes to choosing his goons."

"Doubtful. They got you to come here, didn't they?"

She shrugged, then tensed her shoulders once again. Not wanting to give her time to pull away or realize what he was doing, Braeden slid his hand closer to the curve of her neck to absently stroke the soft flesh beneath her ear.

Alexia shivered at his touch, but remained still.

"Even though you weren't harmed, once your town house was blown up and you had possession of the pages, where else would you go except here?"

She admitted, "I don't know. There isn't anywhere else I could go."

"Exactly. He wanted you with the rest of the manual

and here you are." Braeden wanted to know if she worked with Nathan, but he wasn't a fool. He knew she'd never answer that direct a question. Even if she did answer, would he believe her?

"What are you saying?"

Braeden picked up on the slight change in the tone of her voice. If she wasn't already, she would soon be too suspicious of his actions for him to easily continue.

He realized that in the end, she was going to be livid, but the safety of Mirabilus and those at Dragon's Lair were worth far more than Alexia's rage.

Slowly turning her chair around so she faced him, he took her hands and pulled her up from her seat. He urged her closer. Holding her surprised stare, Braeden briefly touched his lips to hers. "I don't know, Alexia, what am I saying?"

Alexia pushed away from him. She couldn't think rationally when he was this near.

To her amazement, he let her go, but followed her, then asked, "What have you done to convince me that you aren't involved in this whole scheme?"

"Me?" She spun around. "What about you?"

Braeden stopped mere inches from her. "What *about* me? You already know it wasn't my Phantom outside your town house. It wasn't my voice you heard inside your mind. How do I know you aren't working with Nathan?"

She couldn't believe the questions coming out of his mouth. Did he know her so little? Hadn't he learned anything about her during their marriage?

Unable to hold his piercing stare any longer, she turned away. Alexia desperately needed space to breathe and to think. She needed him to back off. But when she parted her lips, to her horror the one question she never wanted to ask slipped out. "Why didn't you ever come after me?"

He came up behind her, refusing to give her the space she'd been seeking. "You told me not to."

"When did you ever listen to me?"

"Until then? Rarely."

At least he was being honest. She could always count on Braeden to tell her the truth, no matter what. "Why, then?"

"Because I thought that by doing what you'd asked, you'd eventually come back."

Alexia sighed. It was amazing how two animals of the same species could interpret things so differently. She'd written the note telling him to leave her alone because she'd been certain he wouldn't do so for very long. When he never came, she resigned herself to the choice she had made.

"I always figured you were happier without me."

"I was."

His response knocked the breath from her. Sometimes his honesty was too brutal. She sidestepped away from him. "I'm sorry, I shouldn't have come back."

"Oh, no, you don't." Braeden grabbed her shoulder, stopping her retreat, then spun her around and lifted her chin with the side of his hand. "I was angry. I still am. But that never meant I didn't want you back or that I didn't care."

His glittering gaze spoke of passion, not anger. It promised fulfilled desire, not rage. Frightened of the deep longing welling up inside her, she put her hand against his chest to push him away. "Braeden—"

His lips closed over hers, cutting off her plea for him to stop. He caressed the back of her head, holding her close. The arm he'd wrapped around her held her steady.

Alexia leaned against him, surrendering to the magic that was Braeden. She didn't want him to touch her. Yet at the same time, she needed to be engulfed by the strength of his will, the demands of his lips and the feel of his body against hers.

She moaned and crumpled his T-shirt beneath her fingers. He answered her near-silent response by steadily moving her across the office until the back of her thighs hit his desk.

Her heart raced unevenly like some skittish virginal bride's on her wedding night. This was no stranger sweeping the papers and other objects from his desk before pushing her down onto the smooth solid top. It was her husband. She knew every inch of his body. Maybe not as well as he knew hers, but there was nothing unfamiliar in his touch.

He cupped a breast and stroked his thumb across the nipple. Without hesitation her body reacted, tightening, pebbling beneath the contact. Everything about their relationship had been spontaneous. From making love within hours of first meeting to their headlong rush to the altar.

And her pain at his cold anger had been just as spontaneous.

She desperately wanted him to strip her naked and take her with wild abandonment.

But she couldn't face the level of hurt that would soon tear her apart. The absolute pleasure she could gain from him now wasn't worth the agony she'd have to live with day after day when she left Dragon's Lair.

He didn't love her anymore. He didn't trust her. That much had been made clear. Lust drove him now. A lust she recognized and admittedly shared. But she wanted, needed more than just a few moments of passion and the brief thrill of a soul-stealing release.

Her breath caught in her chest and Braeden broke their kiss. He rested his forehead against hers and gazed into her eyes a moment before asking, "Did I treat you so badly that you felt justified in putting our family in danger?"

Alexia gasped and tried to twist free of him. This was a conversation that could only end badly. She slid her back along the desk while trying to keep her tone firm. "Please let me up."

Braeden quickly found a way to hold her still on the slippery desktop. He nudged her legs apart and rested between them. Then he slipped his forearms beneath her shoulders, pressing her breasts impossibly tight against the hardness of his chest and leaving her the option of either putting her arms around him or letting them hang at an odd, uncomfortable position on the desk.

"Answer me."

The harsh tone of his voice commanded her attention. His hard glare blazed like fire. But the hands holding her head in place were gentle. The caressing touch against her scalp and along her cheek somehow conveyed warmth and safety to her swirling senses.

She held his stare, but could only manage to whisper, "You're too angry."

"I've been angry for years. I'm not going to hurt you."

He was referring to physical harm. That was not what she feared from him. He might demand and act like the dragon he was named for at times, but Braeden would never do anything to physically harm her.

Her attention flew to the gashes on his cheek. She closed her eyes against the guilt she felt. Obviously, between the two of them, she was the one who'd managed to cause physical harm.

"Open your eyes and answer me."

She looked up at him. His lips hovered just above hers, and their warm breaths mingled. "Why do you want me to look at you? Are you going to take the answers you want?"

To her amazement a seductive smile curved his lips. He readjusted one hand and gently stroked the soft spot below her ear. When she shivered involuntarily beneath his touch, he said, "I won't need my powers."

She froze. He was going to *seduce* the answers from her? Alexia frowned. "That's not fair."

"Worried I might win?"

Worried? No, more like terrified. She knew without a doubt he would succeed.

When she still didn't answer, he slid his other arm from beneath her shoulder and stroked his fingertips down her side. At the same time he lowered his lips to the free side of her neck, and the instant his tongue glided along the sensitive flesh, she knew she'd already lost.

Quickly, before she did anything foolish like moan or gasp with the desire uncoiling in her belly, she said, "I had no choice."

Cool air from the unheated office brushed against her suddenly naked legs. She didn't need to look to realize what he'd done. "You said you didn't need your powers. Give me my jeans back."

The heat of his palm burned a trail down her leg. "I lied. Sue me." He shifted, then hiked her leg up over his hip. "You were saying?"

Alexia's eyes widened and her heart somersaulted as he teased the back of her leg. "If I didn't do the paper on the manual, I wouldn't get a grade."

Like a loser in a game of strip poker where Braeden set all the rules, her blouse vanished. "Braeden, please. I'm not lying. I…" Her breath hitched as his touch slid beneath the edge of her panties. Drawing in a ragged breath, she fought to complete her thought before the raw lust clawing at her made thinking impossible. "I needed that degree. I wanted it. Can't you understand that?"

"Not counting your socks, you have two items of clothing left." His lips brushed against her ear. "If you don't want to lose them, you better finish your explanation quickly."

"I'm trying. But you don't believe me."

"I didn't say that." Her nipples swelled as her bra disappeared. "I'm waiting to hear the whole story before making up my mind. But you're taking forever." He moved down her body, his gaze raking the breast mere inches from his mouth. "I might start to wonder if you're doing it on purpose."

"No."

He laughed at her hoarse response and locked his gaze with hers before trailing his tongue around the tip of her breast.

Alexia closed her eyes, then arched into his touch. "I hate you, Braeden."

The barrier of her panties now gone, he stroked the heat between her legs. "You are such a bad liar."

"Then you know I'm not…" She couldn't keep her thoughts centered on the conversation. "Braeden… please."

He nearly growled when he moved back over her and claimed her mouth with his.

She tugged at his T-shirt. He got the hint and beneath her touch the material was replaced by his heated skin.

This was insane. But stopping him now would be even more insane. It was useless even to try convincing herself that she didn't want his lips covering hers or his tongue plundering her mouth. It would be even more of a lie to say that she wanted him to stop the teasing between her legs, or that she didn't like the circling touch that stroked inside her.

A moan raced up to her throat, only to be cut off by the sound of Cameron's voice over the intercom, now lying on the floor.

"Braeden, we have trouble at the keep."

Braeden emitted a harsh curse. One Alexia mentally echoed.

In less time than it took to blink, he pulled away and instantly their clothes covered their bodies. The loss of contact and the protection of clothing made little difference. Her body still screamed for more.

Braeden extended his hand to help her up from the desk. Before she smacked it aside, she noticed that he was shaking nearly as much as she. Without looking at him, Alexia moved off the desk to the other side, asking, "Did you get everything you needed?"

"No." His voice was rough, his expression hard and closed. "But I will."

A frisson of rage swept away any lingering passion. She pointed at the door. "Just go."

He paused by the worktable, turned over a couple of pages, then looked over his shoulder at her. "You might find this interesting."

The desire to see what he was talking about warred with the need to keep her distance. "I probably will." Alexia placed her palms on the desk. "After you leave."

When the entry door closed behind him, Alexia drew in a long, trembling breath and fell into the oversize executive chair behind her.

Somehow when it came to Braeden, she had to find her backbone. She needed to stay angry with him, which wouldn't be too hard to do. And she desperately needed to keep him more than an arm's length away. She wasn't sure how, but she needed to figure that out before he returned.

The urge to wallow in her memories and fears was overwhelming. She looked at the pages on the table. There was one sure way to set her wayward emotions aside—work.

The pages of the grimoire suddenly called to her. She could feel them breathe warm and inviting against her ear. Curious and more than willing to do something to take her mind off Braeden, she rose and crossed to the worktable.

Alexia whistled softly. "I'll be damned."

She gingerly touched the top page, turned it over, then another and another. Each one was now filled with words, sentences and paragraphs, instead of unreadable gibberish and empty space.

A vision of her and Braeden on his desk, kissing, caressing, filled her mind. The spell on the book was the two of them—together.

The blank page beneath her fingers magically filled with words before her eyes. Just thinking of Braeden and his kiss, his touch, had transformed the manual into something she could read.

Was that why Nathan chased her here? Did he know about the spell?

Chapter 10

His wild lust sated and the seeds of his next steps planted, Nathan leaned back in his office chair and studied Aelthed's small, wooden prison. "You are full of surprises, Uncle. I never would have expected that the words were physically unseen on the pages. I thought the Dragon and his love would have to work together, side by side, each offering their own expertise, to translate the grimoire."

He smiled to himself. Actually, in the end, this only made it easier. Braeden would be able to leave his wife alone to do her work while he headed to Mirabilus. Meaning the Dragon wouldn't be around to protect his mate.

Nathan opened his desk drawer and dropped the cube into its cubbyhole. "Rest well, Uncle Aelthed."

Braeden left his office and headed back to his suite. While news of another break-in at Mirabilus didn't surprise him, the conflicting reports of a whirlwind and a winged beast did. There was no doubt in his mind that Nathan was involved in these latest events.

Since a little girl was missing and another worker injured, he'd have to make a quick trip back there. It was his responsibility to safeguard Mirabilus and its inhabitants. His attempts of recent weeks had been far from successful.

While he didn't begrudge the people of Mirabilus his time, he also needed to concentrate on opening Dragon's Lair and seeing to it that Alexia finished translating the manual before she ran away again.

And she would. He knew it as well as he knew the sun would rise in the morning. The first time things got too complicated or too hard she would be gone.

Braeden entered his suite and leaned against the doorway to his private office. Alexia was so deep in her work that she hadn't heard him enter.

He cleared his throat in warning before saying, "You need to pack up the pages and whatever else you need."

"Why?"

"There's been another break-in. We're going to Mirabilus."

Alexia shook her head. "No." She turned to look up at him. The last thing she wanted to do was relocate to Mirabilus with him. Alone.

She feared what Braeden could do to her heart more than she feared Nathan. While there really wasn't anyone at the Lair who could protect her from Braeden, at least she'd be in the States. The idea of having no one to turn to and nowhere to run if need be, on an isolated foreign island, was something she'd rather avoid as long as possible.

"I'll be fine right here. You can take care of the island without me."

"I can't protect you, as well, if I'm not here."

Alexia glanced pointedly at the desk. "I'll be safer with you gone."

"That reminds me." Braeden walked closer. "We haven't finished our discussion yet."

Her pulse lurched. She held up a hand to ward him off. "Don't. Just don't. Why don't you go to Mirabilus and leave me alone to work?"

He leaned against the edge of the table. "Have enough words appeared for you to work with, or do we need to create a little more…magic for it to be worth your time?"

Wary, she leaned away from him. "There are plenty of words. Nothing important, just more information about your family. There isn't anything that would prove useful to Nathan."

"And if that changes?"

Alexia sighed. They both knew the answer. "If it changes, I'll call you. I swear, Braeden, if the grimoire starts to reveal anything other than what it has so far, I'll call you."

"If you're still here."

"What does *that* mean?"

He shrugged. "You excel at running away. How do I know that the minute I'm gone you won't do so again?"

She rubbed her temples. His distrust was beginning to make her sick. "I said I'd translate the manual. Even I know that I owe you at least that much. I won't leave until the job is done."

To her surprise Braeden said nothing. He left the office for a few minutes, then returned. "I have an hour before I need to leave. We'll have dinner together."

"I'm not hungry."

"Right. Then it's time for a break." He pulled her chair away from the table. "Dinner is waiting in the maze."

"Maze?"

"Of course. Doesn't every castle worth its battlements have a maze?"

She peeled off her gloves, jotted some notes on her pad, then stood up. "I haven't been in enough castles to know."

Braeden drew her from the office. "Then you'll have to trust me on it, won't you?" Pausing at the double doors, he flipped off the overhead light, then extended his hand into the room.

She watched in amazed silence as a glimmering orb surrounded the worktable. Sudden concern prompted her to ask, "It won't harm the pages?"

"No. It'll just keep them safe from anyone's prying eyes or thieving hands."

He pulled the doors closed and locked them before ushering her to the entry door. "Ready?"

Her stomach branded her a liar by growling. "Sure."

After they left the suite, Alexia tried to make small talk. "Did you and Cameron ever decide on someone for chief of security?"

"We hired one."

She glanced up at him. "You say that like it's not a good thing."

"I don't know if it is or not. There's something…off about the guy."

"Then why did you hire him?"

"Cam's in charge of hiring. He wanted the man."

"Yeah, but—"

"But nothing. He hasn't been wrong so far. I'm not going to second-guess him now."

They walked out onto a flagstone patio in the center courtyard. Braeden pointed toward the line of waist-high bushes. "Through there."

"How can it be a maze if you can see where you are?"

"I'm told the plants will grow."

Alexia touched a half-dead shrub. "You sure about that?"

"No. Which is why Cam's trying to find us a full-time gardener. The last one came nose to nose with a black bear and quit."

"I see." She sat down at a small, wrought-iron table laden with food. "I thought you said dinner. Is someone else joining us?"

After removing the domed covers from the plates, Braeden sat across from her. "No. It's just us. I wanted a decent meal before I left."

"Will you be gone long?" She looked forward to some time alone and wondered how much she would have.

"I'll be back late tomorrow night, or early the next morning. Cam and Sean are moving into the suite next door to mine until I get home. The security chief starts tonight. And you know that if you need anything, all you have to do is call me back."

"I'm sure everything will be fine."

"So tell me, what happened to the professor who coerced you into doing the paper?"

Alexia stabbed a fork into her salad. He just wasn't going to give up. "He died in a car accident the night I turned everything in."

Without missing a beat, Braeden said, "He'd served his purpose."

"You think it was intentional?" She'd never thought twice about the man's death. "They ruled it an accident."

"The timing was a little coincidental for an accident."

"Perhaps." Alexia set her fork down and folded her hands in her lap. "Braeden, do you believe me about this? I never would have done a paper on the grimoire if I hadn't been forced."

"Why you did the paper is the least of my concerns right now." He nodded toward her plate. "Finish eating."

She toyed with her food. There was something he wasn't saying. She really didn't want to know what, but asked, anyway. "Then what is your concern?"

"Whether or not you're working with Nathan."

Alexia gasped and leaned back in her chair. "Have you lost your mind? Why would I do anything that low or that dangerous?"

"Why? Where would you like me to start? You thought I blamed you for your accident. You were angry and upset that I didn't come after you. I'd think either reason would be enough for you to consider getting even."

Her stomach tightened. Alexia's fork clattered onto the plate and she pushed the food away. "You know me better than that."

"I thought so, too, at one time. But now? You've given me little reason to trust you."

She slapped her napkin on the table and pushed her chair back. "Have a wonderful time at Mirabilus."

The chair jerked back toward the table. Braeden tossed his napkin on his empty plate. "If you disagree with my assessment, tell me how."

He was all business, acting and sounding as if this topic was nothing more than another contract to be discussed. "I brought you the pages. I told you about Nathan."

"You brought me the pages because you had nowhere else to go. You told me about Nathan under duress."

Braeden leaned back in his chair, studying her, debating. Finally he asked, "Why should I trust you, Alexia?"

To her own chagrin, she had no answer to give him. "I don't know. Maybe you shouldn't."

"You're not going to argue the point?"

"No." What was there to argue?

"And you've nothing to offer in defense of yourself?"

"No." Now she was on trial?

He stared at her, holding her gaze in a searing jewel-toned trap. And Alexia wondered if the pain and doubt she saw in his eyes were reflected in her own. Why were they doing this to each other? To themselves?

She stretched an arm across the table. With her palm up, she asked, "Truce? Can we just declare a truce until the manual is translated?"

He clasped her hand, turning it to entwine their fingers. Braeden lifted her hand and directed his gaze briefly to the amethyst-and-diamond wedding set she still wore. "What then, Alexia?"

"Then?" She paused, determined not to give life to the emotions tearing her apart. "I'll leave."

"Is that what you want?" He released her hand.

No, that wasn't what she wanted. She wanted things to be the way they used to be. She wanted to go back to the beginning and start all over.

But life wasn't like that, not even life with a wizard. There were some things even he couldn't give her. "I thought that's what you wanted." She tossed the decision back to him.

"I did say that, didn't I?" Something unfamiliar flitted behind his eyes and rang odd in his voice. Alexia couldn't put her finger on the emotion.

Braeden shifted on his chair. "I should get going."

She delayed him, hoping to figure out what he was hiding behind that expressive gaze. "Was anyone hurt in this break-in?"

He blew out a low breath. "A little girl is missing."

The food she'd eaten rushed toward her throat. "Oh, my God, Braeden, I am so sorry. Anyone else?"

Her guilt rang loud and clear in her strained voice. And while some of the guilt did rest on her shoulders, Braeden realized she wasn't entirely to blame.

After seeing the magic contained in the Dragonierre's Manual, he wondered if his suspicions about her might be misplaced. "Yes. A groundskeeper was also injured."

"I don't know how to undo what I've done. I—"

"Alexia, don't." He reached out and placed a finger over her lips. "There are some things about the past that we can't change. Your paper can't be undone, no matter how much you wish it. All you can do now is translate the manual and see if there's anything in there that could help us."

She looked down at her plate. "I doubt it." Her words were little more than a sigh. "So far it's still more like a diary than a grimoire."

"Maybe that's all it is."

"Will I be able to get through that bubble you put over it?"

"Of course." Braeden rose to leave, adding, "Cam will undo the spell once you get back to the suite."

"Good." Alexia picked up her glass of water, took a drink, then set it down, saying almost to herself, "Iced tea would be nice."

He stared at the glass she'd set on the table. The clear liquid turned a golden brown. Tea? Braeden focused his senses on the perimeter of the maze, seeking the power behind that transformation.

To his amazement the only power present came from Alexia. Impossible. There was no way she could have possessed any ability all this time without his knowing it. Yet he still sensed no one else around and no other powers at work.

There was another possibility—the Dragon's curse. Was Alexia draining his powers? Wouldn't he know if that was happening?

Instead of drawing her attention to the glass, he sat back down and asked, "What kind of tea? I'll have the kitchen bring some in."

"White tea, with raspberry."

The tea in her glass lightened. Raspberries floated between the ice.

She took another sip and paused to smile at him. "Thank you. Shouldn't you be leaving?"

Was it possible she didn't realize what she'd done? "No problem. Anything else you'd like before I go?"

Alexia shrugged. "A slice of chocolate cake might be nice."

Braeden waited a second to make certain one didn't materialize before signaling for the waiter lounging just beyond the dining area. "A slice of chocolate cake for Mrs. Drake."

While they waited, Braeden wondered if the prophecy was true. He'd always thought it was nothing more than another of his aunt's stories.

The waiter brought the cake and asked, "Anything else?"

"No, thank you."

When the man left, Braeden said, "Now, I really have to be going."

Alexia slid her chair back. "I'll walk you to your car."

"Car?" He frowned.

"To get to the airport?"

"I'm not taking the jet. I'll…"

"Just zip on over?"

"Something like that, yes." He paused and looked down at her. "Alexia, if you need me, at any time, call me. Just close your eyes and concentrate. I'll be here."

Chapter 11

The light streaming in the window dragged Alexia from her slumber. She squinted and held up a hand to shield her eyes, wishing she'd remembered to close the draperies before going to bed.

Unable to get back to sleep, she rose, showered and dressed, tugging on a pair of jeans and a sweatshirt.

In the kitchen, she pulled out the toaster and popped a couple of slices of bread into the slots. She made coffee and pulled butter and jam from the fridge.

While the bread was toasting, she wandered into the office to look at the pages waiting for her. She wasn't surprised to see the detail they contained. The changes were incredible.

She heard the toaster pop and returned to the kitchen. After spreading the slices with some butter and jam, she took them with her cup of coffee into the living room and stood in front of the sliding doors that led onto the balcony.

With the sun shining down on them, the mountains were breathtaking. Brilliant splotches of color scattered here and there made the view worthy of an artist's oil painting.

The fine hairs on the back of her neck rose. Alexia held her breath. Someone was watching her. She could feel it in the pit of her stomach, and in the icy chill skittering goose bumps up her arms.

"Who's there? Show yourself." Her whisper echoed in the room.

She looked around and saw no one, yet the feeling remained. When she turned back around, she caught a brief glimpse of a shadowy form retreating from the balcony.

Alexia blinked, but when she opened her eyes she saw nothing. Slowly bringing her face closer to the glass, she stared hard but still saw nothing.

Had she been anywhere but Dragon's Lair, she'd have brushed it off to a trick of the light. But she wasn't anywhere else, so the fear and uncertainty remained.

Alexia jumped at the sound of someone knocking on the door. Laughing at her nervousness, she opened the door. Her smile froze on her face. "Danielle, come in."

What she really wanted to do was slam the door in the woman's face.

"Please, sit down." Heading for the kitchen, she asked, "Do you want some coffee?"

"No. What I want is you gone."

Alexia sighed while she poured Braeden's aunt a cup of coffee. Whether the woman wanted it or not, she could at least sit here and pretend to drink it while she explained.

And she was going to finally explain.

Alexia walked back into the living room and handed Danielle the cup, suggesting, "Just pretend."

Danielle set the cup on the end table. Alexia couldn't help but notice the woman was dressed to kill, so to speak. Full makeup, hair slicked back into a severe bun. She wore a loud, black-and-red paisley printed suit, matching red blouse—so the blood wouldn't show as much, perhaps?

Alexia swallowed her sarcastic thought, then asked, "So, why the visit, Danielle?" The woman's timing was so obviously planned. She'd never have stopped by if Braeden were here.

The woman frowned, tipping her head and looking at Alexia as if something were dreadfully wrong. Finally she shook off whatever was bothering her and asked, "Do you care for my nephew so little that you are willing to risk his life?"

"He doesn't seem to be too concerned about my coming here."

"I'm not talking about the damn manual or the danger you brought with you."

"Then what?" Alexia groaned before answering her own question. "The curse."

"Of course."

"Give it a rest, Danielle."

The older woman's face reddened. "You really don't care." She nearly shook with anger. "Are you plotting his death?"

Concerned, Alexia stared at Braeden's aunt. "Have you lost your mind?"

"Why else would you intentionally tempt the Fates?"

"Oh, yes, the Fates." Alexia sipped her coffee, hoping the caffeine would give her enough energy to hold this insane conversation. "I don't have any powers. None. And if I suddenly started draining Braeden of his, don't you think he'd notice?"

"He's too bewitched to notice."

"Bewitched?" Alexia shook her head. The whole idea of Braeden being that distracted because of her was ludicrous. "When it comes to me, the only thing Braeden is bewitched by is the translation of the manual and getting me out of here."

Danielle's lip curled into a near snarl. "Can you blame him?"

It was all Alexia could do not to slam her coffee on the table. Instead, she wrapped her fingers more tightly around the cup. "If he was so damn anxious to rid himself of me, why didn't he just file for a divorce? Then none of this would matter."

"A divorce?" Danielle gasped as if Alexia had suggested Braeden shoot himself. "He can't divorce you."

If the woman was going to throw the ruler-of-Mirabilus, High-Druid-wizard stuff out as an excuse, Alexia swore she'd scream. Obviously eager for self-torture she asked, "And why is that?"

"Dragons mate for life."

Alexia watched the coffee cup fall from her hand to the carpet as if in slow motion. It was odd, really. One heartbeat, her fingers were wrapped around the thing. The next, the cup simply sailed to the floor and bounced twice, then rolled in a semicircle before stopping. She hadn't even felt her hand relax.

She stared at the spreading coffee stain, wondering how she'd get it out of the off-white carpet. Without responding to Danielle's inconceivable statement, Alexia rose, went to the kitchen, then came back with towels and a pitcher of cold water.

While she knelt on the floor trying to sop up the coffee, Danielle asked, "You didn't know that?"

It wasn't so much that she didn't know it, it was more along the lines of being so far-fetched she was having a hard time believing anyone would say something so outrageous. "This is the twenty-first century. If for some reason he can't file for a divorce, I can."

Danielle picked up the used towels and carried them out to the kitchen, saying, "A civil divorce won't make any difference. It goes beyond legalities." She came back with a couple of dry towels.

Alexia shook her head. "Look, this is between Braeden and me. It really isn't any of your business."

"So you say. But what happens to this family once the manual is translated and you've taken all his powers? He'll be defenseless against any evil you release."

"Just pretend for a moment that I buy into that whole draining-of-powers concept. What would stop me from defending him?"

"Do not take this lightly."

"Oh, I'm not." Well, that wasn't quite true, but it seemed easier to humor Danielle than to argue with her. "I'm just curious. If all this is true, why didn't you mention this before Braeden and I were married? That might have been a more opportune time."

"Nobody knew you were going to hook him so quickly."

"Thank you. I'm glad to know you think your nephew is that weak-willed." Alexia rose and tossed the remaining towels onto the bar. "You knew from day one that I was mortal. If the curse about the eldest dragon marrying a mortal could prove so destructive, why didn't you talk him out of seeing me then?"

Danielle glared at her. "I tried."

For some reason she couldn't explain, the knowledge

that Danielle had absolutely no control over Braeden made Alexia breathe easier. "So that's why you've hated me from day one—because Braeden chose me over your objections?"

"Even without the threat of the curse, it was all too fast. You don't meet someone and marry them less than a month later."

"I guess in our case that wasn't true." Actually, her sister had voiced the same worries at the time. "So, you intentionally tried to drive me away?"

"Yes. It was the only way to show Braeden how unworthy you were and how little you truly cared for him."

"*Cared* for him? Danielle, I fell in love with him the moment I saw him from across the room. I was carrying his child—our child—and you sent a magical beast to run me off the road?"

"That wasn't me. I didn't even know you were out in the car that night—" Danielle froze and stared at her. "A *what* ran you off the road?"

Alexia waved the question away. She'd already said too much. "Doesn't matter. What's done is done. But you won't get the chance again."

Danielle's eyes were wide. "You don't understand. I can't conjure up anything. I can only communicate intuitively by sending and receiving thoughts. That's all the natural ability I possess. And no potion, no spell, is going to permit me to conjure up a beast."

Great. Alexia had never once thought Braeden was responsible. But she *had* suspected his aunt. If it wasn't Danielle, could it have been Nathan?

Had he been around even then? She remembered the overwhelming fear at seeing the dragon in her rearview mirror. It was the same type of fear she felt whenever

Nathan invaded her mind—a cold, sickening dread she was unable to control. Why had he been following her back then?

"You must leave here." Danielle stood up and came over to stand before her. "I was right, you are dangerous. Braeden will die if you stay."

From the forcefulness of her words, there was little doubt in Alexia's mind that Danielle Drake actually believed that. However, Alexia didn't.

"I'm not leaving, Danielle. I don't believe your curse is true, and even if it were, why would you assume for one second that Braeden couldn't be protected by means other than magical?"

"You just admitted that you were run off the road by a beast, and you could have been killed. What if it had been Braeden?"

Alexia was surprised at the level of worry Braeden's aunt displayed. She was also surprised that the woman seemingly believed her without question. She'd always been certain Danielle would accuse her of making it all up.

"Look, for one thing, Braeden has this innate sense that warns him of danger. For another, he wouldn't have been as terrified as I was and probably wouldn't have jerked the wheel so hard." She didn't have the heart to tell his aunt about the dragon coming out of the book. It would only upset her more. "Danielle, he'll be fine."

"You can't know that."

Alexia couldn't find the words to ease Danielle's fears. "What can we know for certain? Nothing."

"If anything happens to him…" The woman stopped abruptly, her gaze directed out the glass doors.

"What?" Alexia turned around, looking over her shoulder. "What do you see?"

"Nothing. Mist. Shadows. Nothing that would interest you." She spun around and headed toward the door. "I should go."

"You don't have to. Stay, check out the manual with me." Alexia paused. What was she suggesting?

"No. I have a meeting to attend."

Relief flooded through Alexia as the door closed behind Danielle. She didn't know what she'd have done if the woman had taken her up on her offer.

She went over and opened the balcony door. Braeden's aunt had seen something, leaving Alexia's senses even more on edge.

Alexia leaned back from the computer monitor, rubbed her eyes and stretched. Since Braeden wasn't home, she'd turned down his brothers' invitation to dinner so she could work on the book some more. After a while, though, putting this diary together was rather boring.

And typing up her notes, if anything, was even more boring.

"Alexia."

She froze. There was that voice again—Nathan.

"What have you learned?"

"Nothing. Go away."

"Not until I get what I'm after. Then—" He laughed. The sinister sound made her hands shake. *"Then maybe I'll go away."*

Alexia leaned over and reached for the phone to call Sean or Cam. Before she could touch it, the receiver flew across the room as if thrown.

"No, no, my dear. We don't need anyone else."

Trying hard not to panic, she said, "The book is nothing but a diary. That's all it is. Look for yourself." She pointed at the monitor, then choked on a scream. A ghostly image stared back at her from the screen.

"No, I don't believe you. No one would waste the time and energy involved in creating that grimoire to use the pages for a simple diary. I will get the truth, Alexia."

With her feet Alexia shoved the chair as far away from the desk as possible, screaming, "Leave me alone!"

With any luck her brothers-in-law might hear her.

He laughed again. Alexia covered her ears to no avail. While the face on the monitor appeared to laugh with evil humor, the sound still came from inside her head.

"No. You're going to tell me what I want to know."

An invisible force slammed her arms down onto the chair. Unseen bindings held her wrists securely to the chair arms.

Frantic, she tried jerking free. Without thought, she cried, "Braeden, Braeden, I need you now!"

But Nathan's laughter grew louder, drowning out her cries. Had Braeden heard her?

"No. I'm afraid he didn't. It's just you and I."

A cold, nearly frozen finger stroked down her cheek. *"I'd nearly forgotten how soft, pliable and defenseless human skin feels beneath my touch. It's been far too long."*

Alexia leaned as far to the side as the invisible binds would allow. Fear closed her throat, cutting off any further cry for help.

Her struggles proved useless. The unseen finger trailed further down her neck, rimming the edge of her sweatshirt.

He pressed one finger at a time against her throat, dragging her upright in the chair. *"This may hurt a bit, Alexia, but only for a few moments."*

Slowly he tightened his grip. *"At first you'll panic. See, even now your eyes grow wide."*

A little more pressure against her windpipe. *"Then*

you'll struggle to breathe. Can you hear your own gasps for breath? Or does the sound of your heart pounding in your ears drown out the sound of your lungs begging for air?"

Her throat convulsed against his hand as she desperately tried to pull in a breath. Alexia's eyes welled with tears. She didn't want to die like this.

The rush of his hot breath against her ear drew a strangled whimper from her. *"And now—now you'll feel lightheaded, the room will turn hazy, out of focus. Soon, very soon, Alexia, your limp, nearly dead body will be mine to do with as I please."*

The room spun. Her heartbeat slowed. And her body felt strangely weightless.

Again his evil laugh resounded in her head. *"Don't fear overmuch, though. I will not kill you. This is only a warning. The next time, you will give me the answers I seek."*

As if no longer inside her own body, Alexia watched from across the room as a murky shadow hovered over her physical self, now slumped in the chair.

Had he killed her? Or was she hallucinating? Either way, she was quite obviously here, not over there in her body. She couldn't be certain, but she didn't feel dead.

What she felt was anger. No, it was more like rage and she'd be damned if she was going to stand here and do nothing.

There was no way she could take on Nathan alone. If there was the slightest chance she still lived, she needed to get help. Quickly. She raced across the room for the door.

He didn't appear to see her or sense her. Grateful for that bit of luck, she ran through the living room to the front door and grabbed the doorknob. Her hand slid through it as if the knob was no longer tangible.

Alexia stared at the knob, her hand and finally at the door, whispering, "This is either going to hurt really, really bad, or it'll work."

She stepped toward, then through the door and stood in the hallway. With a brief glance behind her, she smiled. "Not bad." But who would she get to help? Even if she could just walk into the suite where Sean and Cam were, would she be able to communicate with them?

Danielle's voice floated down the hall from the dining room. The woman was singing to herself. Alexia realized there was one person nearby who could hear her thoughts. She rushed in that direction, all the while shouting inside her mind, "Danielle, get the boys. I need help, now."

The sound of glass shattering echoed around the corner. As Alexia rounded the last turn in the hallway, she saw Danielle standing in the kitchen with broken glass at her feet.

"Danielle, please, it's Nathan. He's going to kill me. Help me." She tried grabbing the woman's arm, but again her hand touched nothing.

However, Danielle's eyes widened and she jerked her arm away.

Frustrated, Alexia shouted, "Damn it, woman, go!"

In a flash, Danielle ran for Sean and Cameron. She beat on the door to the suite, and when they answered, she gasped, "Alexia needs you—now."

Cam grabbed a key card from the entryway table and headed out the door with Sean on his heels. Alexia followed as they entered Braeden's apartment, each going in a different direction to find her.

"She's in here!" Sean yelled from the office. Cam and Danielle joined him.

Alexia stared in amazement. She was passed out on the floor. Hopefully she was just passed out. No sooner did that thought enter her mind than the room went hazy, then spun wildly and she felt herself fall limp to the floor.

"Alexia, Alexia, can you hear me?"

Arms were around her, shaking her gently. She opened her eyes and stared up at Cam. "Yes. Can *you* hear *me?*"

Her voice was hoarse and it hurt to talk. Her throat felt swollen.

"Of course I can," Cam said. He slid an arm beneath her back and helped her to sit up. "I'm going to take you into the bedroom, then call Braeden."

"No." She grasped his shirtsleeve. "Don't call him."

Sean stood at Cam's side looking down at them. "Lexi, there are red marks on your throat. If they turn to bruises, it's going to be a little hard to hide. I think he needs to know that someone attacked his wife."

She shook her head. "No."

Cam agreed with Sean. "We have to call him. Otherwise he's going to be ticked when he finds out later."

Alexia stared at Danielle, willing her to listen. *"Someone was hurt during this last break-in at Mirabilus. He has enough to deal with there. I'm not badly hurt, so don't let them call him. He'll only rush right back here into what could be even more dangerous."*

Danielle nodded in obvious agreement, then stepped into the conversation with her nephews. "No. Alexia's right. Don't call Braeden."

The lush green forest of the Isle of Mirabilus stretched endlessly before him. The island was approximately 150 square miles, and nearly three-quarters of it was wooded, making the search for the missing girl all that much harder.

Some of the witnesses claimed a tornado had streaked from the sky. Others swore they saw a dragon diving from the clouds. Either way, a little girl was missing. According to the island's historian, nothing like this had happened in more than four hundred years.

Braeden leaned on the stone wall surrounding the keep while waiting for the last search team to return. Throughout the night, they'd hit one dead end after another. Not even the power of his magic broke down the barrier preventing them from locating the little girl.

Finally, toward dawn he'd seen the briefest snippet of a vision and had sent the teams to the caves. With luck she'd be in one of them. And with more luck they'd find her alive.

Braeden glanced over his shoulder at the gate towers and was satisfied to see his orders were being followed. A line of cars and trucks drove through the gates. Around sunrise, frustrated by their fruitless search and dreading another abduction, he'd ordered the island's constable to send everyone with children to the apartments inside the walls of Mirabilus.

He wasn't about to chance another child being abducted. The safest place, the only place to ensure that wouldn't happen, was inside the walls.

Protective magic had been woven into the wall. For countless centuries his ancestors had strengthened the intricate spell that kept the castle and its inhabitants safe from dark powers.

Unfortunately the spell didn't safeguard against the mortal dangers attacking Mirabilus of late. But at the moment, Braeden's main concern was keeping his people safe against Nathan.

He heard footsteps approaching and felt Rolfe, one of

the groundskeepers, draw near. "Mr. Drake, we found Cindy."

He didn't turn around as he asked, "Alive?"

"Scared half to death, but outside of a few scratches and bruises, she seems well enough." From the corner of his eye, Braeden saw the older man's hands shake. Composing himself, Rolfe finally said in a near whisper, "She could have been killed." His voice rose. "She's just an innocent child, barely seven. Why would anyone kidnap her?"

Braeden placed a hand on Rolfe's shoulder trying to offer comfort. "Where is she now?"

"The doctors are checking her over just to be sure. And Beatrice is there, too."

"Good." Braeden's sigh of relief *whooshed* from him. Beatrice was the island's healer. While it was unlikely the woman could do much to assist in healing any physical injuries, she was one of the few who'd be capable of soothing the girl's fears. "Where was she found?"

"In one of the lower caves."

A couple of more hours and the tide would have taken the child out to sea. "Her parents?"

Rolfe leaned against the wall alongside Braeden. "I picked them up in the four-wheeler and brought them here. They're with Cindy and the doctors now."

"Good." Braeden looked at his man. Lines of fatigue marred Rolfe's face. Dark circles beneath his eyes made him look older than his seventy years. "You're exhausted. Go home, get some rest."

"If you don't mind, sir, and if there's room, I'd like to bring my wife here."

They'd recently added more apartments to the complex within the walls. There were now enough units to house every family living on Mirabilus. With the uncertainty in today's world, it was the only way Braeden and his brothers knew of to keep the inhabitants safe without having to drain their powers.

The residents had their own homes and their own lives, and until today they'd never been ordered to move inside the walls. Braeden was thankful that the few families who'd argued against the move had been easily convinced to do it.

"Rolfe, you're more than welcome to bring your wife here. No need to ask."

"Thank you, sir. I'll be on my way, then."

Well aware that Rolfe was exhausted, Braeden knew he'd be walking nearly a mile to his small bungalow. "Let me."

The man's sigh of gratitude as he disappeared under the spell echoed into the night.

Braeden leaned back against the wall and searched his mind for every little detail he knew about Alexia. A cold, sinking feeling in the pit of his stomach nearly screamed the obvious at him.

He'd been wrong.

She wasn't involved with Nathan. Even though she'd possessed no magic until recently, she'd always been intuitive. If her mind hadn't recognized Nathan's vileness, the cringing of her spirit would have sent her running in the opposite direction.

He owed her an apology. Braeden closed his eyes against the distasteful thought. It might stick in his throat, but it was owed.

As he'd done throughout the night, he mentally opened the curtain of time and space between Mirabilus and Dragon's Lair.

But this time, Alexia's presence was nowhere to be found.

His heart plummeted. Before the fear could wrap him
in cold dread, he took himself back to the Lair and stepped
into his office suite.

Chapter 12

The surf pounded against the rock wall below the cave's entrance, sending a cold spray of seawater across Nathan's materializing form.

His senses picked up the lingering trace of intruders. He swung away from the entrance, his eyes piercing the darkness of the cave as he searched for his prey.

The girl was gone. Nathan's lips curled over his bared teeth. Gone. While he'd toyed with the Dragon's mate, someone had taken the girl from his lair.

He should have killed her, but the terror in her eyes and her screams of horror had lent so much strength to his powers that he'd thought to feed off her fear once again.

Nathan waved a hand before the rock wall, bringing Mirabilus into view. Curses dripped from his tongue. The child still lived, but the residents of the isle were moving into the keep where they'd be safe from his powers.

For now.

He closed that view to focus on Dragon's Lair and the manual spread out on the table. Soon he would possess enough power to break the spells wrapped around Mirabilus.

Nothing would keep those on the island safe. He groaned in delicious anticipation.

Once he attained the level of Hierophant, he would see to it that the Drakes paid for all the crimes committed against him and his father. The revenge he'd taken out on Aelthed was not enough. He wanted all the remaining Drakes to pay.

He would wipe their existence from this earthly plane. They would die at his command—slowly and in agony. He would siphon their magic, adding it to his own as he drained them of life.

Soon. Soon all would be his.

Braeden froze in the doorway to his private office. Alexia sat on the floor holding her head in her hands, Cameron, Sean and Danielle all gathered around her. Braeden's stomach twisted in knots and he heard his aunt say, "No. Alexia's right. Don't call Braeden."

"What would they not call me about?" He pushed Sean out of the way to stare down at Alexia. He snarled a curse as he knelt beside her, then took her from Cam, gathering her into his arms.

The intensity of the fear snaking through him took him off guard, shaking him to his core. Braeden shook the ice-cold emotion from himself and studied the red marks around Alexia's throat. They looked oddly like handprints.

He gently touched her neck. "You thought you'd hide this from me?"

"It's nothing." Her voice rasped. "I'll survive."

Braeden covered her lips with a fingertip, ordering, "Be quiet." He glanced up at Cam. "What happened?"

His brother shrugged. "We just got here. As far as we've learned, Nathan attacked her."

Braeden swore again, then ordered, "Call for the car, she's going to the hospital."

Alexia shouted, "No!" But not a sound left her lips. Her eyes flew open with surprise and she asked, "What did you do?" While her mouth moved, she remained mute.

She glared at him.

"I told you to be quiet." He shrugged. "Since I know you never listen, I took care of it myself." Braeden narrowed his eyes at her, hoping to bully her into accepting his decision. "You *are* going to the hospital."

But she shook her head and shot a plea toward Danielle.

"Braeden, she'll be fine." His aunt's tone was soft, cajoling. "Anyway, how are you going to explain the marks on her neck when the police are called?"

He'd meant to laugh in disbelief, but it came out as more of a snicker. "They won't be called. Nobody will remember she was there."

Cam asked, "Do we really want to start doing that here? It's only going to take one receptive person to eventually start wondering."

Sometimes his family's being right was irritating. Braeden rose, lifting Alexia in his arms. "Then we won't start any speculation—*here*." He stepped away from the circle of his family. "I'll call you later."

Alexia grabbed at his shoulders. He looked down at her and she pointed frantically at the worktable.

Braeden rolled his eyes. She *would* think about work before herself. "Gone." Instantly, the manual, her notes, tools and computer disappeared.

Before relaxing in his arms, Alexia looked at Danielle and mouthed, "Thank you."

Alexia's lips had barely formed the words when Braeden whisked them to their private bedchamber at Mirabilus.

They'd spent their wedding night here in this very chamber. Her marriage gift to him, an oil painting of a medieval warrior being knighted by a beautiful queen, still hung on the wall.

He crossed the room and placed her on the high bed. "Stay there. I'm going to go call the doctor."

She grabbed his arm. "No. I'm fine." Her voice was back. He'd released the spell holding her silent. "Please, just let me rest awhile."

Since she seemed to be all right, outside of her scratchy voice, he'd take her word for it. But he wasn't going to leave her alone. "Move over." He stretched out alongside her and pulled her into his arms.

She froze for a moment, then relaxed against his chest. "How did you know I needed you?"

"I couldn't feel your presence." He wasn't about to lie to her. "When I was unable to touch your mind, I knew something was wrong."

She tipped her head back, brows hiked above her luminous blue eyes. "You what?"

He pulled her head down against his shoulder. "You heard me. Yes, I broke my word." And he felt no guilt for doing so. "I intruded on your thoughts repeatedly through the night. I kept my eye on you as best I could. And when I couldn't find you, I came home."

Her gentle breath breezed lightly against his neck. "Thank you, Braeden."

It took a minute for him to realize that the reason she didn't rail against his intrusion was that she was exhausted. He knew that once she had some rest, they would argue again.

He tightened his embrace briefly, ordering, "Go to sleep."

Certain she'd ignore him, Braeden stroked her cheek with the back of his fingers. "Go to sleep, Alexia. All will be well. Just sleep." He caught a glimpse of her drowsy gaze just before her eyes closed.

Regardless of what she thought, he didn't hate her. He couldn't deny his anger at her return. At first, just seeing her had been like opening a festering wound with a jagged knife, and he'd burned with rage.

But seeing her on the floor, with handprints around her throat, made him realize that no matter how hard he tried, there was one thing he couldn't deny. Right now, this impossible woman was still his mate.

He'd known that from the moment they'd met. How had he let himself forget?

He didn't trust her to confide in him. He didn't trust her to always tell him the truth. Yet, as illogical as it seemed to his brain, he would do everything within his power to keep her safe, whether she liked his methods or not.

She could rant all she wanted after she woke up, he didn't care. They had a manual to translate, an enemy to defeat and a danger to vanquish. Everything else, including the decision about their marriage, could wait.

Right now, he wanted a night of peace. Tomorrow would be soon enough to resume snarling at each other. Tomorrow they could renew their mutual distrust.

But tonight…tonight he would do nothing more than hold her, stand guard and keep her safe.

Braeden shifted into a more comfortable position on the bed. He felt Alexia shiver, but he didn't want to get up, didn't want to let her out of his arms. It'd been a long time since he'd held a woman so close. He just wanted to relax quietly and enjoy the silence.

Having powers was perfect for just such a moment. He reached toward a rack in the corner of the room and willed a quilt to his hand. After pulling it around her shoulders and tucking it in, he closed his eyes.

Alexia blinked awake. The arm around her tightened briefly and she froze for a second before remembering where she was, then relaxed against Braeden's side.

"How do you feel?" His deep voice broke the dark silence of the room, surrounding her in warmth.

She swallowed, testing her throat first. "Fine."

He settled his head more deeply into the pillow. "Good. Go back to sleep."

The sudden urge to run a hand across his chest surprised her. She didn't want to want him, didn't want to let herself need him. But she couldn't deny the safety his arms provided. "I'm not tired."

Braeden rolled to his side, drawing her closer into his embrace. At the same time soft light bathed the bed. "Then tell me what happened."

Her pulse quickened. "I don't want to argue."

"Neither do I. At least not tonight." His lips brushed her cheek. "But I need to know what happened."

Alexia leaned away. "Are you planning on using seduction to get answers again?"

"I hadn't considered it. But there'd be no interruptions this time…"

She quickly changed the subject, asking, "How is the little girl? Did you find her?"

"Yes. And other than being frightened out of her wits at being kidnapped by a monster, she's unharmed."

"Kidnapped?" She knew the answer, but had to ask. "By whom?"

"Nathan." A shudder rippled the length of his body before he added, "I'm amazed we found her alive."

A child. Nathan took his anger out on a child. Alexia swallowed the bile clogging her throat. "Oh, dear God. I am so sorry. I never should have—"

"No." Braeden quickly threaded his fingers through her hair and jerked her head back. He stared hard into her eyes, forcing her to look at him. His eyes glittered like gemstones in the flickering light. "Listen to me. This wasn't your fault. While you slept, I made certain that she won't remember a thing—not the kidnapping or the kidnapper."

"But my paper…I shouldn't—"

"Stop it." He tugged on her hair, making her wince, before he relaxed his hold, sliding his hand to warm the back of her neck. "Alexia, your paper didn't bring Nathan here. And it had nothing to do with his quest for the manual. It's probably safe to assume that even your professor's accident was caused by Nathan."

"Why?"

Braeden ran his thumb along the rim of her ear. "He wouldn't want anyone else, especially another mortal, homing in on what he considered his property."

"Still, had I had the guts to stand up to the professor, instead of caving like I did, this wouldn't have happened."

"Even if you didn't have the backbone to refuse, you could have come to me. Still, we can't know for certain if it would have made a difference."

"We'll never know the outcome if things had been different." She looked away, trying to hide her guilt. "But they aren't different, and you made it pretty clear that I'm to blame for this."

Braeden's palm was light against her cheek as he turned her to face him. "I was wrong to blame you. Do you hear me? I was wrong."

Shocked to hear Braeden admit he'd done something wrong, she studied him. He didn't appear to be anything but serious.

When she failed to respond, he continued, "I know damn well that there's no way you could ever be involved with a man who would think to harm a child."

Unshed tears blurred her sight. She didn't know if they were from overwhelming relief at his admission, or lingering guilt over the paper.

He caressed her cheek. "No 'I told you so'? Not even as much as a raised eyebrow? A self-satisfied smirk? Nothing?"

She didn't know what to say. She could count the number of times Braeden had apologized for anything on one hand. Each one took her by surprise. This one, however, was more shocking than surprising.

And not altogether pleasant. Why this sudden change of heart?

Too many years of blame, guilt and anger made her wary. Was he up to something?

Alexia studied his face. He didn't waver, didn't flinch. She detected no trace of subterfuge—but this was Braeden Drake. Ruler and High Druid of Mirabilus, and they were on his turf.

She could search his gaze until the end of time and still be uncertain. She would see only what he wanted her to see.

But lying wasn't one of his tactics. He'd sooner say nothing than lie.

"Alexia?"

Uncertain and confused, she sighed in resignation before asking, "What changed your mind?"

"The little girl Cindy." Braeden's light kisses felt like butterflies across her cheek. "I realized that you could never be involved with someone as purely evil as Nathan."

"You do realize that I should be mad at you?" Alexia trailed her fingertips over the rough stubble covering the hard line of his jaw.

"I know." He stroked her arm, bringing her hand to his lips. "But in return I'd have to get angry because you've neatly avoided telling me what happened at the Lair."

"Nothing much." Now who was lying?

He touched her neck. "Try again."

"Since I wouldn't tell him what was in the manual, Nathan wanted to give me a warning so that next time, I'd basically do as he ordered."

"There won't be a next time."

"He seemed to think there would be."

"He's wrong." Not a trace of indecision colored Braeden's tone. "You're staying here. He can't touch you inside these walls."

"No." Alexia shook her head. "I can't stay here."

"Not that I'm giving you a choice, but why is that?"

"It's too dangerous for me here."

Braeden pushed her onto her back and leaned up on one arm to look down at her. "Dangerous? What are you talking about? You're safer here than…" His words trailed off as he tipped his head and leaned closer.

She could nearly see the thoughts whirling behind his eyes. It wouldn't take him long to figure out what she meant. Alexia wondered if she'd ever learn to keep her mouth shut. She knew Braeden was so attuned to her that it took only a look or a few words for him to know what she was thinking or feeling.

A seductive half smile curved his mouth. "Does this

have anything to do with the challenge you issued? The one about not sharing my bed?"

Not wanting to see what she knew would be a look of pure male triumph glimmering in his eyes, Alexia looked away. "It wasn't meant as a challenge." It was meant to keep her heart safe. And now that she'd unintentionally reminded him, her heart might already be forfeited.

Braeden jerked the covers away, then turned her face toward his. Alexia halfheartedly pushed at his chest. "Braeden, don't."

He laughed and grasped her wrists, and holding them loosely in one hand, he leaned over her. With his lips brushing against hers, he whispered, "Tell me to go away. Tell me you don't want me and I'll leave, Alexia."

Of course she wanted him. She hungered for his touch in a way she'd never thought possible. She ached to accept the pleasure he offered, to match him thrust for thrust and to lose herself in the magic of his darkening gaze. That would be all too easy.

But tomorrow…next week…next month, when she once again slept alone, she would remember this night and the memory of what she lost would tear her apart.

When she remained silent, he asked, "Is it that hard to decide?"

She pulled her hands free, placing them on his shoulders. "Yes. Yes, Braeden, it is."

He buried his face in the crook of her neck. His breath against her skin brought a sigh to her lips. "Alexia, I can smell your heat."

When his mouth closed over the flesh between her neck and shoulder, she shivered. Her gasp echoed in the room. "And I can feel your need."

Braeden pulled her beneath him and held her face

between his hands. He didn't say anything. He didn't need to. She knew what he was waiting for, and when she peered up at him, he finally asked, "What's wrong?"

"I can't." She swallowed, fighting to tame the tremor in her voice. "I just can't."

His lips covered hers, parting them, his tongue seeking, stroking, against hers. He deepened their kiss, demanding her response, until she moaned against his mouth and curled her arms around his back.

He pulled his lips away. "You're on fire."

"Yes."

Braeden scraped his teeth lightly across her lower lip, sending her need spiraling nearly out of control. "You want me. You need me."

"Desperately." She couldn't lie. The magical side of him, the side seething with power, knew what she felt.

Resting his forehead against hers, he asked, "Then why not?"

Alexia shook her head. "I…" Unable to give voice to her fears, she clamped her lips closed.

He gathered her into his embrace and lowered his lips to her ear. She froze, knowing exactly what he was about to do. "Braeden, it…isn't… You don't have to…"

Ignoring her, his hot breath against her neck, across her ear, he fanned the desire to a raging, fevered pitch.

Before she could gather her wits, he ensorcelled her with pure, white-hot lust. It raced through her before she could push him away. And it was so much hotter than she remembered, faster than she expected, setting her limbs trembling, her heart pounding as the unbridled passion coursed a burning trail that throbbed between her legs.

Alexia closed her eyes and gasped raggedly. While her mind rebelled against his unfair seduction, her body begged for more. She writhed beneath him as he breathed his spell of desire into her, silently beckoning her to respond to the magic he wove.

"You're so hot." He softly coaxed, "Relax, Alexia."

When a frustrated moan escaped her throat, he hoarsely whispered, "Let it happen."

The bed seemed to fall away beneath her as a shuddering orgasm ripped through her. Braeden caught her cry of release with his lips. He ravaged her mouth, plundering, stroking his tongue against hers until the last tremor ran the length of her spine.

Once she caught her breath, Braeden rose and stared down at her. She recognized the question in his eyes, but was unwilling to give him the answers he sought.

He reached out and traced a fingertip over her lips. "I'll be next door." Without another word, he headed for the door connecting their bedroom to another one.

Alexia's heart took a while longer to settle into a more steady rhythm. While her sexual frustration was temporarily sated, more or less, the knowledge that he couldn't have spelled her that way if they didn't still have a bond tying them together pounded hard through her mind.

And now he was aware of that bond, too.

Chapter 13

As much as she didn't want to come here, one nice thing about Mirabilus was that Alexia didn't sense anything other than what she saw. In the two days she'd been here, nothing had made the hair on the back of her neck stand on end. Not a single wispy form caught the edge of her vision.

The only thing that bothered her was Braeden and his odd aloofness. He still slept in the room next door. She'd rather deal with his anger than his sudden avoidance of her.

When he'd offered to join her on a walk today, she'd accepted immediately. She'd failed miserably at remaining impersonal. And now she didn't know what she wanted from him. It really was maddening to be so undecided.

Alexia sat on a stone bench, stretched out her legs and lifted her face to the bright autumn sun. Even though the breeze coming off the ocean was cool, the sun kept her warm. After being cooped up inside the castle, coming outside was a welcome respite.

She rose and paced the small garden where he'd left her waiting while he took a call from Cameron. She saw that only one path led out of the garden. Braeden was smart enough to realize that she'd take that route. He'd find her when he came out.

Alexia strolled along the well-trimmed walkway into the forest. Not more than five minutes later, she found herself in a small, secluded clearing ringed by oak trees.

A couple of wooden benches had been placed near the center as if surrounding something. Curious, she walked closer.

A flat marble stone, like a headstone to a grave, was set into the ground. The familiar words etched on the face of the stone stole her breath and pierced her heart as surely as any sword.

Here lies the dream that never was. Rest in peace, Matthew Drake.

At the same instant as a moan of agony for the son she'd never held left her lips, Braeden yelled, "Alexia, don't."

The sound of crunching leaves broke through her pain. Then his arms were around her, forcing her away from the memorial, pulling her tightly against his chest, holding her head against his shoulder.

"I was going to bring you here myself," he whispered against her hair.

She shoved against him, trying to break free of his hold. "Let me go."

"No." He tightened his embrace. "Listen to me. I was going to tell you. I was going to bring you here. This is where we were going to come for our walk. I wanted to explain."

"How could you do this?" She despised the break in her

voice. She was beyond this. She'd gotten past this pain, had pushed it down into the deepest recesses of her soul. But now, now it tore free with a vengeance that threatened to overwhelm her.

"How could I not?" He rested his cheek on the top of her head. "We came here for our wedding night. We had plans to move here, to raise our children here, to grow old together here, remember?"

She nodded against his shoulder, but before she could say anything, he continued, "How could I not bring the remnants of our dreams here?"

"Why? You didn't care before, so why bring the stone I commissioned here to remind you of something that held little meaning?"

"Little meaning?" The pain in his voice rasped against her ears. "You think I didn't care? You think my anger, my rage, wasn't because of losing Matthew?" His chest heaved against hers. "I was given no chance to grieve. I had a wife to worry myself sick about."

Alexia cringed at the accusation in his tone. Hadn't she given him time to grieve? She no longer remembered. She'd been so beside herself, so upset, so livid, that she'd never truly noticed what the accident had done to Braeden.

Still, she'd been that way because of his words to his aunt. "You took your aunt's side and left me to look like an insane murderer." She gasped, her breath rushing painfully into her chest. "You blamed me for his death."

"Stop it." He grasped her upper arms and pulled her from his chest. His eyes shimmered suspiciously. But anger hardened his jaw, giving her insight to the emotion raging through him.

"Alexia, we've been through this already. I never blamed you for Matthew's death. Never."

He'd told her that before, but she knew what she'd heard at the hospital. "Why do you say that? I heard you and Danielle."

"Did you? Did you hear us, or were you so full of your own guilt that you heard nothing but those few words?"

She tried to jerk away, but he held her fast. "No. Damn it, this is it, Alexia. We're doing this now. Here. I don't care if it takes a lifetime. I never, ever blamed you."

Unable to chase the scene in the hospital from her mind, Alexia shook her head slowly. "Yes, you did."

"You fool. I blamed myself, not you. None of this would have happened had we not fought. I started that argument. I did. Not you. It was my fault. Not yours."

His voice broke. Alexia's focus swung to his face, stunned at the terrible pain dulling his eyes.

He lifted her hand to his lips and kissed her palm before placing it against his chest, over his heart. "I would have given my own life to save his, Alexia. I would have done it for you."

The truth of his confession pounded hard beneath her hand. She closed her eyes against the pain throbbing in her own chest. "You never believed me. You took your aunt's side."

"Leave Danielle out of this. I didn't want to believe you. If I had, it would have meant that someone was out to kill my wife. I didn't want that to be true. I wanted you to grieve, to heal, to eventually come to your senses."

"Alone?" To calm the hysteria she heard in her own voice she swallowed hard before asking, "You expected me to get over it alone?"

"You were never alone. Never. Alexia, I was at your side every minute until you locked me out of our room."

Defeat settled in her belly. "It doesn't matter."

He shook her. "Yes, damn it, it does matter. This has been between us too long. Alexia, we never got past that day. Don't you think it's time we give Matthew's memory peace? Don't you think it's time we decide if we're going to move on together or just end it?"

The thought of never seeing Braeden again, of never hearing the sound of his deep voice or even feeling the lash of his anger choked the breath from her. She couldn't have stopped the tears from slipping down her cheeks if she'd tried. "You never believed me." She closed her eyes against the humiliating tears.

"Then tell me. Tell me now what happened."

"I was run off the road."

"Lexi, there was no other car. There were no tire marks, no dents on your car to show you'd been hit."

She drew in a shaking breath and nearly screamed, "I was run off the road by a dragon!"

"A dragon?"

Anger helped to erase a small bit of her pain, just as it had once before. "You still don't believe me. Every time I mention being run off the road, you look at me as if I've lost my mind. That's why I never told you. I was afraid you'd have me drugged, or worse."

"A dragon?"

His voice seemed to come from far off. "Braeden?" She stared at him. He frowned in concentration. She repeated, "Braeden?"

"You're right. I wouldn't have believed you." She tried to jerk free. But he held her tight. "I believe you now. After what we've seen, how could I not?"

While her heart still ached, the pain in her stomach lessened. Relief, like someone had removed a huge weight from her chest, flooded through her.

Braeden must have felt it, because he relaxed his near bruising hold and drew her back against his chest. "Alexia, how could I have believed you then?"

Even then, when it had happened, it had seemed impossible to her. So she had no choice but to give him that much. However, there was that little thing called trust. She could have run from his powers in disbelief when he'd first explained the whole wizard concept to her, but she'd trusted him. He could have done the same for her. He could have given her the benefit of the doubt. "You could have believed me because you knew I would never lie to you. I had no reason to lie about the accident. None."

Which in the end is what drove the final wedge between them. Braeden had been working almost around the clock and had no time for her. Alexia no longer remembered what they'd fought about that night. Their countless arguments had all run together in her mind.

She'd left the condo in Boston angry and had taken off in the car during a thunderstorm. His aunt had claimed that she'd driven off the road just to get Braeden's attention.

"No, you didn't have any reason to lie. I never believed for one minute that you had intentionally caused the accident. I just couldn't understand how it happened. And I couldn't accept that you wouldn't let me in, Alexia. You shut me out as securely as any door."

His heartbeat hammered beneath her ear. She hadn't seen it then, but he was right. She *had* shut him out. In her pain she had no room to care for what anyone else suffered. She could barely take care of herself, let alone anyone else.

She stroked his arm. "Braeden, we both made mistakes. I didn't mean to shut you out any more than you meant to not believe me. I needed you. You needed me. And we both chose to reach inside, to suffer our pain alone, instead of reaching for each other. What are we going to do?"

"What do you want to do?" He rested his cheek atop her head. "What does your heart tell you to do?"

"I'm afraid. Braeden, I can't hurt like that again."

"Neither can I. So I guess instead of taking that risk, we end it. Just put our marriage to rest once and for all."

"You mean file for divorce?" Her chest constricted.

"If that's what you want, yes. We both deserve some kind of life, don't we?"

"But…" Did he want a life with someone else? Did he not love her anymore?

"But what? It might be for the best."

"The best?" The best for whom? Certainly not for her.

"Don't you want to start your life over, fresh and free of the memories that chafe like an open wound?"

She would never be free of her memories of Braeden. Never. All of them, the good and the bad, would be part of her for as long as she lived.

"Don't you agree it would be for the best?"

"Dear God, no. No, Braeden." She pulled away, gasping in agony at the thought. "No. I don't want to lose you."

He reached out and cupped her face, gently urging her forward. "Alexia, then start a new life over again with me. Let's see if we can learn to trust each other again, see if we can rediscover what we once shared. Can we do that? Can we try?"

When she'd come to him for safety, she'd known there would be a high price to pay. She'd wondered what she'd have to forfeit to the Master of the Lair.

Alexia now knew that price. Now was not the time to wrap the false bravado of pride and past hurts around her heart. Not when her heart was the price for coming to him. It was time to let it all go. Time to bury the pain of the past with their son.

She came to him slowly, losing herself in his steady amethyst gaze that silently spoke of promises made long ago.

His warm lips were gentle on hers. His arms held her securely against his chest.

Memories of passion shared, of love given and taken, swept through her, leaving a trail of growing desire in their wake.

To her amazement, she trembled as if this were their first time together. She curled her fingers into his shirt, holding on as he parted her lips.

His kiss was sure and demanded a response as his tongue swept along hers. She moaned softly against his mouth.

His lips left hers to trail a hot line to the soft spot beneath her ear. "I want you, all of you." The huskily spoke statement sent a heated shiver down her spine.

She sighed. "And I want you, but we're in the middle of the woods."

"Are we?"

Alexia opened her eyes and tipped her head away from his. To her amazement they were no long surrounded by sunshine or forest.

"Where are we?"

Instead of answering her, he cupped her breast and stroked a thumb across the peak. Even through the layers of fabric, her flesh responded, straining toward his touch.

Where they were no longer mattered. It was fairly obvious now by the stone walls surrounding them that they were in the bedroom. The only thing that really mattered was the flash of hot need building low in her belly.

She tugged at his jacket until he tore the garment off and tossed it to the floor. Hers followed within seconds, her blouse along with it.

A knock sounded at the door. Braeden cursed, then merely pointed at the bedroom door. Alexia heard the distinct sound of a lock clicking in place. She used to find his powers intimidating and a bit frightening. Now they seemed rather useful.

"It could be important."

He reached out and pinched open the front hook of her bra. As he pushed the straps down her arms, he shook his head. "There's nothing more important than this."

Braeden caressed her breasts, alternately stroking and teasing the already hardening nipples. More starved for his touch that she'd realized, she arched into his hands and closed her eyes.

His mouth closed over one tip, and she grasped his shoulder for support as her legs threatened to buckle. His lips trailed fire across her breast, over her collarbone and up her neck.

"It's been too long."

She agreed. The heat pooling between her legs begged for his touch. Alexia slid her hand down his chest and stomach to rest against the length of his erection. "Yes, it has."

She tugged at the hem of his T-shirt, pulling it free from his jeans and up his chest. "Braeden, stand up."

When he leaned away from her, she stripped it over his head in a flash before sliding her fingers into the top of his jeans and flicking the metal button free.

He brushed her hands away. Slowly trailing his fingertips along her collarbone, he paused to gently trace the outline of her breasts before chasing the shivers down her torso.

His touch drew her forward. "Braeden."

With a low, seductive chuckle, he only pushed her back and continued his slow exploration. He skimmed the top of her jeans, thumbing open the snap.

Anxious and wanting to feel his flesh beneath her fingers, Alexia reached out and tugged his zipper down. She pushed his jeans partway down his hips and slid a hand beneath the waistband of his briefs.

He was hot and hard beneath her touch. She whispered, "I want you now."

Her back hit the mattress before she fully comprehended that they were moving. Like a whirlwind with a single purpose in mind, Braeden had them on the bed, naked.

The first ragged sigh of anticipation hadn't even fully left her lips, making her wonder if she'd been that distracted or if magic had been involved.

But his seeking hand skating along her leg, parting her thighs, made her wonder if any magic could feel as sensual or exciting as his fingers stroking her heated center, slipping between the slick folds.

No mystical powers could be as warm and alive as the body stretched alongside hers.

Nothing borne of the elements could possibly melt her bones and make her shiver the same way his lips against her neck did.

She gasped at how quickly her body responded to his caress. It had been too long. Far too long. She'd slept alone too many nights with only memories, which often awakened her from her dreams, feverish with need.

His kisses, his exquisite caresses, were torture. As enjoyable as she knew it could be, right now, she wanted him on her, in her, wrapped around her senses and body, filling the lonely spaces she'd come to accept.

Alexia grasped at his shoulder, breathlessly begging, "Braeden, please."

He rolled atop her, supporting his body on his elbows and forearms. She moaned with pleasure at the familiar weight of hard muscles cushioned by softer flesh.

Unwilling to wait any longer, she spread her legs wider and tilted her hips against him. "Braeden, love me."

He came into her with one sure, fluid stroke that drew a cry from her lips.

While his hands on her body were gentle, his thrusts and kisses were not. They were demanding and possessive. Alexia clutched him tightly to her, savoring the shared possession.

She broke their kiss, gasping his name, desperate for fulfillment. He reached between them, finding and stroking the pulsing bud at her core.

"Look at me, Alexia."

His hoarse command left her no option. She stared into the shimmering amethyst gaze of her dragon.

In the twin mirrors to his soul she saw the dragon rise up from his nest, step out of his lair, unfurl his mighty wings and take flight. He soared, strong and free, seeking the one thing that would fill the void in his life.

His mate.

Alexia's breath hitched when the beast found her. They circled each other midair, necks arched, tails whipping back and forth, nostrils flaring as they took in the other's scent.

Soon, in a move born of lust, love and need, the dragon captured his mate, held her fast with steely talons, cloaking her protectively within the safety of his wings.

As the beasts came together, Alexia's stomach clenched, her toes curled. She cried out his name while falling into the spiraling vortex of her orgasm.

Braeden covered her lips with his and answered her cry with a deep, ragged one of his own.

Spent, he fell atop her, breathing hard. He gathered her into his arms and rolled onto his side.

Alexia pressed her forehead into his shoulder and gasped for breath. "The next time I think of leaving, remind me of this."

He tightened his embrace and kissed the top of her head. "There won't be a next time."

She snuggled against him, taking advantage of the content, quiet intimacy. It wouldn't last, it never did. Before she was ready to move, Braeden would be heading for the shower, and she'd do her best to drag her limp body in to join him.

Too soon, he eased his hold and rolled onto his back. She propped herself up on an elbow and drew circles with her finger on his damp chest.

He covered her hand with his. "I—"

She finished his sentence. "Need a shower."

"Yes." His laugh filled the room. Some things never changed.

Chapter 14

Alexia tapped a pencil on the worktable Braeden had requested be brought up to their bedroom. It was no wonder Nathan was angry. His father had been killed in this castle while trying to nab the first Dragonierre's Manual from a fire.

"Anything new?"

She turned and lifted her face toward Braeden for a quick kiss, then told him what she'd discovered, adding, "Nathan had been groomed to step into the role of High Druid after his uncle Aelthed died. But because of his father's deceit, he'd been set aside—for a Drake."

Not that it made Nathan's evilness right, but it explained why the man sought to harm the Drakes.

Braeden hooked another chair with his foot, dragged it over, then sat down. "A tale of revenge. The best kind."

"Unfortunately this tale is most likely steeped in truth."

She could tell from his unconcerned expression that he didn't share her worry. He nodded toward the pages. "Anything else?"

"Not a lot." While she could decode the multiple languages used to create the piece of work, it was time-consuming. "Aelthed had a workroom here in the castle. I don't suppose you'd know where?"

"With the amount of construction and remodeling done through the centuries, it could be anywhere—or not exist at all anymore."

She looked around the room. "If the original building had been done in the twelfth century, there should be at least one hidden room or hallway."

Braeden reached into his pocket and handed her a necklace. A silver dragon pendant with a ruby mounted on its belly hung from a thin lace of leather. "Before you go snooping around, put this on."

"Snooping?" Had her intent been that obvious?

"You know you will."

She slid the necklace over her head. "I take it this is the charm you asked your aunt to make?"

"Yes. She had to wait for the right phase of the moon for the spell casting, so I just got them today." He slid a finger beneath the strip of leather around his neck.

"She made one for everyone?" Alexia studied the dragon. "What's it supposed to do?"

"It won't come to life, if that's what you're thinking. It's for protection against Nathan and his family."

She dropped it beneath her blouse, letting it settle between her breasts. "He's your family, too."

Braeden groaned. "Don't remind me."

"Don't you have a couple of meetings at the Lair today?"

"Anxious to start looking for that workroom?"

"Now that you mention it—" she pointed at the far wall "—those bricks look lighter than the others."

Braeden's eyes widened. "I don't want to come home later tonight and find a pile of rubble, instead of Mirabilus."

Alexia heaved an exaggerated sigh. "Fine. If it upsets you so much, I won't bring in the cranes until you're home."

"Agreed." He checked his watch. "I need to get going."

"Hurry back." She shot him what she hoped was a look of disappointment, then sighed. "Since I can't dismantle the castle, I'll get bored quickly."

"Work." He rose and tapped the table. "You have plenty of work to do. If that gets too boring, go read or daydream or something equally safe."

She laughed. "I'll do that." She pushed at his shoulder. "Now get out of here."

"If you need me—"

"I'll call." She finished his sentence.

He was gone before she could turn to look at him. But the warmth of his presence and the spiced scent of his aftershave lingered in the room.

Alexia turned back to the manual. The last thing she wanted to do right now was to dwell on the way Braeden's warmth made her feel safe. She drew in a deep breath. Nor did she want to admit how the scent of his aftershave made her pulse race.

If he knew how much those little things affected her, he'd laugh. At the moment, light and teasing defined the depth of their relationship. While it was better than glaring at each other with rage simmering near the surface, she wondered how long they'd walk on eggshells around each other.

There was nothing unusual about marriage having its ups and downs. Certainly no husband and wife agreed on everything all the time—at least, she and Braeden never had. Arguing had been a common activity. But would they ever be able to trust each other again?

It was a question she didn't have an answer to. But right now, at this moment, she had work to do.

She stared blindly down at the page she'd been deciphering. Considering how much she enjoyed history and truly loved her job, she felt doubly guilty that she found the manual so exceedingly boring.

This Aelthed droned on and on about daily life. To be honest, she'd hoped that eventually the writing would turn out to be something more than the diary of a man who seemingly had no life.

The entry she'd translated this morning told all about an outing to gather nuts. Nuts, of all things. And this is what Nathan was willing to kill for?

She was tempted to make him a deal. She'd do the translation for him if he'd just go away afterward. But she knew that wouldn't happen. For one thing it was doubtful he'd ever give up trying to rid the world of Drakes, and for another, he'd never believe the book was nothing more than the ramblings of an old man.

Braeden insisted there had to be something more here, something she just hadn't found yet. She hoped so, otherwise, she'd brought danger to him and his family for nothing.

A few hours later, after learning how to tell which nut would have good meat and which would be rotten, which apples would make the best pies or which ones to feed to the horses, Alexia stretched and turned off the computer.

She wasn't hungry and didn't feel much like taking a walk. Since Braeden didn't have a television she couldn't relax in front of that.

Alexia grabbed her notes, plumped up the pillows on

the bed and got comfortable. Maybe Braeden was right. Maybe she had missed something.

She sighed and closed her eyes. It was a little disconcerting to realize her boredom was because Braeden wasn't here. She'd fallen back into the new-love syndrome a little too quickly for her own good.

To constantly wonder what he was doing or what he was thinking rubbed on her nerves. She wasn't some young girl completely infatuated with a new lover.

Oh, but he was such a good lover. A shiver raced down her body. She snickered at herself.

Were Aelthed still alive, he'd say she was besotted. The sad thing was—he'd be right.

For all her confusion about their relationship and worries about being hurt, she couldn't deny that the physical attraction was still there. If anything, it had become stronger.

He'd become so skilled that for a minute she wondered how. But only for a brief minute. Because once the world shattered around them, she really didn't care how.

They'd made love this morning and she could still feel the touch of his hands and mouth on her skin. Could feel his heart pounding against hers. Hear his ragged groan. Taste the saltiness of his flesh on her lips and tongue.

She was amazed at the softness of the hair on his muscular chest, and at the fine line trailing down to the coarser hair on his groin.

Her lips twitched. It wasn't the hair that held her attention. She was far more fascinated by the silky-soft flesh covering the length of his hard erection…

Braeden shifted in his seat and clenched his jaw against the growing fire in his groin. He stared at the Lair's new chef, chef's assistant and kitchen manager seated across the conference table, hoping they hadn't noticed his sudden discomfort.

If he didn't know better, he'd swear someone was making love to him.

From the expert touches of the soft hands finding all the right places and the eager lips roaming freely, he'd say it was his wife.

Impossible.

Yet fingertips trailed across his chest to circle his nipples before stroking down his abdomen. The sensation made him sweat. He could feel the perspiration on his forehead and wiped his palm across the sudden dampness.

Her hand closed around his erection mere seconds before her warm moist mouth covered the tip. Braeden inhaled sharply, drawing everyone's attention to him.

He quickly coughed and cleared his throat. "Sorry. Sinuses are acting up. Please…" He coughed again as her mouth slowly moved down the hard length. "Please, continue."

Cameron leaned forward in the seat next to him and met his gaze. Braeden shook his head slightly, hoping to convince his brother nothing was wrong. But Cam wasn't buying it. Eyebrows raised, he mouthed, "Sinuses?"

Cameron was well aware that Braeden didn't have sinus problems.

When she tightened her lips and eased back up toward the tip, Braeden fought to control his now ragged breathing.

To make matters worse, if that were possible, Cam chose that instant to poke inside his mind. *"What the hell is going on with—"*

Cameron leaned an elbow on the conference table and tried to hide his smirk with his hand while mentally laughing. *"TMI, brother. Way too much information."*

Unable to focus his mind on anything other than the feel of Alexia's hot mouth and swirling tongue, Braeden tore a sheet of paper from the pad before him and wrote, "I have to go. You got this?" then shoved it in front of Cam.

His brother nodded. Now all he had to do was get out of here without anyone else noticing his…condition. Fortunately he hadn't removed his suit jacket.

Not wanting to insult the new staff, he pulled his cell phone from his pocket as if he'd just received a call, then rose. "Excuse me, gentlemen, it's an emergency. Cameron has all the data and can handle this from here."

Before anyone could respond, he forced himself to leave the conference room without sprinting.

However, once the door closed behind him, he dashed for his office. Leaning against the door, Braeden wiped the sweat from his forehead.

His pounding heart lurched when he felt her legs straddle his hips. He couldn't have stopped his groan from escaping if his life had depended on it.

Forcing his concentration on Mirabilus, Braeden closed his eyes and swore that if she made him ruin this brand-new suit, he was going to be really annoyed.

"Stop it!"

Alexia jumped and opened her eyes to stare at Braeden. "What? I'm not doing anything."

"Like hell you aren't." He nearly ripped off his suit jacket and tossed it toward the chair. To her utter surprise he ignored the fact that he'd missed. Fear slinked down her spine. Something really had to be wrong for Braeden to leave a tailor-made suit jacket on the floor.

She came up to her knees and stared at him. A sheen of perspiration on his flushed face prompted her to ask, "What's wrong?"

"Wrong?"

She took in the blazing eyes and ragged breathing. "Obviously something is."

"What were you just doing?"

At least he'd said *doing* and not *thinking*. "Nothing. I was just sitting here."

"Right." He wiped a shaking hand down his face. "What were you just thinking?"

Alexia bit her lip to hold back a groan, but the action did nothing to stop the hot flush from covering her face. "I...was...thinking about nothing."

"Really?" He leaned against the door and crossed his arms over his chest. "Let me show you how to think about...nothing."

"What?" Alexia shook her head. What was he up to? What had she done?

"Relax, Lexi." A smile curved his lips. "Sit down and just breathe."

"All right." She did as he suggested. "I'm sitting." Although his demeanor did little to help her relax.

"Comfortable?"

"Sure." Something wasn't right. His smile was far too smug. His tone bordered on sarcastic. Her pulse kicked up a notch.

But a notch was nothing compared to what her heart did when an unseen hand caressed her breast. A callused thumb stroked across the hardening tip only to be replaced by the moist warmth of a tongue.

This was totally different from when he spelled lust into her blood. This felt more as if someone invisible were making love to her. And she didn't like it.

Her eyes widened. "What are you doing?"

"If you're going to play, Alexia, you need to know how it's done."

"But I didn't…" She gasped as his hand slid between her legs, stroking, caressing, edging steadily higher. Brushing past curls, slipping between soft folds of flesh.

"Braeden, don't."

"What? I'm not doing anything. I'm just standing here." His voice was ragged. "Tell me you weren't thinking of us making love."

Even though her body responded to his mental touch, her heart and mind rebelled against this intrusion. Tears burned behind her closed lids. She felt…used. Alexia opened her eyes and stared at him. "Yes. Yes, I was. Braeden, please, stop."

"Damn it, Alexia." He crossed the room and pulled her roughly into his arms.

His heart pounded riotously against hers. He buried his face in her neck. "We need to get you some training real quick."

"For what? I don't understand."

He lifted his head and stared down at her. "I was in the middle of a meeting with the new kitchen staff when I felt someone making love to me. I knew from the touch it was you."

"Impossible." She shook her head. "I don't have any powers."

"No, not impossible. Trust me, I know what I felt. It seems you've been gifted with powers."

"No." She pushed away. "I don't want them."

Braeden nearly snorted. "You think you have a choice?"

"Yes. Take them away."

"I didn't give them to you, so I can't take them away."

She thought he could do almost anything. "Then find out where they came from."

He turned to glance at the table. "The book."

Now that, she knew for a fact, was impossible. "It's just a boring diary."

"Obviously you're wrong." He sat down on the edge of the bed. "Do you remember our dinner in the maze?"

"Yes."

"And the water turning to iced tea?"

"Of course I do." She'd wanted raspberry tea and it had appeared on the table. "I thanked you for it, too."

"I didn't do it."

"You had to have done it."

"No."

She didn't believe him, but asked, "Even if that's true, how do I go from changing water to tea to…" Alexia paused. What was it called?

"Projecting?"

"Sure, projecting."

"It would take a strong spell for that to happen." Braeden spoke softly, as if he was talking to himself.

"There you go, then. That manual is nothing more than an old man's ramblings." She didn't want any powers. While she loved Braeden, she had no desire to be like him. There were days when it was all she could do to handle being normal. She didn't need or want to add anything to her plate.

He rose and retrieved an empty glass from the table. "Want something to drink?"

"A glass of water would be nice."

Ice cubes and water filled the empty glass.

He shrugged. "It wasn't me." Then he upended the glass over the bed.

Alexia jumped, shouting, "No! Don't get the bed wet!"

The water and ice hung suspended in midair. Not one drop touched the bed.

With her mouth open, speechless, she blinked.

Braeden tipped his head to the side. "Personally, I couldn't care less if the bed gets wet. There are other beds. So this is because of your wishes, not mine."

A sinking feeling filled her. What was she going to do now?

Braeden handed her the glass and asked, "Want to put the water back into the glass?"

"How?"

"Try thinking it. Visualize the water and ice in the glass."

She did as he suggested. To her chagrin it worked.

Braeden laughed as he took the glass from her and set it on the night table. "It isn't a curse, Alexia."

"Easy for you to say. It sure feels like one."

With nothing but a glance, his hand stroked her belly, then slid around to caress her hip. "You sure about that?"

She looked at him and narrowed her eyes. He was teasing her.

"Come on, Alexia, you can do it."

She shook her head.

"I dare you to try." He leaned against the far wall.

Heat fired her cheeks. But the glint of passion in his eyes and the challenge in his voice were more than she could ignore.

She leaned back into the pillows propped against the headboard. Closing her eyes she envisioned making love to him.

She trailed her fingers over his face, as if touching him for the first time. Stubble covered his cheeks, the hard line of his jaw and chin.

His lips were full and smooth beneath her touch. She jumped when he swirled his tongue around her finger before closing his lips over it and drawing it into his mouth.

Alexia marveled at the sensation of dampness on her finger, as if he'd physically sucked on her finger. His laugh brushed hot against her cheek.

"The mind is powerful." He stroked a hand beneath her shirt, drawing circles on her belly. "It can be a tool." He snapped open her bra, then caressed one breast, thumb teasing the nipple before moving to the other one. "Or a weapon. It's up to you to choose."

Alexia loosened his tie, pulled it free, then dropped it on the floor. The buttonholes of his crisp new shirt were stiff, and in frustration she visualized his shirt already open. To her satisfaction she instantly found skin beneath her hands.

Braeden shook his head. His lips beneath her ear, he whispered, "That's cheating."

Her lips against his flat nipple, she only moaned in response.

The moan stuck in her throat as he slid his fingers beneath the waistband of her jeans, flicked the snap open and slid down the zipper. To her amazement, it felt as if her jeans were being pushed down over her hips and legs. Cool air brushed her flesh, intensifying her amazement.

She unbuckled his belt, fumbled with the hook closure of his waistband before sliding the zipper down and letting his pants fall.

Alexia tugged his silk boxers down over his hips. She kneaded the tight muscles of his ass, laughing when he clenched them beneath her hands.

His chuckle turned to a ragged groan when she caressed the hot, hard length of his erection.

His hand slid between her legs, touching, teasing, caressing, until she breathlessly rested her forehead against his chest. Alexia gasped when his touch slid inside to stroke the already burning fire hotter.

Suddenly this…projecting wasn't enough. She grazed his chest with her teeth, silently crying, "Braeden, please."

The cool air of the chamber raced against her body as her clothing disappeared. Strong hands clasped her ankles and pulled her down onto the bed. No longer in control, Alexia sighed with anticipation.

Braeden covered her body with his own, came into her and caught her cry with his lips.

She clung to him, shifting to curl her legs around his hips. He was obviously as turned on as she, because there was nothing slow or gentle about his thrusts. They were fast, hard and deep, bringing her quickly to release.

Alexia cried out and Braeden groaned above her, shuddering with his own release.

Once her heart slowed to a more normal beat, she stroked his damp hair from his face and asked, "Wasn't that cheating?"

Braeden rose up on his elbows, kissed the end of her nose. "Complaining?"

She stretched languidly beneath him, tracing his leg with her foot. "Never."

Chapter 15

Braeden rolled off her with a sigh and rose. "I hate to do this, but I need to get up."

He stretched a hand out to her clothes on the floor.

"No." Alexia stopped him. "I don't need your help, I can do it myself. Just get dressed."

She couldn't decipher the look he shot her, but since he said nothing, she let it go.

He retrieved his clothes from the floor on his way to the bathroom, while she got up from the bed and pulled on a robe.

Braeden came out of the bathroom and picked up his suit jacket from the floor. Shrugging into it, he said, "I need to get back to Mirabilus for another meeting. Do me a favor, though."

"What?"

"Don't think about me."

She knew what he was saying. He didn't want a repeat performance of earlier. "Will you be gone long?"

"I'll be back later tonight." Braeden hesitated, then added, "Don't wait up."

He was gone before she could respond.

Alexia blew out the breath she didn't realize she'd been holding and headed for the shower. It didn't take much to figure out Braeden was ticked off.

She never would have intentionally teased him that way, especially when he was in a meeting. He couldn't seriously think she'd done it on purpose.

And he couldn't be upset because she suddenly had these magical powers. It wasn't as if she'd asked for them. In fact, he'd been the one who suggested using them.

Could they have come from the book?

Quickly finishing her shower and dressing, she sat down in front of the table and flipped the computer on, then pulled the last page she'd translated closer.

Once again more words crowded the page. She was getting used to that happening. She stared harder at the new sections, sighing in frustration. Wonderful, now Aelthed was imparting a recipe. Not for a spell, but for a tart.

Two things were at the forefront of her mind. One—medieval cooks didn't usually put measurements into their recipes. Two—even if they had, why would anyone put a cup of salt into a fruit tart?

Alexia rechecked her translation. Now it called for two cups. It made no sense whatsoever.

She pulled the next page closer. More recipes filled the space. The first one was for cassia soup. She shuddered at the thought of a cinnamon soup made with chicken. It called for a pound each of finely ground cinnamon, clove and ginger.

Frowning, she wondered at the measurements. She wasn't a chef by any means, but it didn't take a lot of thinking to realize that a pound of any finely ground spice would be far too much.

She pushed the page away and leaned back in her chair. While finding recipes in the book was new, this wasn't the first time Aelthed had mentioned spices or cooking.

Alexia's heart did a quick tap. She shoved away from the table, raced out of the room, down the stairs and into the kitchen.

She came to a groaning stop. It was possible that in Aelthed's time the kitchen wasn't even attached to the main living quarters.

She picked up the phone and dialed the caretaker's cottage. "Mr. Brightworthe? Hello, this is Alexia and I was wondering if you knew where the castle's original kitchen was located?"

"Yes, ma'am. It was destroyed in a fire years ago. The only section of it that still exists is what we use as the storage shed."

She looked out the side window. "The one attached to the pantry?"

"That'd be it."

Before she could thank him, he asked, "You aren't thinking of going in there, are you?"

"I'd planned to, why?"

"It's isn't safe."

Then it fit in perfectly with her life of late. "Could you expand on that a little? Do you mean structurally?"

"Yes, ma'am. I'll be right over."

She didn't get the chance to tell him not to bother. He'd hung up and she saw him stomp across the yard toward the castle.

He opened the side door. "I'll go with you."

Anxious to discover what she could, Alexis didn't argue. She followed him to the storage shed.

At first glance the wooden structure looked sound, but when Mr. Brightworthe opened the door, she realized what concerned him. On closer inspection the building had been maintained on an irregular basis. The entire thing appeared to be in dire need of demolition. It wasn't just the peeling paint. The rotted and uneven boards couldn't possibly last much longer.

He stood aside, then handed her a flashlight. "Watch your step. I won't be having Mr. Drake breathing fire at me because you got hurt."

Alexia opened the creaking door slowly and stepped through the wood-framed doorway onto the hard-packed dirt floor. Yard tools—rakes, shovels, hoes—lined the walls on both sides. The shelves on the far wall held cans and jars, some with nails or screws, others with garden chemicals.

Gingerly walking further into the shed, she directed the flashlight at the walls. The two sides were nothing more than what they appeared—old, crumbling, wooden walls. The back wall was stone.

"What's behind that wall?"

The caretaker scratched his head. "The pantry."

She moved closer. Reaching past a stack of paint cans, she poked at the wall. "How thick do you think this is?"

"What are you looking for, Mrs. Drake?"

"A secret room."

Mr. Brightworthe snorted and stepped outside. He returned in a few minutes. "From best guess, I'd say that wall is a good six feet thick. If there's a room back there, it's mighty small."

Alexia touched one ancient fieldstone, then another. None of them moved, but she hadn't expected them to. She grabbed a paint can and set it behind her. "Help me clear these shelves."

Once the shelves were emptied, she took a small garden trowel and poked between the stones. After what seemed hours, one stone finally gave way beneath her poking. She stuck a finger into the hole and felt air. While there might be six feet between here and the main building, this wasn't a solid six-foot-thick wall.

"Here, ma'am, let me." The caretaker managed to remove a few more of the stones, giving them a large-enough hole to shine the flashlight into. He whistled before muttering, "Well, I'll be."

"What?" Alexia reached for the flashlight. "Let me see."

Heart racing, she looked inside. Against the far wall a long narrow table held an assortment of old jars covered by cobwebs and a thick layer of dust.

Between the two of them, they were able to remove enough of the stones to permit them entry. "Just a minute, Mrs. Drake." The caretaker grabbed the shovel and pulled a second flashlight from his jacket pocket before entering the room first.

The beam from Alexia's flashlight shook as her hands trembled. She directed the light over the jars on the table, trying not to shiver at the sudden brush of an icy breeze across the back of her neck.

She'd been safe at Mirabilus so far. There was no reason to think otherwise. The trepidation she felt now was from the excitement of their find.

The room they'd discovered was just a hallway of sorts that slanted down to open out into a larger circular room. She stood in the center of the room and slowly spun. "Where are we?"

Mr. Brightworthe shook his head. "I'm not certain. I've never seen anything like this before."

Rough-hewn wood bookcases were still intact. They housed jars, small pots, and an odd assortment of items unidentifiable beneath the dust.

Off to one side of the room on the floor was a circle of stones. Atop the circle rested a large metal cauldron. Near the other side of the room was a table with a rickety-looking chair before it.

Alexia circled the room and studied the items on the table. Gemstones and bits of metal were scattered here and there as if someone had been in the process of making a piece of jewelry or a charm.

She fingered the one around her neck and took comfort from the protection it offered.

Mr. Brightworthe shone his flashlight across the table. Beneath the dust something sparkled. Drawn to the object, Alexia reached out and brushed the layers of grime away with a fingertip.

Beneath her touch the sparkle grew to a shimmering glow of emerald.

Mr. Brightworthe backed away. "Ma'am?"

Hearing the uncertainty in his voice, she paused and studied the object. Nothing real or imagined warned her of danger. "It's all right."

But when she turned around, it was obvious that her words held little meaning to the man. He visibly shook. The last thing she wanted was for Mirabilus's older caretaker to have a stroke.

With a sigh, she scooped up the object, dropped it in her pocket, then headed toward the door. She'd come back here with Braeden. "That's enough for now, Mr. Brightworthe."

When they got back up to the shed, he asked, "What should I do with this hole in the wall?"

Alexia frowned. She didn't want to risk someone getting inside and disturbing the items. Some of them had to be artifacts of value. She needed to get Braeden to put one of his spells on the shed. "For now, just lock the door. I'll have Mr. Drake take care of it later tonight."

The caretaker appeared more than happy to leave it in Braeden's hands. He locked the shed, then headed back to his cottage.

Alexia grabbed a sandwich in the kitchen and headed up to the bedroom with it. After finishing the sandwich, she pulled her find out of her pocket and laid it on the table.

While the strange glow was now gone, it still had a shimmer. She retrieved a toothbrush from the bathroom and lightly drew it across the object, trying to remove the layers of grime.

Her eyes widened as first one wing and then another, and finally a body and a tail, were uncovered. She worked quickly on the head, freeing the emerald dragon pendant from the dust and grime that had hidden the beast for who knew how many years.

She flipped through her notes. Aelthed had mentioned an amethyst and a sapphire pendant, but had written nothing about an emerald one. If the twins had owned the other two, who owned this one?

Alexia held the pendant up to the light and cursed when the beast blinked at her. Instead of freaking out, she ordered, "No. Stay a pendant."

To her relief it worked. Or the blinking had been nothing more than her imagination. But she wasn't counting on that any longer.

A chill breeze blasted her back. She jumped from the

chair. A swirl of mist spun by the door. The pendant in her hand hissed.

Nathan. Alexia swallowed and fervently wished she could be at Braeden's side.

"The head of housekeeping will be here in a couple of minutes. You plan on attending this meeting?"

Braeden hit the intercom button on his desk phone. "Yes, Cam, I'll be there in a minute."

He signed the last two invoices on his desk, then headed for the conference room. Thankfully this would be the last meeting today. Since everything else had been taken care of, he could return to Mirabilus shortly.

Although he still hadn't had a chance to figure out what to do with Alexia. If these new powers of hers were going to be a permanent part of her life, she needed to learn how to control them.

And he wasn't certain he was the one to teach her. If this afternoon was any indication, the lessons could get a little dicey.

He met Cam in the hallway. Before his brother could ask anything about the earlier meeting, Braeden gave him a glare that stopped any questions. The pair paused in front of the conference-room door and Braeden asked, "Are they here?"

"Yes. Dani gave them the grand tour, then brought them here."

Braeden opened the door and caught Alexia as she stumbled into his arms.

"Damn it, Alexia."

Cam edged around the two of them and waved a hand toward the horrified employees. Their gasps of shock froze as they all turned to mute statues.

"What the hell is going on?" Danielle bolted from the table.

Alexia held up her hand. A green dragon shimmered on her palm. "I found Aelthed's workroom."

Braeden released his hold. "No cranes?"

"No. Just a trowel."

"So how did you get here?"

Alexia leaned against him. "Nathan was in our room and I wished I was at your side, instead of there."

Dani clutched her chest. "You *wished* yourself here?" She looked at Braeden. "When did this happen?"

He wasn't sure whom to attend first—the frozen employees, Alexia or his aunt. He looked at his brother.

Cam raised an eyebrow. "I'll take care of the employees. You get the family members."

Braeden muttered, "Thanks," then led both women back to his office.

Once there, Dani leaned against the closed door and slowly ran her hard gaze from the top of Alexia's head to the tip of her toes. Alexia clenched her fists at her sides, visibly bristling at the inspection.

Aunt Danielle grumbled something under her breath that Braeden couldn't quite hear, but it sounded as if she called one of them an idiot.

He didn't have time for this, so he asked outright, "What are you doing?"

Danielle tapped her chin with one long, red fingernail. "Trying to decide how many babies she's carrying."

Braeden thumped down onto the chair behind his desk. This couldn't be happening. Not now. Not yet. What had they been thinking? He shuddered inwardly. They hadn't been *thinking* at all.

Alexia jerked to attention. "I beg your pardon?" The

flush that had covered her cheeks disappeared, leaving behind a ghostly-pale mask of shock. "What are you talking about?"

"You'd think I was talking about a couple of kids who didn't know any better than to have unprotected sex, wouldn't you?"

"Danielle…" The warning tone in Braeden's voice was enough to make his aunt mutter an apology.

Then she stepped forward, shrugging. "Obviously this marriage is back on, regardless of the harm it may cause."

"We're working on it," Alexia answered. Braeden's eyes widened at the defensiveness in her voice and stance. She looked as if she was ready to do battle.

"You may have *worked* a little too hard and fast," Danielle said, her tone dripping with sarcasm. "Don't you think it might have been wiser to wait until Nathan was gone before bringing more Drakes into the world?"

Alexia frantically reached behind her. Braeden waved a finger toward the chair, moving it until it nudged her hand. She spun it around, then sank onto it, digging her fingernails into the leather covering the arm.

Instead of answering his aunt, she turned to him and shot him a look filled with so much fear and worry that he broke his oath and reached inside her mind. *"Be easy. Tell me what you fear, Alexia."*

"What if Nathan finds out?"

"I don't plan on calling him with the news, do you?"

"No, but eventually he'll figure it out."

"Then we need to defeat him quickly, don't we?"

"But—"

Braeden shook his head. *"No. We will defeat him. Trust me."*

When she nodded and relaxed her grip on the chair, he

turned his attention back to Danielle. "Let's table this discussion. Alexia and I will talk later. Right now there are other things that need your attention."

Danielle took him at his word and let loose with a barrage of questions that he had no answers to just yet. So he raised a hand and waited until she got the hint to stop.

"We don't know how Alexia got the powers. They were given to her." He hated to resort to guessing, but in this instance had no other answer. "Probably through the manual somehow. My best guess is that Aelthed wove his spells into the pages in such a manner that whoever translated it would absorb the magic."

"Are you certain it's not because she's carrying your offspring?"

Alexia had turned the water to tea before they'd made love the first time. "No, her powers started before that possibility arose."

In a near whisper, Danielle asked, "What about *your* powers?"

She worried about the old prophecy. He really hated to point out an error in her interpretation but… "My powers are all still intact. So either the prophecy was wrong or…" He let the insinuation hang.

Quick to pick up on his unspoken thought, his aunt said, "Or I was wrong."

Alexia jumped to her feet. "Braeden, Nathan is at Mirabilus. We need to—"

"*We* need to do nothing." He pointed at the chair. "You need to sit down."

He rubbed the back of his neck. "The two of you aren't going to like this much, but I need you to get along with each other."

"Why?" His aunt crossed her arms.

"Because Alexia is my wife. And because someone needs to teach her how to use these powers. I can't do it. We'd only end up harming each other."

"I would never—"

He frowned at Alexia, bringing her declaration to a fast halt. "No. I mean physically harm each other. You have no control over your abilities, Alexia. Our emotions around each other run a little high, don't you agree?"

She nodded. He continued, "The higher the emotion, the more uncontrollable the power."

"Oh."

"So you want *me* to train her?" Danielle sounded incredulous, as if he'd just suggested she set off a nuclear explosion.

"Who better? You trained three boys without too much grief. And you won't much care if she gets upset. So there won't be double the emotional energy."

Who knew what would happen if *he* tried training her? His wife was as headstrong in her own way as he was in his. He couldn't even imagine the firestorm that might occur the first time they had a disagreement about methods or application.

Finally Danielle sighed in what Braeden knew was resignation. That taken care of, he turned back to Alexia. "Now, tell us about the workshop."

She told him about the hints Aelthed had put in the manual and how she and the caretaker had found the round room.

Braeden whistled. "It was there all this time."

"You should see the items in there." She looked at Dani. "You would be impressed. There are jars of stuff all over the place. And it looks like he made charms at the table. There were gems and bits of metal—and this."

Alexia opened her hand. She glanced up at Braeden as he rose and came around the desk. "It's like the one in the book. Watch." She stroked a finger gently down its back.

Braeden quickly stepped closer in case she couldn't put it back to pendant form. There was more to protect now than just his wife—there was a baby to safeguard. To his amazement, the thought fed his ego. He resisted the sudden urge to puff out his chest and strut. He turned his attention back to the pendant.

The emerald glittered, then shimmered to life. The wings spread and fluttered as if stretching from a long sleep.

Dani's eyebrows rose. "Do you have any idea what you're doing?"

"No."

"Then quit playing with the thing. It isn't a toy."

To his surprise, Alexia did as she was told. She held her other hand above the dragon, settling it back down into a shimmering inanimate emerald on her palm before slipping it into the pocket of her jeans. Maybe she'd take her training from Dani without too much trouble.

Alexia asked, "What about Nathan?"

Braeden looked out the office window. The presence of evil was strong. "He's already followed you back here." He looked at Alexia. "You would have been safer staying at Mirabilus. He couldn't hurt you there."

"But he was in our room."

"Was he?"

She frowned. "I saw a swirling mist."

"And that's all you would have seen. He can't materialize there. A spell exists in the mortar and stones of Mirabilus that he can't break."

"I didn't know that." She rose. "Should I go back?"

In unison, Braeden and Danielle shouted, "No!"

Braeden put a hand on her shoulder and pushed her down on the chair. "You have no clue where you'll end up. You were damn lucky to get here."

"I wanted to be at your side."

"Yeah, and instead you ended up in a conference room full of nonbelievers."

Her eyes widened. "What will you tell them?"

"Nothing. Cam will wipe the event from their memory and make some sort of excuse for me not being at the meeting."

"Speaking of a meeting…" Dani rose. "I do need to be there. If we're done here…?"

He nodded.

Danielle paused at the door and stared at Alexia. "You and I need to have a talk real soon. Until then, try not to do anything with your gift. Just sit there. Don't think. Don't play."

"I'll try."

"And one more thing." Danielle pointed at Alexia's stomach. "It's twins."

Once they were alone, Alexia glanced up at him. "Are you still angry about earlier?"

"Angry?" She was intentionally avoiding what they needed to discuss—her pregnancy. "It was a bit…disconcerting to feel your hands and lips on my body in the middle of a meeting."

He walked behind his desk and sat down. Alexia fidgeted. First she smoothed out imaginary wrinkles on her sleeve. Then she pushed unseen strands of hair behind her ear.

Her furtive movements were so erratic and ungraceful that a stranger would recognize her nervousness. For him the motions were no longer necessary. He was as attuned to her body as he was to his own. He could hear the unevenness of her breathing and feel the rapid tempo of her pulse.

Unwilling to let her off the hook so easily, he reminded her, "And now you're here, instead of safe at Mirabilus where I left you. I should be angry."

"It's not like I zapped myself here on purpose."

While he'd found the unwanted lovemaking unsettling, his wife's powers more than simply bothered him. If the speed at which her powers increased were any indication, she'd soon be as strong as he.

And then why would she need him any longer?

Whether she needed him or not was a moot point. She was carrying the next generation of Drakes. The option of her leaving once the manual was translated and Nathan was vanquished no longer existed.

He wasn't about to let her run off and have his children by herself. What if something happened? They'd already lost one child. He wasn't going to chance that happening again. She was staying. Period. He needed to make her aware of that now.

She would probably argue. But he wasn't changing his mind.

Braeden rested his arms on the desk, leaned forward and captured her darting glance with a steady glare. "You were wrong, Alexia. We aren't *working* on keeping our marriage together. We are staying married."

Chapter 16

Speechless, Alexia stared at him.

"Did you hear me?"

They were going to stay married simply because she was pregnant? A wave of anger and defiance rushed through her. "I heard you just fine."

"Good. As long as we understand each other."

"Understand each other?" She bolted from her chair. "There's nothing to understand. We'll make this decision together. Later, after everything settles down."

His jaw tensed. "The decision has been made."

Where had this sudden high-handedness come from? But she knew the answer. It had always been there, just waiting for the right time to make its appearance. "Who do you think you are?"

His gaze lowered to her belly. "The father of my children."

Not the father of *our* children, and most definitely not the man who loves you, Alexia thought. She placed her shaking hands on the desk and leaned closer to him. "Ever hear the term 'single mom'? I don't need you, Mr. Drake. I don't need your money or your name and I most certainly don't need your attitude."

She kept her voice low and even, desperately trying to hide the lies behind her words. "I can raise *my* children without your help."

Quicker than a blink he reached out and grasped her wrist. "That's where you're wrong, *Mrs. Drake*." The name rasped like a hard curse against her ears. "These children will be raised by *both* their parents. Under the same roof."

Alexia watched the play of fierce emotions rushing across Braeden's face. Something stronger than anger drove him.

She tried to tug her arm from his grip. "You're hurting me."

"No, I'm not." He released her.

Actually he *was* hurting her. Not physically, but... "What is wrong with you, Braeden?"

"I tell you that we're staying married and you act like I'm condemning you to hell. What could possibly be wrong?"

"So you decide to sacrifice yourself and do the honorable thing, and I'm supposed to what? Fall on my knees with gratitude?"

"You aren't leaving."

"Don't tell me what to do." She turned and headed toward the door.

"It wasn't a request."

Alexia fisted her hands at her sides before turning back to face him. "I'm well aware it was a demand. Too bad for you that it's not the twelfth century and I don't have to obey."

"Don't push me."

His darkly issued threat only fired her anger more. She made a flourish with one arm and bowed. "No, milord, I would never think to do so."

She straightened, then reached for the door.

"Where are you going?"

Alexia looked over her shoulder at him and answered, "Out."

He narrowed his eyes and moved a hand.

"Don't you dare…" Before the warning fully left her lips, Alexia found herself standing in the middle of the bedroom of his suite.

She screamed a curse while marching toward the open bedroom door. Before she reached it, the door swung closed with a slam. The sound of the lock clicking into place echoed in the room.

He'd gone too far this time. Alexia's shoulders rose with the breath she pulled into her lungs. She trembled with the outrage coursing through her, then used that unleashed anger to whisk herself right back to his office.

To her amazement and relief, she actually ended up next to his desk. "Nice try."

Braeden stood at the window and turned to stare at her. His hard, angry expression didn't so much as flicker at her reappearance. "I'm not going to argue with you about this."

She crossed her arms defiantly. "Since I'm not going to take orders from you, you don't have much of a choice, do you?"

"My power alone couldn't protect you and Matthew. You've just begun to taste your own power. What makes you think I'm going to let you waltz out of here by yourself now?"

His eyes blazed, but she wondered if he was as angry as he tried to sound. Was he perhaps as concerned about her pregnancy as she was? The idea of putting a baby…two babies…their babies in peril made her ill.

What would she do if Nathan found out? Braeden said he could protect them. Maybe he could now that he was aware of Nathan's presence, but could he also protect himself at the same time?

"Braeden?"

He turned away to look out the window, and Alexia's heart stuttered in a vaguely familiar way. They'd been through this before. He was going to shut her out—again.

Uncertainty made her hesitate. What was she going to do? She couldn't go through this again. Why couldn't he just talk to her? Why did he feel it necessary to order her around?

Alexia needed time to think. She didn't want to stand here wondering and worrying. If he decided to talk to her, to hash this out, he would.

Until then… She crossed the office, stopping with her hand on the door. "Braeden."

Without turning around, he asked, "Leaving?"

She knew what he meant. He expected her to try to leave Dragon's Lair, to run away. While a part of her wanted to do just that very thing, she had no intention of doing so.

She had more to think about than herself. They were going to be parents. It was pretty obvious he was correct. She resigned herself to the fact that the decision about their marriage had been made for them. She truly wasn't about to try raising two Drake children alone.

If this magic passed through their DNA, they would need their father's guidance more than they would require their mother's love. The thought stung. This wasn't how it was supposed to be. She'd never had these worries over Matthew.

Alexia glanced back at Braeden, wishing the decision had been based on his feelings for her, instead of honor. She frowned. Is that why he was so angry? Did he feel as if he'd been forced into this against his will?

Instead of giving voice to the thought, and with unfounded accusations dying to spew from her mouth, she said, "Only this room, Braeden."

Alexia didn't wait for his response. She needed to get out of the Lair as quickly as possible. Somewhere away from the threatening memories of yesterday and the crumbling hopes she'd had for tomorrow.

In the short time she'd been at Dragon's Lair, she'd somehow managed to fall back in love with her husband. That wasn't the plan. She was supposed to keep this impersonal. So much for good intentions.

And now she was carrying their children. She placed a hand over her stomach. Babies. Her babies. Would they be like their father? Would they be born with magic in their blood, or would they grow into it later?

Magic. To top off everything, she'd been given magic. Alexia pushed through the entrance door into the coolness of the night. As far as she was concerned these powers weren't a gift—they were a curse.

And regardless of what Braeden had declared earlier, he obviously thought the same thing. Or at least, he acted as if it was a curse for *her* to have powers.

Her anger beginning to find renewed life, she stomped around to the side of the Lair and ran into Sean. Literally.

"Alexia, careful." He grabbed her by the shoulders before she stumbled into the bushes.

"Sorry." She shook off his hold and noticed he wasn't alone.

"Alexia, this is Sam Wilson, the new Chief of Security. Sam, this is Braeden's wife, Alexia."

She shook Sam's proffered hand and frowned at the prickly sensation running the length of her arm. Staring up at the man, she asked, "Have we met before?"

"No, ma'am."

"I'm just showing him around the grounds." Sean leaned closer. "Are you all right? You don't look well."

Alexia took a step back, wiping her palm across her jeans. "I'm fine. See you later." She resumed her walk, stopping just before she reached the corner of the building to stare back at Sean and Sam Wilson.

She knew him. *From where?*

At that moment the man looked over his shoulder and caught her stare. He held it and smiled before turning his attention back to Sean.

Alexia's chest contracted. She gasped for breath. Oh, she knew him all right. He was the man who'd accosted her in the museum parking lot. He may have worn a full mask, but she'd recognize those eyes and that evil smile anywhere.

She leaned on the wall. Closing her eyes, she fought growing panic. She needed to warn Braeden.

Concentrating on his office, she sent him a message and hoped he'd hear it. *Braeden, we're in danger.*

Nathan laughed to himself. It couldn't get any better than this. Alexia Drake was outside, away from her husband's protection, and his own henchman was nearby.

Granted, the man was with the youngest Drake brother. But that posed little problem.

With nothing more than a wave of his hand, he knocked Sean Drake to the ground, unconscious. The new security guard jumped back and looked around until he saw Nathan.

"I see you got the job." Nathan ran his gaze up and down Sam's uniform.

The guard pushed out his chest and answered, "Yes, yes, sir, I did."

"Good. Then it's time for you to go to work."

"So soon?"

Nathan notched an eyebrow before reaching out to squeeze the man's neck. "You were recognized, fool."

The guard's eyes bulged from lack of oxygen, but he managed to nod slightly.

Nathan released him, then patted his shoulder. "Good, man. Now, you hike into those woods and wait for Mrs. Drake."

"She's going for a walk in the woods? At night?"

Nathan sighed, but when he again reached his hand toward the man's neck, the guard stepped back. "I'll go wait in the woods. Then what?"

"If she won't give me what I want, I'm going to chase her into the woods. You'll be hot on her trail. Once you capture her—" Nathan pierced the guard with a glare "—and you *will* capture her, you'll hold her until I get there." He waited a moment for his orders to sink in, then asked, "Have you got all that?"

The guard nodded. "After you chase her into the woods, I'll catch and hold her for you."

"See how easy that was?" For added measure, Nathan warned, "If you screw this up, I'll kill you, instead."

Certain the man completely understood, Nathan left to do his part.

The bricks against her back were cold, but Alexia was too afraid to move away from the building. A soft laughter was building in her mind. It got louder and louder until, unable to stand it anymore, she slapped her hands over her ears.

The laugh was soon replaced by an icy-cold touch against her cheek. *"You thought you were rid of me? Oh, Alexia, my dear, you won't be free of me until I have the translation."*

She erected a mental shield around her mind, hoping it would block Nathan, and took a deep breath before stepping away from the building to head back into the Lair.

But her next step brought her up against an invisible, solid wall. Alexia sidestepped to get around it, but no matter where she stepped, the wall stopped her.

"Let me by!" She beat her fists against the solid air.

"So, you've learned how to block me from your mind." The vile laughter resumed as Nathan took form next to her. "But you won't be able to block me now." He grabbed her hair, tugging her closer. "The translation, Alexia, then this will all stop."

Even if she *had* any information to give him, she didn't believe for a second that he'd go away.

"How many times do I have to tell you, there is nothing in that book of any value. It's just a diary. Aelthed played a joke on you."

"I don't believe you." Nathan pulled harder on her hair. She gritted her teeth against the pain of her burning scalp.

Why had she left Braeden's office? She wished she could be back there now. This time her wishing did no good.

Nathan shook her. "Give me what I want."

Alexia swung her fist and kicked him, shouting, "Let go of me."

Nathan jerked away as if someone had grabbed him and tossed him aside. She screamed as more than a few strands of her hair went with him. Looking around, she saw no one, but didn't pause to figure it out. Instead, she took off for the woods.

Since she'd been unable to wish herself back to Braeden's side or contact him mentally, she wondered if she could touch him. Right now, anything was worth a try.

Her ability to concentrate hampered by trees and bushes, Alexia did her best to envision her husband. He'd probably still be in his office, so she pictured him there, seated behind his desk.

He was relaxed, eyes closed as if he was thinking about something. Alexia slowly approached him and opened his shirt, button by button, trailing her fingertips down his chest as she worked steadily lower.

She swiveled his chair away from the desk and leaned over to kiss him. Braeden shivered beneath her teasing touch as she ran her tongue along the seam of his lips.

Alexia stumbled over a log and reached out to stop her fall by clutching at a tree trunk. She paused a moment to catch her breath, but then heard the faint sound of someone behind her.

She ran blindly, her chest burning, eyes filling with tears. "Braeden, please." Once again she focused her attention on her husband.

Her hands shook as she threaded her fingers through his hair and straddled his lap. Alexia leaned into him, pressing her breasts against his chest. She wound her arms about his neck and rested her cheek against his.

Braeden jerked upright in his chair and pushed away from the desk. His skin tingled from the feel of Alexia's fingers trailing down his chest. He shivered as her tongue traced the seam of his lips. Her breasts were soft against his chest, her tears hot against his cheek.

He bolted from the chair and spun around to the window. Where was she? Had she gone outside? He scanned the area with his mind.

Instead of finding Alexia, he discovered Sean prone on the pavement outside the Lair. Where the hell was Wilson? They'd been together. Sean was supposed to be showing him the grounds.

There was nothing around that provided any clue as to what had happened. Braeden lingered over his brother's body long enough to check for signs of life.

Certain Sean wasn't dead, he sent his mind around the resort. Alexia wasn't on the grounds. He went further into the woods. Trees and bushes raced by beneath his search.

Braeden could hear the frantic pounding of her heart and her ragged breaths. She was running blindly in the forest. He scanned the area behind her and saw a uniformed figure following her tracks.

Now he knew where Wilson was.

Without hesitation, Braeden pulled out his cell phone, hit the intercom, then ordered, "Cam, go to the entrance. Now."

He didn't wait for Cam to respond. Once Cam found Sean on the ground, he'd understand the call.

Braeden took one step toward the window and fought off the mind-numbing fear for his wife and the new life she carried. He sped through the dense forest.

He paused, listening for Alexia. He heard the crashing of her flight before he saw her. As she came through a stand of trees straight toward him, he reached out, looped an arm around her waist and brought her hard against his chest.

Before she could alert Wilson by screaming, he covered her mouth with his hand, then whispered in her ear, "I'm here."

She sagged against him with a choked, frightened cry. Braeden turned her around in his arms and held her close. "Shh, baby, it's okay. I've got you."

"I tried to call you." She curled her fingers into his shirt. "But you didn't hear me. Then I tried to wish myself to your side, but it didn't work. I didn't know what else to do."

"It's all right, Lexi. You did the right thing." She needed to learn how to call on her magic quickly, even when she was frantic or under duress. The problem was they didn't know what sort of powers she did or didn't have.

The sound of snapping twigs made her press more tightly against him. "It's Nathan."

He smoothed a hand down her hair, trying to keep her calm. "No. It's the security guard."

"He was one of the men who tried to kidnap me at the museum."

Braeden cursed softly. Even though hiring was Cam's job, he should have followed his instincts about this man and kept his brother from bringing Wilson aboard.

"Lexi, can you hang on a few minutes? Do you trust me?"

Hesitantly, she asked, "Why?"

"I want to see if we can catch this man. You won't be harmed—I need you to believe that."

She nodded against his chest.

The beam of a flashlight traveled over them. "Isn't this sweet? The two of you together."

Braeden looked over Alexia's head and noticed the gun in Wilson's hand. A spell meant to disarm the man didn't work.

Wilson possessed no magic of his own. Apparently Nathan had set a protection spell around his goon. Fine.

Braeden would simply find another way to capture the man while keeping Lexi safe.

He hoped to stall for time and maybe catch Wilson off guard, so even though he already knew the answer, Braeden asked, "What are you doing? Who do you work for?"

"Obviously not you." In his cockiness, he stepped closer.

Braeden held out a hand. "Stay right there. Don't come any closer."

"Why?" Wilson waved his gun. "What are you going to do?"

"I'm unarmed, so not much. I just don't want you frightening my wife any more than you already have."

"Too bad. I'll be doing more than just frightening her before the night is over."

Alexia shivered and Braeden tightened his hold. He rested his forehead against hers for a brief moment so he could more easily convey information. *"When I relax my hold, fall to the ground. Got it?"*

She pressed her forehead against his. He hoped that meant she understood. Then he turned his attention back to Wilson. "Why did you come here?"

"Since you won't be alive much longer. I see no harm in telling you. My boss ordered me to. Seems he wasn't happy that we botched the job at the museum, so I was sent here to set things right."

"You do realize your boss isn't exactly human, don't you?"

"Of course I do. I'm not stupid."

Don't bet on that. Braeden kept that thought to himself. However, from Alexia's gentle shaking against his chest, he knew she'd heard him.

"What do you plan on doing with us?"

Wilson came another step closer. "Just hold you here until the boss arrives."

Braeden had no intention of waiting around for that to happen. He relaxed his hold.

Alexia dropped to the ground.

Wilson hesitated just long enough for Braeden to extend his arm and throw a ball of energy in Wilson's direction. The force knocked the man down.

But before Braeden could conjure a length of rope to secure the unconscious man, a bolt of lightning flashed through the trees straight through Wilson's chest.

Alexia screamed as the stench of charred flesh filled the air around them. Braeden bent down and grabbed her up from the ground. He relaxed his hold a little only when they were standing in their bedroom at Mirabilus.

Chapter 17

She leaned against his chest, clinging to his suit jacket for support. Otherwise, she'd have collapsed on the floor. "Hold me."

He tightened his embrace. "I am holding you."

"I can't feel you." She pressed harder against him, wishing she could burrow beneath his jacket and shirt.

"That's because you're shaking." He sat down on the bed and held her across his lap. "It's over."

She shook her head. "No, it's not over. Nathan is still out there. He isn't going to stop until he has that damn book."

"Unfortunately I doubt he'll stop even then."

Tremors moved down her body. They were so hard her clenched jaw hurt.

Braeden rubbed a hand up and down her back. "Alexia, you have to stop this. He can't harm you here. He's powerless at Mirabilus."

"I can't stay inside these walls forever."

"It isn't forever. It's just until you can be trained how to protect yourself."

"Fine, as long as you stay with me until then."

"Alexia, I can't. I have to get back to the Lair."

"No!" she nearly screamed. Softening her tone, she said, "Then I'm going with you." She was adamant. "Braeden, I'm not leaving your side."

"I need you to stay here."

"No." She repeated. "If you leave, I'll only follow. I came to you for protection, so damn it, protect me."

"I can only guarantee your safety here."

His curt tone warned her that he was losing patience. She didn't care.

She was acting like a frightened two-year-old. Again, she didn't care.

There was magic out there more powerful than anything she ever could have imagined in her wildest dreams, and she wasn't going to be left alone. He could get as angry as he wanted.

Braeden tried to pry her away from his chest, but she wouldn't budge. "Sean was hurt," he said. "I need to get back there and find out what's happened."

"Did you let Cam know?"

"Of course I did."

"Then he can take care of it." She cringed at her own selfishness.

"Alexia."

Hysteria bubbled close to the surface. Tears welled in her eyes. "Don't leave me alone. Please."

He rocked her back and forth on his lap. "You'll be fine here."

"No. You don't understand." She pulled away from his

chest and stared at him. Unchecked tears blurred her vision. "They've tried to kidnap me once and kill me twice. I have this…this magic that doesn't work when I need it to. But I make dragons come to life." Her fear and hysteria burst over the dam. "I'm afraid. I'm afraid for me and for our children. Braeden, please, don't leave me alone."

Speechless, Braeden stared at her. Everyone had their breaking point and obviously his wife had reached hers. He had to give her credit—Nathan had thrown nearly everything in his arsenal at her and so far she'd stood her ground. She'd held up far longer than most would have.

He couldn't begrudge her a moment of weakness, not when she'd earned it. And getting angry with her now would most likely only make matters worse. Although he wasn't sure how much worse anything could get. Nor did he want to find out.

He turned and laid her down on the bed. "Shh, Lexi, I'm here. I'm not going anywhere. I'll be here as long as you need me. I promise." As he stretched out alongside her and gathered her into his arms, he hoped he could keep that promise.

He held her tightly as she sobbed against his chest. His heart twisted until he thought it would break.

It wasn't more than a couple of hours ago that he'd wondered what would happen when she no longer needed him. Perhaps that day was further away than he'd thought.

Regardless of whether that day came tomorrow, next week, next month or next year, right now she desperately needed him. Almost as much as she'd needed him after the accident and losing Matthew.

He closed his eyes, swearing he wouldn't let her down again. Because he knew damn well if he did, he would lose her for good.

That was a risk he was suddenly unwilling to take.

When her sobs lessened, he threaded his hand through her hair and coaxed her face toward him. She tasted of salty tears. He gently kissed them from her eyes and cheeks before covering her lips with his.

She leaned into the kiss with a strangled moan that sounded more like a terrified kitten than his wife. Seeing her like this made him angry—at Nathan, at the situation and at himself.

He was planning to pawn her off on Danielle for training. That wasn't fair to either woman. Lexi needed to be in control *now*, not next week or next month or whenever his aunt found the time. Alexia had to believe she could protect herself and the babies if need be as soon as possible.

She was pliant in his arms, the tremors slowly subsiding beneath his touch. Braeden's memory was in excellent working order. He knew this docile mood of hers wouldn't last.

Once the fear wore off, she'd be contrary, vacillating between her need for protection and her anger because she needed the protection. It had been the same way before— one moment she'd want comforting, then in a heartbeat she'd be outraged that anyone thought to offer her the comfort.

It had made no logical sense to him whatsoever and he'd given up in frustration. This time it would be different.

He nudged her onto her back and rolled on top of her, resting his weight on his elbows. He kissed her slowly, thoroughly, trying to convince her that she was the most important thing in his life.

She slid her arms around him and returned his kiss. The

moan he drew from her now contained no fear, only growing desire.

Braeden lifted his head and stared down at her. Satisfaction swept through him as he watched hunger replace the terror in her eyes.

Something tapped against the window. Nothing supernatural or magical. It could have been a bug, a leaf or a twig blown by the autumn wind. But the sound caught Alexia's attention. When she brought her gaze back to his, Braeden saw the tiny glimmer of fear.

He touched his lips to hers. "Give me your nightmares. Let me hold your terrors."

When Alexia blinked and hesitated a moment too long, he removed their clothing with nothing more than a thought.

Before she could comment, he said, "It wasn't a request."

He smiled at the flush of beginning anger tinting her cheeks. As she parted her lips to give voice to her thoughts, he covered them with his own.

At first she remained motionless, but he was well aware that she'd soon give up her anger beneath his onslaught. He fought back a grin of triumph when she tightened her embrace and returned his kiss.

Braeden shifted to her side and stroked a hand across her belly and up to cup a breast. Slowly, as if memorizing her body for the first time, he circled his thumb around the swollen peak and caressed the soft fullness.

When she arched into his touch, he pulled away and sat up on the bed. "Hold out your hand."

He gave her a minute for the haze of desire to fade slightly before grasping her wrist to raise her arm. "Open your palm."

She frowned, but did as he requested. Braeden released her wrist and held out his hand. A ball of luminescent bright blue swirled and shimmered on his palm.

"This is energy. It is power and protection." He dropped the swirling mass on her outstretched palm and covered it with his hand. "I freely give it to you."

Alexia shook her head, but he said, "This gift doesn't decrease my own powers. It is just a small drop for you to nurture. Close your eyes and pull it into your body."

The frown didn't leave her face, but she closed her eyes. Braeden pressed lightly on the ball. It melted into her hand.

She shivered, then opened her eyes. "What do I do with it?"

"Right now, nothing." He stretched alongside her again and circled a fingertip over her belly before leaning in for another kiss.

Once he was certain he had her full attention again, Braeden swept his hand down the length of her torso, across a hip, then traced a line up the inside of her thighs.

He nudged her legs apart to tease and torment her while their mouths sought more of each other. Alexia quivered beneath him, ready for more than a touch.

Again, Braeden sat up on the bed. When the desire faded from her face this time, it was replaced with building anger.

He ignored it and said, "Show me your power."

"What?" Her passion-laden voice was laced with outrage.

She could get as mad as she wanted, but he wasn't budging on this. "Hold out your hand and show it to me."

Alexia stuck out her hand. "There's..." Her words trailed off as a ball of shimmering blue wavered on her palm.

"Good." He held out his hand, and when it filled with an orb of blue, he tossed the orb in the air and let it settle around him. "Now, see if you can poke a finger through."

She reached out and tried. The shield held fast, not permitting her to touch him.

Braeden waved away the shield. "Now, you try."

Once she had her protective shield settled around her, he rose and crossed the room. Before she could realize what he planned, he grabbed a paperweight from the desk and threw it at her.

Alexia shouted, raised her arms and ducked. After the paperweight bounced off the shield, she straightened on the bed and glared at him. "Cute, Braeden."

He chuckled. By the time he was done with her today, she'd be good and mad. But at least she'd be able to protect herself, and that was the important thing.

From inside her wavering ball, she poked at the sides, asking, "Now how do I get rid of this?"

"Until you get used to doing it, hold out your hand and will it back into your body."

Without taking her hot stare off him, she slowly followed his suggestion. He knew by her look what she was thinking. She was going to try using the shield to keep him away.

Braeden waited until the shield was almost gone from sight, then he lunged across the room, tackling her and putting her beneath him on the bed.

She pushed at his shoulders. "That's not fair."

He ignored her and concentrated, instead, on the soft flesh where her neck and shoulder met. When her struggles ceased, he resumed his teasing.

Alexia gasped. "Tell me there aren't any more lessons."

He shifted, bringing his body over hers, and slowly kissed his way down the length of her torso and belly to come to rest between her legs.

She lifted her head slightly and looked at him. "You can't keep this up."

He twirled a finger in her damp curls, parting them before asking, "Want to bet?"

When he stroked her with his tongue, Alexia fell back onto the pillow, sighing weakly. "No."

"Good." She trembled beneath his intimate kiss. He paused to add, "Because you'd lose."

Although, he was so hot and hard right now he wasn't sure he'd make it through this final session.

Forcing himself to have patience, he kissed and teased until her fingers curled into the sheets beneath her. Braeden slid a finger deep into her. When her body tightened around him, he eased away.

Their groans collided as he once again rose on the bed. This time, his breathing was as ragged as hers.

She tried to laugh, but it came out more as a strangled chuckle. "It serves you right."

He took a breath, willing his heart to steady, ordering his burning body to wait.

Once he had himself under control, he held out his hand and grasped the hilt of a medieval battle sword that had just appeared. "This hangs with its mate in the Great Hall. It's a real blade. Do you remember where they are?"

Alexia nodded.

He opened his hand and the sword disappeared. "Focus on the weapon and call it to you."

She closed her eyes.

"No." He reached out and grasped her chin. "Alexia, never close your eyes when drawing something dangerous to your hand."

She opened her eyes and he released her. "Just hold your hand out as if you were going to shake someone's hand. Visualize the *hilt* landing in your hand, not the blade."

He stayed at her side, ready to grab the weapon if she drew it to her incorrectly.

Alexia took a long, slow breath and held out her hand. Within a matter of seconds the sword materialized in the correct position, and she curled her fingers around the hilt.

The corners of her mouth curved up in a smile. She raised one eyebrow and shifted to the other side of the bed. "Now we're done."

He could easily guess her intention, but she'd earned her fun. Opening his eyes wide, he innocently asked, "We are?"

Alexia pointed the weapon at his chest. "Lie down, Braeden. On your back."

He did as she ordered, trying hard to swallow his own smile.

Once he was stretched out on the bed, she directed the sword back to its mate and then straddled him.

"I think it's my turn to play."

He shook his head. "I don't think so."

"No?"

Braeden slid both hands up the inside of her thighs. He paused at the top and stroked a thumb through the hot folds of flesh. "No."

Alexia gasped and rose up slightly on her knees. Before settling down atop him, she whispered, "Fine, this time you win."

He wrapped his arms around her tightly, drawing her down against him. "Are you sure this is what you want?"

She ground her hips against him, unable to find the movement she wanted. "No. No it's not."

"Hang on."

Braeden rolled them over until she was beneath him. It

took less than a heartbeat for them to find the pace that satisfied both of them.

Alexia curled her legs around his hips and dug her fingernails into his back.

He deepened his thrusts and brought them quickly over the edge to fulfillment.

Alexia went lax beneath him. Once her breathing evened out, she smacked his arm. "That wasn't fun."

Nearly unable to move, he whispered against her ear, "I don't know, I kind of enjoyed it."

"You weren't the one being tortured."

"I don't know about that. I feel like I was."

She sighed, then pushed at his shoulder. "You're getting heavy. Go take a shower."

He slid to her side and wrapped one arm around her rib cage. "Later."

She plucked at his hand, trying to remove his arm. "What are you doing?"

"Nothing."

The way he said *nothing* made her realize he had something on his mind. "What?"

Braeden slid his palm down to cover her stomach. "Twins?"

"So says your aunt."

"How do you feel about that?"

Alexia's heart pounded. She didn't want to give strength to the fears she harbored by talking about it. "I've actually tried not to think about it."

"Why?"

"You know why."

Braeden angled his chest over hers, and resting on his elbows, he captured her gaze. "Nathan won't hurt them. Trust me, Alexia. He won't get the chance."

Her throat seemed to close, but she forced the fear out into the open. "As much as you want to, you can't guarantee that. Braeden, what if…what if we lose them, too? I don't think I could bear it again."

His fingertips ran soothingly over her cheek. "Shh, baby, don't look for trouble. We'll all be fine. Trust me. Trust us. We can get through this."

He'd said *we* as if the two of them were some kind of team. But they weren't. Not by mutual choice. As far as he was concerned, they were only together because he'd ordered it. And he'd only done so because of the babies. Alexia choked back the emotions building in her throat.

Still holding her gaze, Braeden frowned, asking, "Lexi, what are you thinking about?"

She shook her head. "Nothing."

"Don't." His voice lowered to a warning pitch. "Don't do this now."

"What? I'm not doing anything." She tried turning her face away from his burning glare, but he grasped her chin, holding her in place.

"Tell me what you're thinking about."

She narrowed her eyes. "Like you tell me what you're thinking about?"

He matched her expression. "Falling back into old habits isn't the way to start things off."

"Start what? You mean our marriage? The one you ordered me to keep?"

"This is a waste of our time." Braeden pulled away and sat up. "Why don't you just go file for a divorce and be done with it?"

Shock, loss and unbearable heartache slammed against her all at once, taking her breath away. Alexia slowly sat up, drawing whatever slender thread of strength she could find inside along with her. "You'd let me do that?"

He didn't turn around, but answered, "If it's what you want, yes."

She reached out hesitantly to touch him, then pulled her hand back. "Braeden, I…"

Alexia didn't know what to say, what to think. She only knew that the dark emotions raking her heart were unbearable.

He glanced over his shoulder, then sighed as he turned to face her. "Alexia, file for a divorce so I can hunt you down and court you all over again."

She kept her attention riveted on her knees. "Why?"

"So you know that my intentions aren't directed solely toward the babies." He lifted her chin with the side of his hand. "While their existence may have forced the issue, it's their mother I want, not just them."

"Are you certain?" She closed her eyes for a minute before adding, "Because I'd rather raise them alone than force my presence on you."

"Force your presence on me?" Braeden shook his head before sliding his hand across her cheek to thread his fingers into her hair and pull her closer. With his lips against hers, he whispered, "I want *you*. Babies or no babies. You. Can you believe that?"

Alexia slipped her arms around him, holding him tightly. He hadn't said that he loved her, only that he wanted her, and she wondered if that would be enough.

When he finally broke their kiss, she sniffed, fighting to gather her courage, and blinked away the gathering tears before pushing him away. "You need to go make certain Sean is all right."

"Are you sure?"

"Yes, I'm sure. If I could summon that protection shield while my mind was hazy with lust, I'm certain I could do the same if I was afraid."

"I don't have to go."

"No, Braeden. I'm sorry I acted so weak. Go."

He studied her eyes and found no fear, no nightmares haunting her gaze. "There's nothing weak about you." He captured her lips for another kiss before heading to the bathroom for a shower.

Chapter 18

Alexia slid up the bed, propped her back against the pillows, then tipped her head back and closed her eyes. Now that her heart didn't pound with fear—or desire—she wanted nothing more than a nap.

Even though she was thoroughly exhausted, she had to admit that Braeden's unorthodox method of training worked. Although, if he ever mentioned training someone else she'd have to object—violently.

"Alexia."

She sat bolt upright, opened her eyes and looked around the room.

"Alexia."

It was Danielle's voice. Why would she be trying to contact her, instead of Braeden?

A vision formed in her mind. Alexia frowned. Danielle was chained to a wall in…a dungeon? She shook her head. Why would that image appear?

"Alexia, help me."

Danielle tugged at the manacles around her wrists. Alexia heard the clank of chains.

She leaped from the bed, scrambling to gather her clothes while yelling, "Braeden!"

He swung open the bathroom door. Shampoo was lathered in his hair, water sluicing from his body. "What?"

While pulling on her jeans, she said, "It's Danielle. She's in trouble. She's…" Alexia paused trying to make sense of what she'd seen. "It looks like she's chained up in a dungeon."

He rubbed his temples. "You concentrate while I rinse off."

She sat on the edge of the bed tugging on her socks and shoes. Unable to call the vision back, she whispered, "Danielle, talk to me."

The woman's voice was weak and Alexia had to strain to hear it. *"Help me. It's Nathan."*

Braeden came out of the bathroom wearing jeans and a shirt. He looked at her. "You aren't coming with me."

Alexia got to her feet. "Nathan has Danielle. You can't face him alone."

Braeden grabbed her shoulders. "Listen to me. Cam is more than able to help me. I don't need to be worrying about you and the babies while I'm trying to rescue Aunt Dani."

"You have no reason to worry about me and our babies."

"Why? Because you've learned a few tricks? Danielle is far more experienced than you are, yet she's being held captive by Nathan."

"And Danielle admitted herself that she has no powers other than those enabling her to communicate telepathically and cast a few spells."

"And you think you're stronger than she is?"

Alexia nodded. "I know I am."

Braeden sucked in a breath, then whistled low and soft. "You've gotten a little arrogant in the past few minutes, haven't you?"

She jerked back as if slapped, but held her ground. He was trying to piss her off so that she'd stay here. A couple more comments like that and he'd succeed.

"Damn it, Alexia, promise me you'll stay here."

She pretended to give in. Willing to play along—for now. "Fine. I promise…"

He disappeared before she finished her sentence. "…not to make you worry about me."

Braeden paused at the head of the stairs leading down to the basement of the Lair. Cam stood behind him.

Luckily Sean had suffered nothing worse than a split lip from hitting the pavement facedown. Right now he was up in his suite nursing a bruised ego, completely oblivious to what was happening.

Both Braeden and Cam preferred it that way. By the time Sean was ten, he'd refused to finish his lessons, claiming magic and wizardry existed only in fairy tales. They'd given him a hard time about it for years. But lately, neither of them bothered anymore.

The last thing they needed right now was an uninitiated wizard anywhere near Nathan.

Braeden glanced over his shoulder. "Ready?"

Cam nodded. The two of them transported themselves to what they knew was a dark corner of the basement behind a partition.

Braeden glanced around the makeshift wall and saw Danielle seated before a table. If she'd been chained to a wall, she wasn't now. Two men flanked her at the table.

Nathan was nowhere in sight.

Cam whispered, "I don't sense him."

Braeden agreed. The wizard wasn't there. So what was this about?

"I have no idea where she is." Dani's voice rose with anger. From her animated hand gestures, it was obvious her patience had reached its limit.

The one man grabbed the front of her blouse and jerked her up from the chair. "You better get her here. Now."

Braeden swallowed a growl. These idiots wanted his wife? That wasn't likely to happen.

He stepped out from behind the partition. "Get your hands off her."

Both men pulled jewel-encrusted daggers from their boots. It was a fair guess that Nathan had sent them. If one wanted to kill a wizard, a nice, sharp, spelled blade would be the perfect weapon.

The blade would not only cut through flesh, muscle and bone, it would also cut the wizard's powers. As Drakes, Braeden and Cam had known that from the time they were old enough to learn their lessons. Which is why they were well trained in the use of blades.

And there was no doubt it was the same with the Learneds.

Braeden heard the rush of air behind him as Cam procured weapons.

He held up his hand and flinched with surprise when Cam slapped the hilt of a battle sword against his palm.

"Overkill, don't you think?"

Cam stepped to his side. "Why waste time with little toys?"

Braeden snorted. His brother had been longing for a sword fight for some time. But every time they so much as mentioned a mock battle, Danielle went into hysterics. Obviously Cam wasn't about to miss this opportunity.

They approached the two men. Braeden asked, "Did Nathan send you?"

The shorter man nodded. "Yes, our uncle asked for our help."

Excellent. Not only did these men work for Nathan, they were most likely wizards, too.

To prove that as fact, the taller man shook his dagger, and it was transformed into a sword.

Cam made a noise that sounded suspiciously like a growl. Braeden resisted rolling his eyes and held out his sword. He beckoned the men forward with his free hand. "Let's see what you've got."

Danielle bolted from the table and rushed toward him and Cam. "No, don't do this."

"Are you trying to get yourself killed?" Braeden grabbed his aunt's arm and swung her behind them, out of harm's way. "Stay out of this." He pointed toward the steps. "Go upstairs."

The rebellious look she shot him before heading for the stairs spoke volumes, but with the other two men approaching, he didn't have time to be distracted.

Braeden stepped away from Cam, giving both of them room to move. Prepared for the blow, Braeden only laughed when the taller of the two men swung his sword and made contact.

He heard Cam defend himself against the other man. Sword clanging against sword echoed in the nearly empty basement.

His own opponent was defeating himself by using brute force to strike at Braeden again and again. At this rate, the man would soon be winded.

Until then, Braeden had only to dodge the blade and keep the man moving.

Apparently the man came to the same realization. He stretched out his free hand and a ball of fire rose from his palm.

Braeden shook his head. "You need to do better than that." In the next heartbeat he set the sprinkler system on high. The heavy spray of water put out the fire.

A curse ripped from the lips of Cam's opponent as he slipped and fell on the now wet concrete. His curse turned to an agonized scream followed by the clatter of a sword falling, then bouncing on the floor.

The taller man's eyes narrowed and his lips thinned as he rushed Braeden. Ready for him, Braeden sidestepped and used the hilt of his sword to whack the man on the back of his head as he rushed by.

Braeden glanced at Cam, who shrugged. "This wasn't all that fun."

Both of Nathan's nephews disappeared.

Braeden headed toward the stairs. "Don't be too disappointed. I don't think this is over."

"Where are you going?" Cam was on his heels as they sprinted up the steps.

Danielle and Sean met them at the top. "He's here." Dani looked away, hesitating.

Sean said, "He has Alexia."

Braeden's heart stumbled. "That's not possible. She's at Mirabilus. He can't materialize there."

Cam put a hand on his shoulder and looked at Danielle. "She's here, isn't she?"

Dani nodded.

A string of curses ripped out of Braeden's mouth before he asked, "Where?"

* * *

Alexia materialized at the edge of the woods behind the Lair. She swore. Braeden had warned her that she could end up in the wrong place.

Nathan's laugh rippled across her cheek before he whispered, "Finally."

She turned around and stared at him, ignoring the sudden racing of her heart. He wore a long robe that billowed around him in the night's breeze.

The light of the full moon illuminated his eyes, making them appear to glow an evil shade of gold.

"What do you want?"

"Why, Alexia, I want what I've always wanted. The translation to the grimoire."

She held out her hand. A sheaf of papers appeared. "Here, take them."

He snatched them from her hand and quickly scanned the first page. With a bark of vile laughter he tossed it to the ground. Then did the same with the next page and the next.

Finally he threw the rest of the pages at her, letting them blow across the open yard. "Is this your idea of a joke?"

She shook her head. "No. I told you before it's nothing more than a diary."

Nathan glared at her. His eyes narrowed. As if just realizing what she'd done, he asked, "Where did you get powers?"

Alexia shrugged. "We don't know. The book maybe?"

He pulled a small wooden box from the inside of his cloak. Holding it up to the moonlight, he asked, "Aelthed, what trickery is this?"

She stared in amazement as the cube levitated slightly and spun just above Nathan's hand.

"It is no trickery, you fool."

A voice she'd never heard before rang loud and clear from the box.

"That was the secret, Nathan. My powers were woven into the pages of a seemingly useless grimoire. It was never an instruction manual. It was nothing more than a vehicle, a storage place to hide my powers until one deserving of them came along."

Nathan pointed a shaking finger in her direction. "And you gave them to *her?* A mere mortal? A woman is more deserving than I?"

Alexia could feel his rage at being thwarted yet again. She stepped back from the heated anger emanating from his body.

"I will not have it, Aelthed. They were mine. They've always belonged to me."

"It is too late, Nephew. They have been given to one far more deserving than you."

She wasn't at all certain about the deserving part.

Nathan screamed, "No! They are mine."

He turned to her. "I will take them from you. I will drink your death and have what is rightfully mine."

Drink her death? He'd lost his mind. Alexia turned to run, but he grabbed a handful of her hair and jerked her backward so hard she fell to the ground.

Moonlight glinted off a dagger in his raised hand. Her breath stuck in her throat.

The little wooden box spun out of control and slammed against the side of Nathan's head. He instantly released his hold. Just as quickly, Alexia scrambled to her feet and raced toward the Lair.

Her pulse pounded in her ears. Her breath came hard and ragged from her chest. A spot on her upper thigh burned like fire.

Without stopping her race for safety, she reached down and felt the spot. The dragon pendant in her jeans pocket was burning her flesh.

She pulled the emerald beast from her pocket and gasped. It glowed.

"Alexia!" She stopped running as Braeden came to a near-breathless halt at her side.

He grasped her wrist and she lifted the pendant. "Wait. I think he wants to help."

Braeden stood behind her, his strong arms wrapped protectively around her as they turned to face Nathan, who was still a few yards away. Holding out her hand, she placed the dragon face up on her palm and gently stroked the beast with a fingertip.

The wings unfurled as the beast stretched its head, back and tail.

Alexia pleaded with the growing dragon, "Faster, please. Before he gets here."

Braeden cupped one hand beneath hers and whispered over her shoulder, "Let me help."

She leaned harder against his chest, willingly accepting his offer.

"I am the Dragon, little beast. My power is yours. Use it." At Braeden's command, the dragon shook itself, then quickly rose up from her palm and took flight.

Braeden's hold around her waist tightened and they watched the beast together.

The dragon grew until it towered at least twelve feet. Its wingspan was enormous. And while Alexia knew any sane person would be terrified, she was awed at the beauty and power before her.

Nathan had stopped dead in his tracks and now stared up at the dragon making slow circles around him. It dove toward him once, made another circle, and on the next graceful dive, reached out with long, sharp talons and grabbed the wizard.

Nathan's screams echoed across the yard as the dragon carried him away.

Danielle snapped back to reality first. "What the hell was that?"

Alexia smiled. "My dragon."

Sean whistled. "Sweet."

Danielle cleared her throat, then asked, "*Your* dragon?"

"Well, I did find him." Alexia looked up at Braeden. "Do you think Nathan is gone now?"

When Braeden didn't answer, Cam said, "I'd rather have seen the beast eat him. Then we'd know for sure."

Braeden finally leaned down and whispered in her ear, "Mrs. Drake, you and I need to talk. Now." He turned, and with her still held tightly at his side, headed toward the Lair.

They got as far as the door before Cam shouted, "It's back."

The dragon landed lightly in the yard and stared at her. She tugged at Braeden's arm. "Please, let me go." He released her. And she went to stand in front of the beast.

It lowered its head, opened its mouth and dropped the small wooden cube at her feet. Alexia ignored the cube—she could study that later. Right now she was fascinated with the mythical beast that by all accounts didn't exist.

It leaned its great head forward and blew hot air against her ear before rising to full height and shaking itself like a wet dog.

Uncertain what it wanted at first, Alexia finally stretched out her hand, palm up. The dragon blinked at her, folded its wings and shrank.

When it was small enough to hold, she picked it up and

placed it on her palm. Holding it close, at eye level, she said, "Thank you." Then she cupped her other hand over it. "Be a pendant again, my beast."

She slid the emerald pendant back into her pocket, picked up the wooden cube and turned to Braeden. "You wanted to talk?"

Chapter 19

Braeden stared at his wife from across their bedroom at the Lair. He was torn between two urges. Make love to her—or lock her away in a nice, safe, magic-proof cell somewhere.

It was a tough choice.

"You intentionally disobeyed me."

"Disobeyed?" Alexia's eyebrows rose. "As in you lord, me servant?"

"Don't get flippant. I told you to stay at Mirabilus. You promised me."

"No. You didn't stick around long enough to hear my promise. I promised only to not give you cause to worry."

"And you think watching you confront Nathan wasn't cause for worry?"

She looked around. "I'm here, aren't I?"

"With a little help," he reminded her. "You had no idea you'd end up the victor. He could have killed you. What would I have done then?" He wanted to gag on his own words. He sounded like an old woman. Where had his logic and backbone gone?

"Braeden?"

"What?"

She smiled at him. In the next moment she was naked. Alexia slowly approached him.

His worries dissipated, along with his anger. She'd put herself in danger needlessly. He should be angry, outraged.

Not burning with desire.

She stopped before him and placed a hand on his chest. Meeting his gaze, she asked, "Braeden, we made a good team, didn't we?"

She was right. They did make a good team. He doubted if there was anything the Dragon and his mate couldn't accomplish together. But somehow he knew that life with her at his side was going to prove more than he ever could have imagined.

Throwing all caution to the wind, he gathered her in his arms. "Yes, my love, we made a good team."

She peered up at him from beneath her lashes. "Your love?"

She was so obviously toying with him that he couldn't resist shrugging before saying, "Unless, of course, you still want that divorce."

Alexia frowned as if in deep thought, then replied, "I would, but I'm not really sure I can raise two wizards alone. They may occasionally need their father's guiding hand."

He rolled his eyes in mock disbelief. "Their mother needs a guiding hand more than they ever will."

She gently swung her hips from side to side, brushing intentionally against him. "Then if it's okay with you, I may as well stay. I really don't have anywhere else to be."

It wasn't as if he'd ever let her go. Without touching her, he leaned forward and gently kissed her lips. "That depends."

She slid her breasts against his chest. "On what?" Her low and sultry voice nearly broke his will.

"Will you finish the translation?"

Alexia sighed. "If you insist."

"I do."

"Then, my love, for you I will."

"Will you take your bankbook out of my desk?"

"I suppose. There are a few things I need to buy. Cribs, diapers and, you know, other little things."

He grasped for more illogical questions. Anything to keep her attention off the fact that he was backing her steadily toward the bed.

"Will you litter-train that beast of yours?"

She laughed. The sound raced across his ears, nearly drawing a smile from him. "It's going to take a big litter box. But I'll try."

Just before the back of her legs hit the bed, he asked, "And will you obey me?"

She grabbed hold of his shirt and fell backward onto the bed, pulling him along. "Never in a million years."

He laughed and cupped her head between his hands. "Yes, Lexi, it's okay with me for you to stay. To be my wife. To be the mother of our children. And to be the love I can't live without."

She leaned up and kissed him. "There's only one condition."

He shivered in mock fear. "And that would be?"

"That you love me forever."

He nuzzled the side of her neck. "I've loved you from the moment we met." He rained kisses on her eyes. "I love you now." He brushed his lips across hers. "You are my mate. I will love you throughout eternity and beyond."

From across the room, in the cube Alexia had set on the table in a dark corner, Aelthed sighed. Soon he would be released from this box. His soul would be free to pass on.

But first there were secrets the Drakes needed to know. Secrets he'd yet to weave into the book.

Crossing his legs, he leaned against the corner of his cell and began adding pages to the grimoire.

The Dragon's love would enjoy discovering that there was much more to this boring old man than recipes.

There were stories about other dragons—amethyst and sapphire ones. And tales of a magic box yet to be told.

Soon all the stories would be told. All the secrets revealed. And then, only then, would he finally be free.

* * * * *

Harlequin is 60 years old,
and Harlequin Blaze is celebrating!
After all, a lot can happen in 60 years,
or 60 minutes…or 60 seconds!
Find out what's going down in Blaze's
heart-stopping new miniseries,
FROM 0 TO 60!
Getting from "Hello" to "How was it?"
can happen fast….

Here's a sneak peek of the first book,
A LONG, HARD RIDE
by Alison Kent.
Available March 2009.

"Is that for me?" Trey asked.

Cardin Worth cocked her head to the side and considered how much better the day already seemed. "Good morning to you, too."

When she didn't hold out the second cup of coffee for him to take, he came closer. She sipped from her heavy white mug, hiding her grin and her giddy rush of nerves behind it.

But when he stopped in front of her, she made the mistake of lowering her gaze from his face to the exposed strip of his chest. It was either give him his cup of coffee or bury her nose against him and breathe in. She remembered so clearly how he smelled. How he tasted.

She gave him his coffee.

After taking a quick gulp, he smiled and said, "Good morning, Cardin. I hope the floor wasn't too hard for you."

The hardness of the floor hadn't been the problem. She shook her head. "Are you kidding? I slept like a baby, swaddled in my sleeping bag."

"In my sleeping bag, you mean."

If he wanted to get technical, yeah. "Thanks for the loaner. It made sleeping on the floor almost bearable." As had the warmth of his spooned body, she thought, then quickly changed the subject. "I saw you have a loaf of bread and some eggs. Would you like me to cook breakfast?"

He lowered his coffee mug slowly, his gaze as warm as the sun on her shoulders, as the ceramic heating her hands. "I didn't bring you out here to wait on me."

"You didn't bring me out here at all. I volunteered to come."

"To help me get ready for the race. Not to serve me."

"It's just breakfast, Trey. And coffee." Even if last night it had been more. Even if the way he was looking at her made her want to climb back into that sleeping bag. "I work much better when my stomach's not growling. I thought it might be the same for you."

"It is, but I'll cook. You made the coffee."

"That's because I can't work at all without caffeine."

"If I'd known that, I would've put on a pot as soon as I got up."

"What time *did* you get up?" Judging by the sun's position, she swore it couldn't be any later than seven now. And, yeah, they'd agreed to start working at six.

"Maybe four?" he guessed, giving her a lazy smile.

"But it was almost two…" She let the sentence dangle, finishing the thought privately. She was quite sure he knew exactly what time they'd finally fallen asleep after he'd made love to her.

The question facing her now was where did this relationship—if you could even call it *that*—go from here?

* * * * *

*Cardin and Trey are about to find out that
great sex is only the beginning....
Don't miss the fireworks!
Get ready for
A LONG, HARD RIDE
by Alison Kent.
Available March 2009,
wherever Blaze books are sold.*

CELEBRATE
60 YEARS
OF PURE READING PLEASURE
WITH HARLEQUIN®!

We'll be spotlighting a different series
every month throughout 2009
to celebrate our 60th anniversary.

Look for Harlequin® Blaze™ in March!

0-60

*After all, a lot can happen in 60 years,
or 60 minutes...or 60 seconds!*

Find out what's going down in Blaze's
heart-stopping new miniseries *0-60!*
Getting from "Hello" to "How was it?"
can happen fast....

Look for the brand-new 0-60 miniseries in March 2009!

www.eHarlequin.com   HBRIDE09

You're invited to join our Tell Harlequin Reader Panel!

By joining our new reader panel you will:

- Receive Harlequin® books—they are FREE and yours to keep with no obligation to purchase anything!
- Participate in fun online surveys
- Exchange opinions and ideas with women just like you
- Have a say in our new book ideas and help us publish the best in women's fiction

In addition, you will have a chance to win great prizes and receive special gifts! See Web site for details. Some conditions apply. Space is limited.

To join, visit us at
www.TellHarlequin.com.

REQUEST YOUR FREE BOOKS!

2 FREE NOVELS PLUS 2 FREE GIFTS!

Silhouette®

n o c t u r n e™

Dramatic and Sensual Tales of Paranormal Romance.

YES! Please send me 2 FREE Silhouette® Nocturne™ novels and my 2 FREE gifts (gifts are worth about $10). After receiving them, if I don't wish to receive any more books, I can return the shipping statement marked "cancel." If I don't cancel, I will receive 4 brand-new novels every other month and be billed just $4.47 per book in the U.S. or $4.99 per book in Canada, plus 25¢ shipping and handling per book plus applicable taxes, if any*. That's a savings of about 15% off the cover price! I understand that accepting the 2 free books and gifts places me under no obligation to buy anything. I can always return a shipment and cancel at any time. Even if I never buy another book from Silhouette, the two free books and gifts are mine to keep forever.

238 SDN ELS4   338 SDN ELXG

Name _____ (PLEASE PRINT) _____

Address _____ Apt. # _____

City _____ State/Prov. _____ Zip/Postal Code _____

Signature (if under 18, a parent or guardian must sign) _____

Mail to the **Silhouette Reader Service:**
IN U.S.A.: P.O. Box 1867, Buffalo, NY 14240-1867
IN CANADA: P.O. Box 609, Fort Erie, Ontario L2A 5X3

Not valid to current subscribers of Silhouette Nocturne books.

Want to try two free books from another line?
Call 1-800-873-8635 or visit www.morefreebooks.com.

* Terms and prices subject to change without notice. N.Y. residents add applicable sales tax. Canadian residents will be charged applicable provincial taxes and GST. Offer not valid in Quebec. This offer is limited to one order per household. All orders subject to approval. Credit or debit balances in a customer's account(s) may be offset by any other outstanding balance owed by or to the customer. Please allow 4 to 6 weeks for delivery. Offer available while quantities last.

Your Privacy: Silhouette is committed to protecting your privacy. Our Privacy Policy is available online at www.eHarlequin.com or upon request from the Reader Service. From time to time we make our lists of customers available to reputable third parties who may have a product or service of interest to you. If you would prefer we not share your name and address, please check here. ☐

SN08#

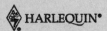
HARLEQUIN®

INTRIGUE®

SPECIAL OPS
TEXAS
COWBOY
COMMANDO

BY JOANNA WAYNE

When Linney Kingston's best friend dies in
a drowning accident one day after she told
Linney she was leaving her abusive husband,
Linney is convinced the husband killed her. Linney
goes to the one man she knows can help her, an
ex lover who she's never been able to forget—
Navy SEAL Cutter Martin. They will have to
work together to solve the mystery, but can
they leave their past behind them?

Available March 2009 wherever you buy books.

nocturne™

COMING NEXT MONTH

#59 IMMORTAL BRIDE • Lisa Childs

Guilt-stricken Damien Gray believes he is losing his
mind—everywhere he turns he sees the spirit of his
beautiful bride, Olivia, whose disappearance is a
mystery. Not willing to lose her again, he seeks to find
a way to connect the divide between the living and
the dead. But first he must battle an evil presence
in the ghost realm, who is determined to ensure
Damien never finds true happiness....

#60 FURY CALLS • Caridad Piñeiro

The Calling

When Blake Richards made the choice to turn
Meghan Thomas into one of the undead, he hadn't
realized just how angry she would be—even after four
years! To win back her love, Blake must show her he's
no longer the rogue she knew. But when a deadly
feeding frenzy overcomes their vampire clientele, can
he convince her that he isn't somehow involved?